"I'll take him!"

In the dim light of the flickering lanterns Dixon bent into a catlike crouch and balanced on the balls of his feet. His black eyes turned darker as the venom in his soul filled them. "Okay, Markie boy," he called across the forty feet that separated him from the marshal, "pick the second you want to die. It's your play."

Mark Young splayed his hand over the .45 on his hip and said, "You're the one who came to town looking for this little party, Duke."

Dixon's hand plunged downward.

No one saw Mark Young move. It seemed that the .45 Colt leaped from the holster into his hand. In the thunder of Young's shot, Dixon quivered like a lightning-struck tree and toppled backward into the dust. His own gun slipped harmlessly from his fingers.

The Badge #1
SUNDANCE

THE BADGE: BOOK 1

★

SUNDANCE

★

Bill Reno

 ™ **BCI** Created by the producers of
Stagecoach, Wagons West,
White Indian, and Winning
the West.

Book Creations Inc., Canaan, NY · Lyle Kenyon Engel, Founder

BANTAM BOOKS
TORONTO · NEW YORK · LONDON · SYDNEY · AUCKLAND

SUNDANCE

A Bantam Book / October 1987

Produced by Book Creations, Inc.
Lyle Kenyon Engel, Founder

ISBN 0-553-26774-4

Published simultaneously in the United States and Canada

PRINTED IN THE UNITED STATES OF AMERICA

KR   0 9 8 7 6 5 4 3 2 1

SUNDANCE

Following the Civil War, as settlers headed west and towns sprang up in what had been a wilderness, civilization had to be won behind the barrel of a gun. In this often chaotic world, one thing stood alone as a symbol of law and order–the badge of the lawman.

At the top of the hierarchy was the U.S. marshal, appointed by the President to enforce federal laws for an entire state or territory. At his disposal was a large force of deputy marshals, who handled the actual field work. Each county elected a county sheriff, who hired deputy sheriffs to help enforce state and local laws. As an individual community grew, it would hire its own marshal to keep the peace.

Together, the federal marshals and local sheriffs and marshals comprised a system of law enforcement uniquely suited to the needs of a vast, ever-changing frontier.

© BOOK CREATIONS INC. 1987

RON TOELKE '86

Chapter One

The vagrant early morning winds skipped across the Black Hills of northeast Wyoming, bending the long-bladed grass and pouring through the shaggy clusters of sagebrush. The summer sun lifted skyward, chasing shadows away and changing the complexion of the pitted, craggy face of the giant rock formation known as Devil's Tower.

The tower lifted its lofty head 1280 feet above the floor of the south Belle Fourche Valley, where the shimmering Belle Fourche River snaked its way through northeast Wyoming, exposing its banks of bloodred clay. The rock-strewn, tree-covered base of the tower rose 415 feet above the valley. The towering sentinel, with its long vertical fluted columns and flat summit, rose another 865 feet above the rounded base, dwarfing the surrounding forest of ponderosa pine, oak, aspen, and Rocky Mountain juniper.

At the base of the giant monolith several hundred campers were rolling out of their blankets, excited about the promise of the new day. It was July 4, 1893, and the crowd had gathered to observe Independence Day. Such celebrations were nothing new to the people of northeast Wyoming. For years they had gathered on July Fourth at the foot of the tower. But this year's event was going to top them all. Newspapers had spread the word all over Wyoming, Colorado, Nebraska, Utah, Montana, and the Dakotas that a man named Bill Rogers was going to provide the thrill of a lifetime—he would defy the cold claws of death by being the first person ever to scale the sheer vertical face of Devil's Tower.

Rogers, a cowhand at the Circle D ranch twelve miles west of nearby Sundance, had made elaborate preparations for the spectacular event. He had come to the tower several days before to begin the crude ladder by which he would scale its face, driving pegs cut from native oak into the vertical crack between two columns on the southeast side. The pegs, sharpened at one end, were twenty-four to thirty inches in length. While the crowd watched below, he would climb the tower, driving in the remaining pegs one by one.

The Crook County Promotion Committee had distributed handbills through towns in a two-hundred-mile radius, promising that there would be plenty to eat and drink on the grounds, with music and dancing day and night. Also, there would be an ample supply of hay and grain for the horses. The committee gave assurance that order would be maintained by county sheriff Jim Naylor. The celebration would be highlighted by Bill Rogers's spectacular climb up Devil's Tower, with bold letters at the bottom of the handbill proclaiming that the event would be even more fun than the ongoing World's Fair in Chicago.

The smell of hot coffee and sizzling bacon drifted along on the morning breeze. Laughing children played among the rocks and trees at the base of the tower, while their parents discussed the daredevil feat that was to be attempted that day. Some who were acquainted with Rogers explained that the lanky young cowboy had been climbing mountains in the Colorado Rockies since he was a boy. Since hiring on at the Circle D and first seeing Devil's Tower, he had felt that climbing the monolith would be the challenge of a lifetime.

Buckboards, buggies, and riders on horseback were pulling in by the drove. By nine o'clock a carnival atmosphere prevailed. A brass band from Cheyenne was blaring out its music, while small groups of Blackfoot, Cheyenne, Sioux, and Kiowa Indians filtered through the gathering crowd, eager to watch the pale-faced cowhand scale the tower. Hustlers had taken advantage of the occasion, with many of them wandering through the crowd, barking their wares. Others had set up crude display stands, around which curious onlookers were gathering.

The most colorful attraction was an old stagecoach that had been painted red, yellow, and green. From up top, Doc Witherspoon was peddling his Indian River Elixir, eloquently proclaiming that it would cure every ailment known to man.

While the band played, people milled about, renewing acquaintances with old friends or making new ones. Groups of young girls giggled coyly at tousle-haired boys who grinned from ear to ear. Babies were crying, mothers shouting at unruly children, dogs barking.

Everywhere, the main topic of conversation was the upcoming climb by Bill Rogers. When Sundance's undertaker, Hector Evans, pulled up in his wagon, someone called out, "Hey, Hec! You come to haul Bill's corpse out of here?" A round of laughter followed.

Sheriff Jim Naylor rode in, having just made the twenty-eight-mile trip from Sundance.

"Hello, Sheriff," said one man. "Ken Eastman with you?"

Naylor shook his head. "Someone's got to keep an eye on the town."

"Guess that's what deputies are for, huh?" The man chuckled.

Naylor nodded with a grin, then turned back to his horse. After loosening the cinch on his saddle he headed over to the hastily constructed platform where the speeches would be made. Three women were decorating it with American flags and red, white, and blue ribbons.

Albert Frye, mayor of Sundance, was seated behind the platform on a tree stump, rehearsing his speech. As he scribbled something on a piece of wrinkled paper, Naylor walked up and said, "Morning, Albert."

Frye looked up with a smile and returned the greeting.

"Things about ready to go?" asked the sheriff.

"Think so," replied the mayor. "Rogers ought to be here shortly."

Naylor looked around for a moment. "Some crowd, huh?"

"Bigger than I expected." Frye nodded. "I'd say there's at least fifteen hundred here right now. With latecomers dragging in for the next two or three hours, it'll probably top two thousand."

"Wouldn't doubt it," said Naylor, still looking over the crowd. "This thing's liable to get more publicity than the Chicago World's—"

Albert Frye heard the sheriff's words cut off. Looking up, he asked, "What's wrong?"

Naylor's gaze was fixed on two men and a young woman who were dismounting from their horses on the fringe of the crowd. He swore under his breath.

"What is it?" repeated the mayor.

The sheriff looked back at Frye. "We may have trouble on our hands, Albert," he said grimly. "It's Butch Cassidy and Harry Longabaugh."

"Cassidy and the Sundance Kid?"

"In person. You sit tight. I'm going over there."

"You going to tackle them alone?" asked the mayor.

"Maybe they'll be peaceful." Naylor grunted. "They've got that schoolteacher with them."

The sheriff hitched up his gun belt and moved slowly through the noisy crowd toward the trio, while Frye watched apprehensively. When Naylor was some thirty feet away and as yet unnoticed by the two outlaws, a young boy ran in front of him and yelled, "Hey, Sheriff! Are you gonna arrest Cassidy and Sundance?"

Suddenly, eyes swung around to take in the scene. Cassidy and the Sundance Kid set their gaze on the approaching lawman. Both stiffened their necks and bristled. The woman with them looked blandly at Naylor.

"Howdy, Sheriff," spoke up Cassidy, forcing a smile. Twenty-eight-year-old Robert LeRoy Parker, alias Butch Cassidy, wore a smirk that looked as though it had been engraved when he was born. He stood a stocky five feet nine inches tall and was known to be tough with his hands and accurate with a gun.

Sheriff Naylor fixed the Sundance Kid with a hard look. Two years younger than his outlaw friend, Harry Longabaugh was an inch taller, more slender of build, and known to be the more dangerous of the two. As a youth he had spent eighteen months in the Sundance jail for horse theft. As a result he had been dubbed the Sundance Kid.

Naylor ran his gaze between the two men and spoke slowly. "What are you two doing here?"

Cassidy curled his lips even more than usual. Looking over the crowd, he said caustically, "You asking everybody the same question, Sheriff?"

"Everybody here is not an outlaw," Naylor snapped.

"You got something on us, lawman, put the cuffs on us," grated Cassidy. "Otherwise, leave us alone."

The sheriff knew he had no proof of the latest escapades of Cassidy and Sundance, hence no excuse to arrest them. Rumor had it that Cassidy had been holding up trains with the vicious Tom McCarty gang, while Sundance had been rustling cattle and horses with some unnamed accomplices.

"These are honest, decent people gathered here today," Naylor said evenly. "Your presence spells trouble to me. I asked you what you're doing here."

"Just came to see that fool cowboy break his neck," spoke up Sundance. "Any law against that?"

Naylor's face flushed slightly. "I don't need your smart mouth, Harry," he said stiffly. "Now, I think it would be best for everybody if you two would just get astraddle of your horses and ride out of here."

"And leave Miss Place all by herself, Sheriff?" the Sundance Kid sneered. "She came here to see the big fool climb the rock. Would you deprive her of our company?"

Before Naylor could answer, Cassidy said, "Sheriff, the three of us are just patriotic Americans, looking to celebrate July Fourth along with our fellow citizens. We ain't bothering anyone."

With a smug look Etta Place said through tight lips, "We are here to enjoy a holiday, like everybody else, Sheriff Naylor. I am not going to start any trouble, and I assure you that, with me here, neither will these gentlemen."

"These are not little boys like the ones you teach in school, Miss Place," replied Naylor. "You can't whip them and stand them in a corner. They are both outlaws and troublemakers, and you know it."

"Look, Sheriff," breathed Cassidy hotly, "are we breaking some law?"

"Not at the moment."

"Then why don't you leave us alone until we do?"

"That's it right there," rasped Naylor. "With you two on the premises, trouble is in the cards."

"Hey," put in Sundance, "Butch and me ain't gonna give you no trouble today, Sheriff. We're here for a good time, like everybody else. Okay?"

Just then somebody in the crowd shouted, "It's Bill Rogers! Hey, everybody! Here he comes!" All eyes turned to the Circle D wagon, which had just crossed the Belle Fourche River and was heading to where the huge crowd had gathered. A loud cheer filled the warming air.

Naylor turned back to Butch Cassidy and the Sundance Kid. He took a deep breath and let it out slowly through his nose. "You can stay for now," he said resignedly. Then he turned his back on the two men and walked away.

At the same time that the crowd was cheering the arrival of Bill Rogers at Devil's Tower, a lone rider moved slowly into Sundance. United States Marshal Mark Young sat straight in the saddle, squinting his eyes against the blast of sunlight as he probed the deserted street. Not more than a half-dozen horses were tied at the hitch rails in front of the clapboard buildings along the length of Main Street.

Young reined in at the sheriff's office, but before swinging from the saddle he turned to gaze southward at Sundance Mountain. The town was butted up against the foot of the rugged mountain, and for a moment Young let his slate-gray eyes trace its outline against the Wyoming sky. Then he dismounted and stepped up onto the boardwalk in front of the sheriff's office.

Deputy Sheriff Ken Eastman looked up from his desk, startled to see the silhouette of Marshal Mark Young standing in the doorway, framed against the glare of the sun-bleached street. Young stood an even six feet in height; his body tapered from extremely broad at the shoulders to narrow hips. Eastman knew Young, knew that he was every inch the man he appeared to be. He was as tough as rawhide and as fast as chain lightning with the Colt .45 that hung low on his right hip. A native of Wyoming, the thirty-year-old federal officer had recently been assigned the Wyoming-Montana area.

The young deputy sheriff stood up behind the desk and grinned broadly. "Howdy, Mark," he said. "Come on in. Guess you know where everybody is."

"Yes." Young nodded as he removed his hat, revealing his wavy light-brown hair. Pulling a bandanna from his hip pocket, he mopped his brow, then wiped moisture from the inside of his hat. "I kind of envy this guy Rogers. There might be a breeze up on top of the tower."

Eastman chuckled. "What brings you to town, Mark?"

"Butch Cassidy," came the marshal's dry reply.

"Cassidy? In Sundance?" Eastman's eyes were wide.

"Trailed him mighty close to here. He's in the area. I figure he just might be curious enough to head for the tower to watch Rogers make the climb. Thought I'd stop and ask if you'd heard any word that he'd been seen around."

"Nope," said Eastman. Furrowing his brow, he asked, "You got something on Cassidy?"

"A warrant for his arrest. I just came from Kaycee. Seems he rode away on a man's horse and forgot to pay for it. If he's still riding the same animal, I'm going to slap Mr. Parker, alias Butch Cassidy, in jail."

Eastman sat down and leaned back, lacing his fingers behind his head. Grinning, he said, "I think there's more to this trip than slapping Cassidy behind bars. Right?"

"Right."

"Don't tell me. Let me guess. You're going to squeeze him for Tom McCarty, aren't you?"

"Like an orange. Cassidy's been running with McCarty as sure as hens lay eggs. He's going to point me to McCarty or rot behind bars at the state prison in Rawlins."

Eastman hoisted his feet up on the desk. "Maybe McCarty's hiding out at the Hole-in-the-Wall."

The famous outlaw haven known as the Hole-in-the-Wall was not really a hole but a barren, lonely canyon in central Wyoming, bordered on all sides by towering red walls. When outlaws made a strike, they would vanish inside the canyon walls as if they had dropped into a hole. There was an unstated threat that any lawman who ventured into the canyon would never come out alive. The threat had never been tested.

Young shook his head. "McCarty's too active in too many places to be hiding there. He's holed up somewhere, planning a robbery very close to where he's at. Butch knows where that is, and I'm going to lean on him to find out."

Eastman studied Young for a long moment and saw the determination written all over him. He had been on Tom McCarty's trail for over a year. The elusive outlaw was a cold-blooded killer. He had robbed, maimed, and killed all over Colorado, Montana, and Wyoming. He had to be stopped, and Mark Young was the man who was going to do it.

"Tell me something," said Eastman. "Butch Cassidy makes such a big thing about having never killed a man. If that's true, why does he run with a killer like McCarty?"

"Easy money," Young replied. "Nobody's raking it in like McCarty and his gang. Their reputation for killing somebody in nearly every robbery has people scared to death. When his gang bursts into a bank or hops aboard a train yelling who they are, everybody shovels money to them like they're happy to give it away. So Cassidy goes on a job with McCarty now and then to keep his pockets full."

"You think the Sundance Kid will join up with McCarty?"

"Longabaugh is too much of a lone wolf, Ken," replied Young. "He'll work with a man or two to rustle some cattle or steal some horses, but he doesn't run with gangs. My guess is that he and Cassidy are going to start working together more. But now that I have a warrant for Cassidy, I intend to make sure that doesn't happen."

"You mean unless Cassidy has already sold that horse and stolen another," put in the deputy.

Young let out a sigh. "I sure hope he hasn't. I need to nail his hide." Clapping his hat on his head, he added, "Well, I guess I'd best be heading for the tower. I've got a feeling old Butch just may be there. Besides, I'd like to get a gander at Bill clawing his way up that rock wall."

"Sure hope he doesn't fall," said Eastman. "For his sake, of course, but also for Mrs. Dunne's. She can't afford to lose any men right now."

Molly Dunne was the twenty-six-year-old widow of Circle D owner Sam Dunne, who had been killed two months ago by an unknown bushwhacker. At the mention of her name, Young's heart quickened pace. "I haven't seen her since Sam's funeral," he said, trying to sound casual. "How is she?"

"It's hard adjusting to the responsibility of running a ranch," Eastman said advisedly. "She never had to handle any of it when Sam was alive. Now, all of a sudden, she has to make decisions on things she knows very little about."

"I assume Cory Bell is still foreman."

"Yes, and Cory has been a real help to her."

"I'm sure that with Cory's help, and with the other hands sticking by her, she'll make it okay."

"I think so. Her younger sister is living with her now. That will help ease some of the loneliness."

Young smiled. "Anna Laura has probably developed into quite a young lady by now. I was hoping to see her at Sam's funeral, but Molly said she couldn't make it."

"You're right about that," commented Eastman. "She's just about as beautiful as Molly."

Changing the subject, Young asked, "How about the killer, Ken? Any clues yet?"

"Nothing. Sheriff Naylor has worked hard on it, but there's just nothing."

"Too bad," said Young. "I'm sure it would help Molly if Sam's killer were caught."

"Doesn't look like it's going to happen, though," remarked Eastman, shaking his head.

Young turned to leave. "Well, I'm glad Molly has Anna Laura there to help ease her pain."

"Someone else is trying to ease it too," said Eastman.

"What do you mean?" Young asked, looking back around.

"I mean a would-be suitor."

Lines of concern etched Young's forehead. "Somebody's trying to romance Molly already? Sam only just died."

Dropping his feet to the floor, the deputy nodded. "I know, but this guy is trying for all he's worth."

Young let out an irritated sigh. "Who is he?"

"Some wealthy land developer from Denver, name of

Walter Smythe. Seems he appeared at the Circle D a short time before Sam was killed. Made some kind of a ridiculous offer on the ranch. Sam just laughed at him. Said if he wanted to give the ranch away, he'd give it to somebody who needed it, and besides, the place wasn't for sale. Wasn't long after Sam was buried that Smythe showed up to offer Molly his condolences and his shoulder to cry on."

Mark Young's lips curved sardonically. "How old is this guy?"

"Don't know—I've never seen him. Smythe has been back several times, and I hear he's asked Molly to marry him."

Anger leaped into Mark Young's eyes; the corners of his mouth pulled tight. "Who does this guy think he is?" he blurted. "Sam isn't even cold in his grave yet." He lifted his hat, sleeved away sweat, and dropped it back on his head, then asked cautiously, "What'd Molly tell him?"

"Are you Molly's keeper or something?" Eastman replied with a nervous chuckle as he rose.

"No . . . of course not. But we've been friends for a long time—since before she met Sam. I care what happens to her, that's all. I asked you what Molly told this Smythe."

"Word is she said she's not marrying anyone for some time. Says she'll get along fine with things as they are."

"At least Molly's got good sense," Young said with evident relief. "I suppose I can't blame this Smythe for asking. She's a lovely woman."

Eastman squinted at the marshal and cocked his head slightly. "You have a special interest in Molly?"

Young swallowed the lump that had come to his throat. "I just care a lot," he said. "I've known Molly for a long time."

The shadow of an old pain touched Mark Young's face. Saying he would see Eastman later, he turned and stepped through the doorway. Halting, he tilted his hat to shade his eyes and he gazed eastward. He could see the stagecoach from Cheyenne entering Sundance at the end of Main Street. Then his vision clouded over as the face of Molly Dunne seemed to hang before him.

Time fell away until he was reliving the day when Molly told him that she was marrying Sam Dunne. He and Molly had seen a lot of each other, even attending some barn dances and holiday celebrations together. But a deeper romance had not blossomed—at least on Molly's part. Their times together were light, easy, and fun. The torch had been lit in Mark Young's heart, but he'd decided to let Molly get to know him better before he told her that he was head-over-heels in love with her. Then all of a sudden Sam Dunne came along and swept her off her feet.

Standing there on the dusty street, Young remembered the pain that had pierced his heart when Molly happily announced that she and Sam were engaged. She expected Young to be happy for her, so he had put on an act while his heart seemed to die within his breast. On the day of the wedding, he'd thought of every excuse in the world to keep from attending. But he knew his absence would hurt Molly, so he endured the agony of watching the woman he loved become another man's wife.

The torch that Mark Young carried for Molly had never gone out. Following Sam's funeral he had decided that when enough time passed, he would go to the Circle D and tell Molly how he felt. But now he faced an obstacle—some wealthy land developer. Suddenly Young knew he must talk to Molly before his assignment in Sundance was finished. But right now he had to head for Devil's Tower.

The marshal looked up as the stagecoach rolled in and squealed to a halt in front of the Wells Fargo building next door to the sheriff's office. As the wind blew the dust cloud away, two well-dressed men alighted from the stage and approached the door of Jim Naylor's office. One of them noticed Young's badge and asked, "Are you Sheriff Naylor?"

Before Young could explain that he was not the sheriff but a U.S. marshal, Ken Eastman came out of the office and said, "Sheriff Naylor is at Devil's Tower for the July Fourth celebration, gentlemen. I'm his deputy, Ken Eastman, and this is U.S. Marshal Mark Young. Is there something I can do for you?"

Both men eyed the marshal speculatively. They had

heard his name and knew his reputation. "I'm Jack Clancy," spoke up the older one. "This is Durwood Peters. We're detectives with the Pinkerton Agency, hired by the Union Pacific Railroad to track down and capture a train robber named Tom McCarty. It's our understanding that McCarty's in this vicinity, and we've come from Chicago to check it out."

Mark Young felt a cold knot in his stomach. These two fancy-pants city detectives could get in his way. McCarty was a lot more than a train robber—he was a heartless killer. He had to be stopped, and Young felt that he was the man to do it. As U.S. marshal assigned to this territory, he intended to bring in or kill the nefarious Tom McCarty.

Stepping close to the two men, he said, "Let me explain something, gentlemen. I have been hired by the federal government to apprehend McCarty. He is wanted on charges that go far beyond train robbery. Why don't you just hop on that stage and go back to Chicago and tell Mr. Pinkerton there's somebody already on McCarty's trail. When I catch him he won't be bothering the Union Pacific anymore."

Clancy eyed Young coolly and said, "Well, Marshal, since all three of us are being paid to bring in McCarty, we had best do our duty. You do yours, and we'll do ours. I expect the early bird will catch the worm."

Young's lips pulled tight. "This is a raw country out here. These outlaws aren't like your city criminals. They're tough and brutal, and this one's meaner than a rattlesnake with a sore throat. Now, the situation here is well in hand. You just go on back to Chicago and let us handle McCarty."

With a sour expression Durwood Peters said crustily, "If that's so, why don't you have Mr. McCarty in custody?"

Young's face flushed with anger. Stepping so close to the detective that their noses nearly touched, he breathed hotly, "You white-shirt-and-tie boys have got it all worked out on paper, haven't you? Let me ask you something. How many outlaws have you apprehended west of the Missouri?"

Peters cleared his throat nervously. "Well . . . uh—"

"How many have you killed?"

"Well . . . uh . . . none, so far. But—"

Young turned to Clancy. "You look a little older, Mr. Clancy. I'll ask you the same questions."

Clancy ran a shaky finger inside his shirt collar but did not answer.

"Just as I thought."

"Now look here, Marshal," said Clancy, finding his voice. "That badge on your chest doesn't give you the right to keep us from carrying out our assignment. We're being paid to pursue and apprehend Tom McCarty, and we intend to earn our money. You have no legal right to stop us."

"Okay, boys," Young said with a gravelly voice, "but don't get in my way. Understand?"

The two men stood in silence as the marshal wheeled around, nodded good-bye to Ken Eastman, and mounted his horse.

The young deputy watched with admiration as Mark Young rode his big chestnut gelding westward out of Sundance. Eastman had long esteemed Young as the epitome of a lawman. Secretly he had begun to pattern himself after Young, trying to develop the same self-assured manner that makes an outlaw think twice before he tests you.

Durwood Peters ejected a low whistle. "So that's the famous Mark Young."

Jack Clancy turned to the deputy and asked, "Is he really as tough as they say?"

"Tougher."

"I've heard about that gun on his hip," put in Peters. "Is he really as fast as rumor has it?"

"Faster."

Chapter Two

On June 30, five days before the big event at Devil's Tower, outlaw Tom McCarty and his gang of eight men were gathered in a hotel room at Buffalo, Wyoming, a hundred miles west of Sundance. Among the group was McCarty's twenty-one-year-old nephew Bob, who was on the floor, leaning against the bed and reading a saucy burlesque magazine.

Young Bob McCarty had started his life in the right direction. He had enrolled in college at Austin, Texas, studying business administration. He had been doing well when, during his sophomore year, his father, Bill, had gone insane, murdering his wife and then killing himself. With both parents dead and no money to continue school, Bob had taken up with his father's younger brother Tom.

Tom McCarty was an educated man with a degree in sociology. Somewhere along the line, while still in his twenties, McCarty had, like his brother, also shown a strange emotional disorder and had done a sudden about-face. Turning his back on society, he'd become a crafty, brutal outlaw and killer.

The outlaw leader, now in his mid thirties, had taken in his nephew as if he were his own son. He'd trained Bob in the use of firearms, knives, and fists. Bob had proven his ability with all three and was developing into a cunning outlaw, which pleased his uncle. But along the way Bob had discovered that he enjoyed killing. He had a weakness for women and had become a brutal rapist, always murdering his victims when he was finished. This aspect of Bob's character concerned his uncle. Even the ruthless Tom McCarty, bloody as he was, avoided killing women. Though McCarty cautioned Bob against needlessly endangering the gang, he was finding his nephew increasingly hard to handle.

Tom McCarty stood just under six feet tall and weighed an even one hundred and seventy muscular pounds. He was strikingly handsome, with a finely chiseled face, a thin mustache, and well-trimmed coal-black hair. One reason he had such a soft spot for his nephew was because Bob looked more like McCarty than he did his own father. Bob even kept himself as well groomed as his uncle.

The McCarty gang was waiting in Buffalo to rob a train coming south the next day from Miles City, Montana. They had word from one of McCarty's informants that in its baggage car the train was carrying a safe loaded with cash. Their plan was to ride out and intercept it some twenty miles north of Buffalo.

The nine men were lounging about the room McCarty had taken under the name Frank Holmes. McCarty held a hand to his jaw, swearing at the pain from a bad tooth.

"You better see a dentist about that tooth," said Ernie Derks. "Train job'll be easier if your mouth don't hurt."

"Guess I should," answered McCarty.

Mike Landy lazily swung his eyes to his boss and said, "Tom, how about fillin' us in on what's doin' with that Circle D situation."

"I'm taking the ranch," McCarty said flatly. "It's that simple."

"What do you want with the ranch?" asked another of the men. "Gonna sell it?"

McCarty swore. "No, I'm going to keep it. Those damn lawyers in Austin swindled me out of my dad's ranch after he and Ma died. I figure the world owes Tom McCarty a ranch, and I'm gonna get me one. That Circle D is some spread and would more than fit the bill."

"Yeah," said Bob, looking up from his magazine. "And

from what I hear, that Dunne woman is some peach. If I were you, Uncle, I'd keep her too."

"Nope," said McCarty. "I don't need her. I'm just a step away from convincing her to marry me. As soon as the knot is tied, the Circle D will become the Circle M. Shortly thereafter Molly will have an accident, and the whole spread will be mine . . . all mine."

Bob eyed his uncle quizzically. "I thought you were against killing women. You're always boasting that you've never killed a woman."

McCarty shot his nephew a stiff look. "Just this one time, Bob. And only because it has to be done. I'm the boss of this outfit, and I don't ever want to hear any more about me killing this one woman, do you hear? Never again." As McCarty said it he ran his eyes over the entire group, pressing his words on each of them.

One of the most experienced members of the gang was a gunman and robber named Elzy Lay, who had run with the best of them in and out of the Hole-in-the-Wall. He was lounging on the feather bed, reading a copy of the *Police Gazette*. To this point he had not been paying much attention to the conversation, but now he lifted his eyes over the magazine and said, "I wonder what that Dunne woman would say, Tom, if she knew you were the one who bushwacked her husband."

McCarty laughed, holding his aching jaw. "She'd probably never forgive me, Elzy!"

Gus Waymore guffawed and said, "Yeah, and she'll probably never forgive you for killin' *her* neither!"

Everyone except Willie Chance joined in the laughter. Small and wiry, Chance had been with McCarty for ten months, and at fifty he was the oldest member of the gang. Though he was good with a gun, he lacked the killer instinct and was the only gang member who had not committed murder. He did not think the murder of Sam Dunne was funny.

As the laughter died down Tom McCarty's gaze fell on the burlesque magazine in Bob's hands. His eyes went hard as flint steel. Snatching the magazine from his nephew's hands, he snarled, "I don't want you reading any more of that trash! It's that kind of stuff that makes no girl safe with you around!"

Bob's cheeks flushed. Leaping to his feet, he said through clenched teeth, "Give that back!"

Without warning McCarty swung his hand and gave his his nephew a stinging blow across the face with the magazine. In reflex Bob lashed out, but McCarty caught his wrist in midair and squeezed hard.

Looking his uncle straight in the eye, Bob hissed, "Give me back my magazine." In response, McCarty let go of his wrist and tore the magazine in two.

For a moment Bob stared incredulously at his uncle. Then a wild, insane look filled his eyes, and he swung a fist at the older man. McCarty blocked it and returned a powerful blow to the midsection, doubling Bob over and sending him careening into the wall. The whole room shook from the impact, which sent a picture crashing to the floor.

The rest of the gang watched impassively as McCarty tore the magazine into shreds while Bob rose unsteadily, fury burning in his eyes. Dropping his head, he charged across the room, catching his uncle in the chest. The two men staggered back against the window, shattering the pane. For a moment they stood locked in a bear hug, but then McCarty lifted the younger man off his feet, turned him around, and knocked his head back against the window frame.

As Bob howled and then sank his teeth into McCarty's shoulder, the older man twisted and spun his nephew around, suddenly unleashing an elbow that caught Bob flat on the nose. Blood spurted from Bob's nostrils as he fell backward, tumbling into two men. They quickly shoved him toward McCarty, who was coming after his nephew in a fiery rage, his face contorted with anger, a thick vein pulsing along the edge of his temple.

With blood running from his nose, Bob lunged at McCarty, his fury surging like a wild river rushing through a narrow canyon. McCarty steadied himself, timed his punch perfectly, and caught Bob flush on the jaw.

Just then the door to the hall was thrown open by the desk clerk, who had run up the stairs after hearing the window shatter. The young clerk tried to move as Bob's reeling form came sailing at him, but he could not dodge fast enough. The impact sent the two men backward, crashing into the railing at the top of the stairs. They went through it and flew over the edge, landing halfway down the staircase.

McCarty rubbed his shoulder where his nephew had torn flesh with his teeth. His anger not yet abated, he charged through the door and down the stairs. Flinging the clerk aside, he pounced on Bob, who was glassy eyed and groggy. Straddling the younger man, McCarty stung his face with several backhanded blows to clear his brain.

When Bob's eyes seemed to focus, McCarty sank steellike fingers into the younger man's hair and rasped heatedly, "I'm the boss of this outfit, sonny boy! As long as you want to run with us, you'll do what I tell you! Being a relation doesn't exempt you, understand?"

Bob was having trouble making his tongue work.

Shaking Bob's head by the hair, McCarty snapped, "I asked you a question! Do you understand who's boss here?"

Gasping, Bob said, "Yes."

Tightening his grip on the hair, McCarty said, "Then listen, kid, and listen good. I don't want you ever putting your hands on another woman. You stay away from the women. Understand?" When there was no immediate response, he shook Bob's head and half screamed, "You're not listening, kid! I said you stay away from the women or get out of this gang!"

Bob's face was sheet white, except for red marks where he'd been slapped and punched. He nodded in assent.

"Don't just shake your head!" snarled McCarty. "I want to hear you say it. You're going to stay away from the women or else. Now, let me hear you say it!"

Bob mumbled the words McCarty wanted to hear, but he wasn't saying it loud enough to suit McCarty, who backhanded him savagely again. "Say it so I can hear you!" he shouted.

Breathing unevenly and rolling his tongue around in his mouth, Bob said loudly, "No more women. I won't touch any more women. It'll be just as you say."

"Good," said McCarty, standing up. "Now let's go back up to the room."

While Bob was stumbling up the stairs, McCarty found the clerk, who had taken refuge behind the front desk, and gave him money to cover the damage, with some extra so that he would not bring in the law. The frightened clerk accepted it, thanking him.

As McCarty returned to the room Bob sat sulking in a corner on the floor. In order to cool the air a bit, Elzy Lay, who was still seated on the bed with the *Police Gazette* in his hands, said, "Hey, Tom, there's an article in here about Mark Young."

"Ask me if I care," McCarty replied blandly.

"You ought to," commented Elzy. "This guy is something. Says here that Young is the number one U.S. marshal in the whole western United States. He's cleaning up Wyoming and Montana like he was using a whisk broom."

"He better use more than a broom when he comes near me," growled McCarty.

"He's no doubt planning to use the Colt on his hip," spoke up Willie Chance.

"According to this article," Elzy Lay continued, "Young's got a draw like a rattler's tongue. Lists eight of the top gunfighters he has put beneath the sod in the last two years. Did you know that he killed Seth Morey?"

"Seth Morey?" echoed Gus Waymore. "I didn't think anybody could outdraw Morey."

"Neither did Morey," snickered Elzy.

"Hey, what's all this gunfighter talk?" said McCarty. "I'm not fool enough to draw against Young. Tom McCarty is no gunfighter. When I kill Young, my gun will already be in my hand."

"Article also tells about Young's rough handling of outlaws with his fists and the barrel of his gun," remarked Elzy Lay. "Gives the names of six outlaw gangs he's broken up in these same two years. Says some are behind bars at the penitentiary in Rawlins. Others are buried in cold, dark graves."

As a subdued silence came over the room, Elzy Lay added, "Fellas, we had best face one plain, hard fact.

Young has made it clear enough that he's after us. Especially McCarty. We'd best be on our toes."

Bob McCarty spoke up from where he sat. "So what's all this fearsome talk? The big-shot marshal is only one man. A single bullet in the right place will take care of him."

"Yeah," chortled McCarty. "The right place is where he wears that badge on his chest. When Young and I meet I'm going to put a hole right through that shiny badge."

"You bet you will, Uncle," said Bob, getting over his pout. "No stupid U.S. marshal is a match for you."

Tom McCarty stood up. Putting his hand to his jaw, he said, "I've got to find a dentist. This tooth is killing me." The gang watched silently as their leader headed out into the hall, closing the door behind him.

The handsome outlaw made his way down the stairs to where the clerk was piling broken pieces of the handrail. Looking up, the young man smiled nervously.

Standing over him, McCarty said, "I assume this burg has a dentist."

"Yes, sir, Mr. Holmes," said the clerk. "Down the street to your left—about half a block, on the other side of the street. Dr. Eli Swafford. He's Buffalo's only dentist."

The outlaw leader thanked the clerk and headed down the street. He found Swafford's office and pushed open the door. The dentist was seated in the chair, reading a newspaper and sipping whiskey from a small flask. Upon McCarty's entrance he snapped the newspaper closed quickly, attempting to hide the flask behind it.

Stepping inside, the dark-haired man said, "Are you the dentist?" As Swafford nodded sheepishly McCarty eyed the man's bloodshot eyes. Noting his foul breath, he asked, "Are you sober enough to pull a bad tooth?"

"Why sure, son." Swafford grinned. "I, uh . . . just use the spirits for medicinal purposes, you understand. Sit right down and let me take a gander at what's ailin' you."

McCarty eased down into the chair and opened his mouth. The dentist stood unsteadily over him and asked, "Now, just where are you feelin' the pain?"

McCarty pointed his finger at the spot on his jaw where the pain was concentrated. Swafford blinked slowly as he examined the place inside McCarty's mouth. "Ah, yes," he murmured. "I see the culprit." Reaching for his pliers, he said, "Won't take but a minute, and we'll be rid of it."

"Hey, hold on, Doc!" McCarty said, straightening up in the chair. "Aren't you going to give me something to ease the pain?"

"Oh, sure," Swafford said, his tongue a bit thick. "Here, take a swig of this." He handed him a whiskey bottle from a small cupboard.

McCarty eyed him warily, uncorked the bottle, and pulled deep. He gave it back to Swafford and settled back in the chair.

"I'll give you some more to wash your mouth out with after the tooth is extracted," Swafford said encouragingly.

Wavering a bit with the pliers, the dentist reached into Tom McCarty's mouth, clamped hard on the tooth, and began working it loose. McCarty gripped the chair, swearing in spite of the pliers. Swafford mumbled something about the tooth having roots that went to his patient's ankles, as he relentlessly swiveled his wrist, uprooting the stubborn tooth. McCarty half screamed another swear word, spraying Swafford with blood as he stiffened his whole body against the excruciating pain.

Suddenly the half-drunk dentist stumbled backward as the tooth came out. McCarty sat up, looking for somewhere to spit the blood. Swafford reached toward a shelf behind him and seized an old coffee can. "Here," he said, shoving it in the patient's hand. "Expect—expectorate in this."

McCarty emptied his mouthful of blood into the can and grabbed the whiskey bottle. For several minutes he took gulps of whiskey, swishing it around in his mouth and spitting it in the can. Finally he quit spitting and turned to drinking the amber-colored liquid.

The dentist threw McCarty's tooth in a wastebasket nearby and said boldly, "That'll be five dollars, sir."

McCarty stood up, swaying slightly. He paid the man and walked out, carrying the whiskey bottle.

At ten o'clock the next morning the gang sat their horses in a wooded spot near the track some twenty miles north of Buffalo. Casting a glance up the tracks, McCarty said, "Train ought to be along any minute."

Elzy Lay said, "This should be a good heist, boss. I wish Butch was along. Train robberies are his specialty."

Tom McCarty, whose mouth was still hurting, commented, "Butch is all right, Elzy, but he has that stupid objection to killing. Man makes a better outlaw if he's not skittish about shedding blood."

Willie Chance spoke up, "I think Butch has a point, Tom. Killing folks in a robbery is not necessary."

McCarty eyed Chance as if he'd just seen him for the first time. "It is necessary, Willie," he said stiffly. "When a gang has a reputation for killing during their robberies, it makes victims more cooperative when you draw guns on them and announce who you are."

"He's right," Elzy Lay told Willie. "You've seen it work since you've been with the gang." Then squinting at him, he said, "Come to think of it, I don't think I've seen you gun anybody down yet."

Willie's features crimsoned. "I've taken as much loot off folks as you have," he said defensively.

McCarty set his black eyes on Chance. "Now that Elzy mentions it, Willie, you haven't even pulled a trigger yet since you've been with us."

"I would if somebody was going to shoot one of us," Willie said, scrubbing a palm over his brow.

"That's not good enough, Willie," blustered McCarty. "I'm making you an assignment right now. On this job today I want you to kill somebody. Got it? But we don't kill women, you understand?"

Bob gave his uncle a dismal look.

"But we do kill men," McCarty went on. "You do it today, Willie."

Willie Chance swallowed hard, nodding his assent. His blood went cold. In all of his outlaw career he had never even shot anyone, let alone killed a person.

Matt Warner, one of McCarty's most reliable men, pointed a finger northward. "Train's coming, Tom."

All eyes turned to see the puff of black smoke on the horizon. Warner set his gaze a half mile north of the spot where they waited and noticed that the train would pass very close to a tall rock formation. He suggested to McCarty that he ride to the rock, climb it, and drop into the open coal car when the train passed by. He could then slide down into the engine and force the engineer to stop the train.

McCarty liked the idea and told Warner to hop to it. Then turning to the others, McCarty said, "Get your masks out, boys."

One by one they reached into their saddlebags and produced the stocking caps they had converted into masks by cutting dollar-size holes for their eyes. McCarty had insisted from the first time he pulled a holdup that his men wear masks. As a result Tom McCarty's likeness had never been printed on a wanted poster, since the law had no photograph or drawing of him. His name was known and feared, but his face remained a mystery.

Less than ten minutes later, as Matt Warner was holding the engineer and fireman at gunpoint and the engine was grinding to a halt, half the gang leaped inside the coaches to rob the passengers. Among them was Willie Chance, his mind locked on the grisly task he'd been assigned.

The other half of the gang, which included Tom and Bob McCarty, ran to the baggage coach, which reportedly contained the money-laden safe. The doors of the coach were locked. McCarty banged on the side of the door, shouting, "Hey, in there! This is a holdup! Open the door!"

There was movement inside, but no response to his command.

Turning to his nephew, McCarty said, "Go get the dynamite." While Bob obeyed, McCarty shouted, "Hey, you inside the baggage coach! We want the money in that safe! Open up or we'll blow it open!"

There was still no response.

Bob came running back with two sets of dynamite sticks. Each set had four sticks wrapped together with heavy twine, with an ominous dangling fuse. McCarty took one of them, laid it on the metal ledge at the foot of the door, and lit the fuse. The men scattered, throwing themselves on the ground. A moment later the charge exploded, the impact rocking over the open prairie. The force of the explosion tore off the doors on both sides of the coach and blew part of the roof to smithereens.

The two men inside the coach were dead as the gang climbed into the smoking mass. They quickly located the safe, covered with sooty film and debris. McCarty told them to clear everything away, then head for cover. Bob handed him the other dynamite packet, which McCarty placed on a box next to the handle of the safe. As soon as the rest of the gang had left the coach, McCarty lit the fuse. With a run and a leap, he hit the ground, ran farther, and went flat.

Again the prairie reverberated with the deep sound of the dynamite exploding. Moments later McCarty and the gang members were back aboard what was left of the baggage coach, stuffing their saddlebags with money from the safe.

When the bags were loaded on the horses, McCarty hollered for his men to mount. Suddenly shots came from inside one of the passenger coaches. Swinging into his saddle, McCarty drew his gun. As the four gang members who were inside dashed out to mount their horses, McCarty saw the conductor look out a window, and he squeezed off a shot, hitting the conductor between the eyes.

McCarty rode to the engine, where Matt Warner was waiting to be the last man off the train. "Okay!" he hollered to Warner. "Let's go!"

As Warner was running away from the engine McCarty shot the engineer and the fireman. One of them peeled out of the engine, hitting the ground. The other crumpled dead on the floor of the cab.

Holstering his gun, McCarty turned to his nephew and said, "You have some more dynamite, don't you?"

"Yeah. Six sticks. But they're not bound together."

"That's all right. Give me one of them "

McCarty took the stick of dynamite from his nephew's hand and rode close to the engine, which stood like a giant hissing beast. Lighting the fuse, McCarty leaned from his horse and tossed it into the cab and up next to the boiler. Swinging his hand, he motioned for his men to follow him. They were eighty yards away when the boiler went. Fire, smoke, and steam blossomed into the sky with a double explosion—first the dynamite and then the boiler itself.

The gang pulled the masks from over their heads and rode away, everyone feeling jubilant except Willie Chance, who had not found the nerve to shoot anyone during the robbery. He felt sick inside as he imagined McCarty's reaction.

The nine robbers rode into Buffalo, pulling up in front of the Gold Nugget Saloon. As the breeze carried away the dust stirred up by their horses, Tom McCarty said, "You boys go on in and start celebrating. I'm going back to see that dentist. My mouth is killing me."

Dr. Eli Swafford was just finishing up with a patient as McCarty entered his office. His eyes were clear this time, and he seemed quite sober. Looking at McCarty, he said, "I didn't expect to see you back."

"Something's wrong in here, Doc," McCarty replied. "I want you to take another look."

"Sure." Swafford nodded. "Be with you in a moment."

Within ten minutes the dentist ushered out the other patient and told McCarty to get in the chair. McCarty slid into it saying, "I've still got the pain I had before, Doc."

Swafford's bushy eyebrows arched. "Really? I don't understand that. Let's take a look-see."

McCarty opened his mouth wide as the dentist probed around the hole left by the tooth he'd extracted the day before. "Oh, dear," he said half to himself.

"What's the matter?" asked McCarty.

"Well, sir," came the reply, "yesterday I took a little too much of my medicine. I wasn't seeing too good."

"Spit it out, Doc," the outlaw said, pushing Swafford's hand away. "What did you do wrong yesterday?"

Clearing his throat nervously, the dentist mumbled, "I pulled the wrong tooth."

McCarty straightened up, shaking his head in disbelief. His nostrils flared. "*You pulled the wrong tooth?*" he bellowed. Jumping from the chair, he began to call Dr. Eli Swafford every profane name he could think of.

The small-framed dentist trembled, his eyes wide. When McCarty ran out of breath, Swafford said in an aggrieved voice, "Well, you needn't tear a man's head off. I really am sorry. I'll pull the correct one if you'll sit down again. There will be no charge."

McCarty swore again. "You bet there'll be no charge, buster!" Dropping back into the chair, he growled, "You better pull the right one this time!"

The dentist produced a new bottle of whiskey from the cupboard and handed it to his patient. While McCarty popped the cork, he held the full weight of his stare on Swafford. Downing a healthy gulp, he said, "Okay, get it over with."

This time Swafford put the pliers on the correct tooth, which began to give way more easily due to its rotting condition. While the dentist worked it loose, fury grew within Tom McCarty. He had lost a good tooth and suffered needlessly because of this man's drunken incompetence.

When the tooth came out McCarty washed his mouth with the raw, amber-colored liquid, swallowed a good amount, and lifted himself out of the chair.

Looking up at him in trepidation, Swafford said weakly, "You can even keep the bottle of whiskey."

McCarty's temper had reached the boiling point. Looking the dentist square in the eye, he dashed the whiskey bottle to the floor, shattering the glass and splattering whiskey all over. Swafford's eyes bulged, and his body jerked at the sound of the impact.

Level eyed, McCarty said in a menacing tone, "Get in the chair."

"Whaa—"

"Get in the chair!"

As he said it, McCarty grabbed the dentist and rammed him into the chair, noticing that Swafford was so frightened he offered no resistance. Holding him in the chair with one hand, the angry outlaw took the pliers with the other. "Open your mouth," he commanded, swinging the pliers to the trembling man's quivering lips.

Eyes frozen wide with fear, Swafford obeyed, and McCarty then clamped the pliers on his two lower front teeth and twisted them from their sockets. Blood spurted, and McCarty laughed as Swafford howled. McCarty opened the pliers, leaving the bloody teeth lying in the dentist's mouth. Dropping the pliers, he cupped a hand under Swafford's chin, clamping his mouth closed.

"Swallow both of them!" he hollered.

Swafford, apparently afraid even to close his eyes, watched McCarty and gulped down the two teeth and a mouthful of blood.

Breathing heavily, Tom McCarty released him and turned toward the door. Pausing in the opening, he said, "Let that be a lesson to you. Don't drink when you're going to be pulling a man's tooth."

Swafford nodded wordlessly, eyes still bulging.

The Tom McCarty gang was in a good mood and laughing boisterously when McCarty entered the saloon—everyone, that is, except Willie Chance. Chance knew that he was in for trouble from McCarty, and he dreaded it.

"Hey, boss!" Elzy Lay greeted him as he sat down at one of the tables. "How's the tooth?"

"Fine. Stupid dentist pulled the wrong one yesterday."

Elzy and the others wanted to laugh, but the look on McCarty's face warned them not to, so nothing more was said.

McCarty ordered a bottle of whiskey and began pouring it down. Within a few moments the pain began to ease. For some time he talked in a low voice of his plan to return to the Circle D and try to woo Molly Dunne into marriage. Periodically he looked around to make sure the bartender was not picking up on the conversation.

As he talked McCarty's eyes fell on Willie Chance, and he thought of the assignment he'd given the wiry little outlaw. "Hey, Willie," he said, keeping his voice low.

Chance knew what was coming. A chill washed over him, and cold sweat beaded his brow. He took off his hat and drew a sleeve across his forehead. Forcing his eyes to meet McCarty's gaze, he said, "Yes, sir?"

Expecting a positive answer, McCarty smiled and asked, "You take care of that little assignment I gave you today?"

The other men looked at each other fleetingly.

Chance swallowed twice. "I—uh . . . no, I didn't."

McCarty's lips turned downward and his gaze grew hot. "Why not?" he demanded.

Chance shifted uncomfortably on the chair. Barely audible, he said, "I just couldn't do it."

McCarty glanced over at the bartender, then turned back to his men and said, "Let's go outside, boys."

The gang filed out into the blazing sunlight and followed McCarty to a vacant lot across the street. Willie Chance's knees were shaking as the leader of the gang turned to face him.

"You deliberately disobeyed my orders, Willie," he said through clenched teeth.

Chance knew there was no use trying to defend himself. He nodded glumly.

A wild expression formed on Tom McCarty's face, much like his men had occasionally seen on the face of his nephew. Stepping close to Chance, he breathed hotly, "Nobody runs with this gang who can't or won't take my orders. We talked about that when you joined up."

"But . . . but . . . when I joined up you didn't say I had to kill nobody," the little man squeaked.

"That goes without saying," blurted McCarty. "This isn't a Sunday school, mister. This is the hottest gang west of the Mississippi! And it's going to get hotter. You don't fit in, Willie."

Chance's face was ashen. He stood like a statue, waiting for the storm that was surely coming. McCarty was going to exclude him from the gang, but it would not come without a beating. McCarty might even kill him.

Fixing the little man with his burning eyes, McCarty hissed, "I'm going to let you live, Willie. You can thank me for that." He waited for Chance to speak. It did not come. "I said you can thank me for not killing you!"

Chance nodded, his body shaking. "Th-thank you, Mr. McCarty, f-for not killing me."

"But you disobeyed my orders," McCarty said, looking insane.

"Yes, s-sir."

"You don't get any cut of the loot from the train we just robbed. You disobeyed me."

"Yes, sir."

"But you do get punished, Willie."

McCarty curled his upper lip into a rabid smile, then

without warning jerked Chance's gun from its holster and clouted him on the head. The little man went down in a heap, moaned, and rolled over. McCarty kicked him in the stomach, then the groin. Finally he kicked him in the face several times until Chance lay still. McCarty then opened the cylinder of Chance's revolver and dumped the cartridges on the ground. Kneeling down, he filled the barrel and cylinder with dirt, then jammed the gun back in the holster.

When Chance began to stir, McCarty picked him up and repeatedly slapped his face until he acknowledged that he understood what McCarty was saying. Then McCarty pulled Chance's face close to his and railed, "Find your horse and get lost, Willie! If I ever see you again, I'll kill you!"

Willie Chance stumbled away toward the livery where the gang had lodged their horses. He was hurting, as well as burning with anger, but he knew better than to try to take on McCarty—especially in front of the whole gang.

When Chance had disappeared from sight, McCarty turned to his men and said, "We pull out in the morning, boys. We'll swing down to Osage, rob the two banks there, then head for Sundance."

As planned, they rode out of Buffalo early in the morning on July 2—two days before the Independence Day celebration at Devil's Tower.

Chapter Three

At Devil's Tower on July 4 the crowd cheered and applauded as the Circle D wagon rumbled to a halt. Two women and a man were in the wagon seat. The hero of the day sat in the back, waving at his admirers. Behind the wagon on horseback rode sixteen of the ranch's cowhands.

The band struck up a rousing tune as Bill Rogers stood in the wagon bed, his tall frame ramrod straight. A lean man in his late twenties, he wore a thick handlebar mustache, which counterbalanced his thinning brown hair. The crowd pushed close, with dozens of voices crying for him to speak. Above the din he shouted that the speech would come as soon as he made his way to the hastily built platform where Mayor Frye was waiting to begin the ceremonies.

Rogers hopped from the wagon, and autograph seekers rushed to him. Elbowing his way through the press of people, he told them to wait until he made the climb. He was not a celebrity yet.

As the crowd followed Rogers to the brightly decorated platform, Cory Bell wrapped the reins around the wagon's brake handle, climbed down, and turned to help the two ladies down. Despite being only twenty-four—and not looking a day older—Cory had been promoted from cowhand to foreman of the Circle D by Sam Dunne six months before Dunne was murdered. He stood five feet ten inches tall and was of medium build. Women generally considered him good-looking in a youthful sort of way, and they particularly admired his thick and curly dark-brown hair.

Cory Bell had been intensely loyal to Sam Dunne and felt the same loyalty for Sam's widow. He'd worked at the Circle D since he was nineteen and through the years had especially looked forward to the occasional visits by Molly Dunne's younger sister, Anna Laura Leslie. Cory had fallen in love with Anna Laura the first time he laid eyes on her, and that love had deepened over the years. He was elated that she now lived at the ranch, but he suffered inward pain when he saw her occupied with other men.

Anna Laura Leslie scooted across the wagon seat and allowed Cory to help her down. At nineteen she was an alluring brown-eyed woman with long strawberry-blond hair. She wore it differently every day, and Cory had yet to see a style he did not like. Anna Laura's fine-featured face and well-developed figure were the talk of the young men in the Sundance area—and the envy of the young women.

"Thank you, Cory," Anna Laura chirped as he eased her slowly to the ground. When her feet touched earth Cory was looking deep into her brown eyes and forgot to let go of her. "I said, *thank you*," came her firm voice.

"Oh, sure," he gasped, releasing her and stepping back. Smoothing her dress, Anna Laura gazed toward the platform, then turned and walked in that direction.

Molly Dunne, still seated in the wagon, smiled as Cory walked around to her side. After he helped her down she said gently, "Cory, just go easy with Anna Laura. I can tell that she likes you better than any of the other young men she sees, but she's not quite ready to settle down yet. Bide your time and I'm certain you'll win out."

"Thanks, Molly," he said, grinning boyishly. "It's just that I don't want to let her slip through my fingers into some other guy's hands."

"You won't, if you don't push her," Molly advised.

Shaking his head, the youthful foreman again grinned infectiously. "I'm trying. But it's hard."

"I understand. Now you run on with Anna Laura, and I'll see you later."

Molly watched Cory move into the crowd and thread

his way toward her sister. The young widow was beautiful in her own right, with thick coal-black hair. At five feet she was an inch taller than Anna Laura and as well proportioned, but there was a trace of sadness in her ink-blue eyes.

She was suddenly aware of five or six women making their way toward her, and as they drew near she smiled a welcome. "Good morning, ladies."

They greeted her, then Dorothy Andrews, wife of a neighboring rancher, said, "How's the boss of the Circle D?"

"As well as can be expected," she responded. "I have some good helpers. Cory Bell has the men all working smoothly, and my sister Anna Laura is living with me now. She helps fill in some of the lonely spots." When the women showed interest in Anna Laura, Molly explained that she had been in Kansas with an aunt since their parents died.

"What's this I hear about you being courted by a handsome, wealthy man from Denver?" piped up Sally Jardine, another rancher's wife.

"You must have Walter Smythe in mind," said Molly, "but he's not courting me. He showed an interest in buying the ranch a short time before Sam was . . . was killed. He's a very kind man. Whenever he's in the area he stops by."

"Are you saying he's not shown some romantic interest?" queried Bertha Mullins, wife of a Sundance businessman.

Molly's face tinted. "Well, yes, he has. But it's all on his part. I have no such interest in him."

"Word is that Mr. Smythe has asked you to marry him," added Bertha.

"He has," admitted Molly. "But it's out of the question. Sam has been gone only two months. I'm not considering marrying anyone at present—and won't be for a long time. Besides, I'm not in love with Mr. Smythe."

Molly's plain talk brought the conversation to an end just as Mayor Albert Frye mounted the colorfully decorated platform. The brass band played a few bars of fanfare, and then Frye raised his hands to gain the crowd's attention. As they grew quiet he lifted his voice and said, "Ladies and gentlemen! We are gathered today for a most momentous occasion! As all of you know, a brave young cowboy from the Sundance community is going to defy gravity and death before your very eyes by performing a feat that has never been done. He is going to scale the sheer rock face of the awesome tower behind me and stand on its very top!"

While Frye was giving the history of the jutting volcanic rock formation and explaining the scientific view as to its creation, Molly Dunne stood at the rear of the crowd and let her eyes lift toward Devil's Tower. The vast, impressive monolith loomed skyward, casting its shadow across the Belle Fourche Valley.

Molly, born and raised in the Sundance area, studied the tower, as she had many times before. She always found it captivating and enchanting. Even at that moment the sunlight was giving it a different appearance from a few seconds before. The tower seemed to change from minute to minute, with the fluted, weather-pocked columns catching light and forming shadows in nearly endless combinations.

Mayor Frye's words caught Molly's attention again as he explained that the climb would be 865 feet up the sheer face of the tower and that when Bill Rogers stood on the top, he would not only be 1280 feet above the valley floor, but 5260 feet above sea level. This would place him just twenty feet short of standing one mile high.

Frye next went into the Indian folklore of the tower, explaining that there were several legends as to its origin. The Kiowa, Cheyenne, and Blackfoot each had their own stories, passed down for centuries by their ancestors. He gave a brief sketch of the Blackfoot and Cheyenne legends, then told the most captivating one—that of the Kiowa.

The Kiowa called the tower *Mateo Tepee,* meaning Grizzly Bear Lodge. According to the Kiowa, their tribe once camped upstream on the Belle Fourche River, where there were many bears. One day seven little girls were playing together at a distance south of the camp. Suddenly a giant grizzly charged out of the forest. The girls ran for their lives as the huge bear chased after them.

When the bear was about to catch them the seven girls climbed up on a large, low rock about three feet in height. They could hear the bear shortening the distance behind them. Frightened, they began to pray to the gods to take pity on them and save them. Suddenly, the rock began to rise up out of the ground, lifting the seven little girls higher, out of reach of the bear. The giant beast began to scratch at the rock, attempting to reach the girls; the bear's claw marks could now be seen as the cracks between the long, fluted columns.

The rock continued to lift the children higher into the sky while the bear clawed, scratched, and roared in frustration. The Kiowa say that the gods then raised the seven little girls into the heavens, where they remain to this day, twinkling in the night sky as the seven stars of the Pleiades in the constellation Taurus.

The crowd applauded the story, although the majority of them had already heard it.

Frye followed with an explanation as to how the tower got its current name. It was called Tower of the Gods by the several tribes that lived in the area before white men first appeared. When the white explorers came the Indians wanted them to stay out of the region. In order to frighten them away, the Indians told them that the towering rock formation belonged to a bad god who was jealous of his tower and the surrounding area. He would kill the whites if they stayed. Hence, the explorers carried away the tale that in the western edge of the Black Hills there was a giant tower belonging to the devil. From that time on, it became known as Devil's Tower.

The mayor swung a hand toward the tall man standing beside the platform. In a bellowing voice he said, "And now, ladies and gentlemen, I present the brave soul who will attempt something that has never been done by mortal man! Before your very eyes he will scale the dreadful, sheer face of Devil's Tower! Let's welcome . . . *Bill Rogers!*"

The lanky Circle D cowboy bounded up the platform steps while the crowd cheered and the band blared out a deafening fanfare. He raised his hands, and slowly the ovation faded to silence.

Rogers carried with him one of the oak pegs he had made. Raising it for all to see, he explained how he would build a ladder up the face of the tower by driving the pegs into the natural cracks between the fluted columns. He turned toward the tower and pointed out that he'd already begun the ladder a few days before so as to conserve time today. The crowd could see the dark stakes dotting the wall, ending about a third of the way up the tower.

"Now," Rogers said excitedly, "I need three volunteers to help me carry the sacks of pegs to the spot on the tower's base where I will climb the ones I've already driven and continue on. Those volunteers will remain at the base through the duration of the climb and send me pegs on a rope as I need them."

Cory Bell stood beside Anna Laura Leslie, a twinge of jealousy pricking his heart. The beautiful strawberry-blond woman was totally entranced by Bill Rogers and the heroic feat he was about to undertake. Cory thought about volunteering but decided against it. It was going to be a long day. He wanted to stay close to Anna Laura.

There was no rush of volunteers; people knew that the men who worked at the base would not have a good view of the climb. Bill Rogers's eyes roamed the crowd as he waited for the first person to come forth. Finally a ten-year-old local boy named Danny Yarrow stepped forward and raised his hand. "I'll help you, Bill!" he exclaimed.

"I don't know, Danny," Rogers said. "You're a little bit young. I—"

"Let him help, Bill!" a husky male voice called out. "I'll come along too!"

Rogers recognized Danny's father, Clint Yarrow, and a smile spread across his lean face. "Okay, Clint! You and Danny come out!" Running his gaze over the sea of faces again, he said, "I need one more, folks! Who will help me?"

Anna Laura turned to the curly-headed man beside her and said in a low voice, "Why don't you do it, Cory?"

Cory's face crimsoned slightly. Not quite meeting her eyes, he replied, "I would rather stay here with you."

Anna Laura smiled, hunched her shoulders, and said, "It's your choice."

Abruptly another voice called from the crowd. "I'll help, Bill!" It was Abe Willard, another Circle D cowboy. Willard moved forward and joined Clint and Danny Yarrow, who now stood near the platform. The crowd applauded.

Mayor Frye stepped to the front of the platform again, placing his hand on Rogers's shoulder. "Bill," he said with admiration in his voice, "we the people of Sundance and the surrounding area are proud of you for what you are about to do. You represent to the young people—and to all of us gathered here—what America is all about. Here in this rugged land of the West we are carving out a new frontier with the same kind of courage and determination that you're displaying before our eyes today. You are the red-blooded example of what America is made of!"

While Frye was making his speech two women approached and mounted the platform. One of them carried a red, white, and blue shirt and the other bore a large American flag.

The mayor told Rogers and the crowd that the shirt had been made by Mrs. Pearl Sanders of Sundance. Smiling broadly, Rogers took the colorful shirt from Mrs. Sanders and held it up for the crowd to see. On the back, white letters against a red and blue background read KING OF DEVIL'S TOWER.

The crowd cheered, and as Rogers put on the shirt, the band played a rousing tune. When he was ready to begin his climb the band swung into the "Star-Spangled Banner." The entire crowd was instantly on its feet. Rogers unfurled Old Glory, allowing the wind to wave it in a dramatic manner. Hands were over hearts, and military veterans stood saluting at attention. Many eyes were filled with tears.

When the anthem had ended, Mayor Frye introduced the Reverend Elijah Hanks, minister of the Community Church of Deadwood, South Dakota. A hush came over the crowd as the minister led them in prayer, asking for Bill Rogers's safety.

When the "Amen" was said a photographer approached

Rogers, asking if he could take a photograph of him alone and with his three volunteers. Rogers complied. Powder flashed as the pictures were taken with the gigantic tower in the background. After taking the second picture the photographer laughed and said, "Bill, will it be all right if I photograph your body when you fall and hit the ground?"

The crowd was silent until Rogers retorted, "Only if you'll come and stand where I can fall on you." Then laughter filled the air.

The band struck up a military march as Rogers, Abe Willard, Clint Yarrow, and young Danny mounted the base and headed for the sheer face of Devil's Tower. At the foot of the ladder Rogers folded the flag and tied it to his back. Then he began the dangerous ascent.

Over an hour later, with Rogers inserting new pegs nearly three hundred and fifty feet up the face of the tower, Harry Longabaugh—the Sundance Kid—shifted his position. He was sitting on a log and had just lit a cigarette. Through the smoke he saw a tall figure ride up to the fringe of the crowd, pull his horse to a halt, and lift his gaze to where Bill Rogers had become a miniature figure against the buff-colored tower wall.

Leaning over to Butch Cassidy, Sundance said in a low voice, "Hey, Butch, we might better clear out of here!"

Etta Place frowned at Sundance, then turned her eyes to Cassidy when he asked, "What are you talking about?"

Sundance looked over his shoulder to make sure he was right, then turned back to Cassidy. "It's Mark Young."

Cassidy suddenly looked as though he'd just smelled sour pickles. "Mark Young? Where?"

Sundance pointed with his jaw toward the spot where the United States marshal sat his horse, and Cassidy focused on him and swore. Snarling, he said, "Why should we run? Young ain't got nothing on us. He can't prove I was in on that Denver train robbery with McCarty—and the only cattle you've rustled in his territory lately have already been sold. Relax, Kid. Enjoy the show. Young can't touch us."

Etta laid a worried hand on Sundance's arm. "Sundance, is Butch right? I mean, Sheriff Naylor is one thing. But a federal man is something else."

Patting her hand, the Sundance Kid looked into her eyes and said soothingly, "Yeah, honey, Butch is right. Young can't lay a finger on us. I just get jumpy when he's around. Those pale gray eyes of his seem to look right through me. It's like he knows what I'm thinking—and everything I've ever done."

Butch chortled. "Hey, Kid, I said relax. Mark Young may be some people's little tin god, but he puts his pants on every morning the same way you do. He can't read your mind, and he don't know any more than any other man. So he's fast with that gun on his hip. It don't matter, 'cause we ain't gonna try drawing against him. Come on, now. Your sweetie here came to see the show. Let her."

The Sundance Kid grinned nervously, put his arm around Etta, and lifted his eyes toward the tower. Etta was shaky. She knew that when Sundance felt cornered he became extremely dangerous.

Sheriff Jim Naylor, a veteran lawman with thirty years under his belt—and a paunch over it—was moving among the crowd when he spotted Mark Young reining in. Young was dismounting when Naylor walked up and said, "Well, if it isn't Uncle Sam's finest!"

The two lawmen shook hands while Naylor asked, "What brings you out here, Mark?"

Young hitched up his gun belt. "I'm looking for Butch Cassidy. He's in the area. Figured he might show up here."

"Well, you figured right," Naylor said, turning to spit something from his mouth. "Butch and his pal Sundance are both here. The Kid's got his teacher girlfriend with him."

Young's eyes brightened. "You talked to them?"

"Yep."

"They give you a sensible reason for being here?"

"I guess you could call it that. Said they are just patriotic. They've come to celebrate the Fourth of July with their fellow Americans."

Young smiled. "I question how much they love this country. The only thing they love is what they can rob, swindle, or bilk from its citizens."

The sheriff nodded in agreement, then furrowing his brow, asked, "You got something on Butch?"

"Might have. Where's the horse he's riding?"

Jim Naylor had seen the two outlaws and Etta Place ride in. With a jerk of his head, he led Young to a spot where three horses were tied to a small pine tree. Laying his hand on the rump of a white-stockinged bay mare, he said, "This is the one Cassidy was on."

The U.S. marshal pulled a slip of paper from his shirt pocket and unfolded it. As he did so he asked, "Do you know where they are in the crowd?" When Naylor nodded, Young added, "Can they see us from there?"

"Nope. They're behind those boulders over there."

"Good," breathed Young as he held the unfolded paper next to the bay's flank.

Naylor saw at once that the drawing of a brand on the sheet of paper matched the brand on the bay. "Stole it?"

"Yes. From a rancher near Kaycee. I've got Mr. Butch Cassidy red-handed."

"How you want to handle it?" asked the sheriff.

"Carefully," responded Young. "I hate to try to take him in this crowd. Somebody could get shot—not that I would mind if it was Butch or Sundance, but I sure don't want anyone else hit. Not even the girlfriend."

"Yeah," Naylor agreed. "Any kind of a scuffle could get her injured—or killed. I don't know why an educated, intelligent woman like her would get mixed up with the likes of the Sundance Kid anyhow."

"World's made up of puzzles, Jim," observed the marshal. "Puzzles me why any man would want to be an outlaw, having to run and hide all the time, looking over his shoulder for the glint of a badge. Most of them spend so much time behind bars, they would make a lot more money if they'd simply work an honest job."

Naylor lifted his hat and scratched his head. "You're right about that, my boy." He chuckled. "But then, what would men like you and me do if there weren't outlaws?"

Mark Young looked up to where Bill Rogers was inching his way up the side of Devil's Tower. "Guess I'd be a rock-climbing cowboy," he snickered.

Young looked the stolen horse over, pondering how to

arrest Butch Cassidy without getting anyone else hurt. Then he said, "Jim, I'll have to catch Cassidy on this mare before I can arrest him. Otherwise he'll deny ever seeing it. I'll just bide my time until he and Sundance decide to leave. Then I'll play it by ear just how to take him."

Leaning down, Young loosened the cinch on the stolen horse. He fixed it so that it would swivel downward if Cassidy tried to ride away but so that he would not notice it if he mounted up in a hurry. Any attempt on Cassidy's part to make a run for it would be foiled.

Just as Mark Young straightened up, he heard the crowd gasp. Quickly he and the sheriff looked toward the face of the tower. One of the oak pegs had suddenly come loose under Rogers's weight, and he was clinging precariously by one hand to another peg, his feet dangling freely. Everyone in the crowd was frozen by the sight. The Reverend Elijah Hanks folded his hands and began praying, his eyes glued to the frightening scene on the face of Devil's Tower.

Rogers flattened himself against the wall while still hanging on by one hand. With effort he lifted his other hand and worked it toward the peg, and within a few seconds he was holding on to the peg with both hands. There were sighs of relief all over the throng. Moments later he'd fully recovered himself and started climbing again. There was a roar of approval from the crowd, along with applause.

The scare over, the vendors began to circulate, selling peanuts and candy. Whiskey bottles were in evidence among the crowd, being shared by the men. Doc Witherspoon had gathered around his converted stagecoach a group of elderly women, who were more interested in his spiel about the youth-providing effects of the Indian River Elixir than they were in Rogers's hair-raising climb.

Mark Young asked the sheriff to show him where Cassidy and Sundance were, and Naylor led him through the trees and around some boulders to a spot where he could get a clear view of the outlaws' position. They were seated on fallen logs with Etta Place between them. The Sundance Kid was taking a swig from a whiskey bottle.

The two lawmen backed out of sight. Young said, "Jim,

will you stay close and keep an eye on them? There's
someone here I need to see."

"Sure." Naylor nodded.

"If they try to leave before I get back, you sing out."

"Will do," the sheriff said with a tight grin.

Jim Naylor watched the broad-shouldered U.S. marshal
pick his way among the boulders and head for the spot
where the wagons and buggies were parked. "Dollar to a
doughnut I know who he's going to see," the sheriff said to
himself.

Chapter Four

Anna Laura Leslie sat beside her sister on the seat of the Circle D wagon and watched with admiration as Bill Rogers scaled mammoth Devil's Tower. Like a puppy, Cory Bell had followed her to the wagon and now sat leaning against the front wheel closest to Anna Laura.

Cory felt more than a touch of jealousy when the strawberry-blond woman said, "Oh, Molly, isn't Bill the very bravest man you've ever known?"

From the corner of her eye Molly saw Cory stiffen. "I don't know if I'd go that far," Molly answered her sister. "Certainly Bill is brave, but there are lots of brave men—and many kinds of courage and bravery. Take Cory, for instance. He's very courageous. How many men his age would have the wherewithal to take on a job like his?"

Anna Laura did not answer, and Cory Bell did not look at her.

Suddenly Molly's gaze fell on the broad-shouldered form of Mark Young ambling toward the wagon. She smiled broadly, lifted her hand to wave, and saw Young smile back and quicken his pace.

"Who's that, Molly?" asked Anna Laura.

"Why, that's Mark Young, honey. You remember him."

"Oh, of course." Anna Laura nodded. "It's been such a long time since I've seen him."

The U.S. marshal greeted and shook hands with Cory.

Then looking up at the widow, he said, "Hello, Molly. Are you doing all right?"

Still smiling, Molly Dunne assured him she was fine, then laid a hand on her sister's shoulder and said, "Bet you don't know who this is."

Mark Young looked at the lovely young woman. "I wouldn't if Ken Eastman hadn't told me in town that your sister had come to live with you. Little Anna Laura! Who would have guessed that she'd turn out so beautiful?"

Anna Laura blushed, but Cory knew she was basking in the compliment. "Why, thank you, Mark," she said coyly.

"Last time I saw you, Anna Laura, you were just a freckle-faced kid."

"Girls do have a way of growing up," put in Molly.

Holding Anna Laura's gaze, Young said, "I'm mighty glad you're here with Molly, Anna Laura. She needs you."

The pretty widow started to climb down from the wagon, and Young hastened to help her. When her feet touched the ground she said, "Can an old friend have a hug?"

As Young took Molly into his arms and held her close, his heart drummed his ribs and his blood raced. There was no question that he was still in love with Molly—and that he always would be. He thought of his plan to propose one day to the beautiful brunette. Then he felt a coldness run through him as he remembered that a wealthy man named Walter Smythe also wanted Molly.

Young's thoughts were interrupted when Anna Laura spoke from the wagon, saying, "Hey, I'm an old friend too. How about a hug for me?"

Cory reluctantly helped Anna Laura down, knowing that she would embrace the marshal. But Mark Young hugged Anna Laura only briefly. As he released her Molly asked him, "What brings you here?"

"Sort of a mix of business and pleasure. The pleasure is seeing you. The business I'll take care of later." Not wanting to announce his plans to arrest Butch Cassidy, he turned toward the tower and said, "Sure hope he makes it."

"He will," spoke up Anna Laura. "Bill's an expert."

Cory Bell felt his stomach go sour, but at that moment Young diverted his attention by saying, "Cory, I've been given a good report on you. Let me commend you for the job you're doing in helping Molly to carry on with the ranch."

"Thanks, Mark," responded the curly-headed foreman. "The Dunnes have always been very good to me. It's only right that I do all I can to keep things running smoothly."

Looking at Molly, Mark Young said, "They have some sarsaparilla over there. Can I buy you some?"

"That would be nice," she said, taking his arm.

As Young and Molly walked away Anna Laura said to Cory, "They make a nice-looking pair, don't they?"

Relieved that Anna Laura showed no infatuation for the ruggedly handsome marshal, Cory said, "Yeah. I hope she'll find somebody like him when her mourning time is over. She's too young to spend the rest of her life alone."

Anna Laura had yet to meet the land developer from Denver named Smythe. Curious as to Cory's reaction to him, she said, "What about this Walter Smythe?"

"I don't like him," came the young man's quick reply. "There's something about him I don't cotton to. Besides, he just doesn't fit with Molly."

Watching the couple disappear into the crowd, Anna Laura said, "Mark used to have it bad for Molly. Even as a little girl I could see it in his eyes. I think maybe it's still there." She smiled politely at Cory, then turned her attention back to Bill Rogers.

At the refreshment stand Mark Young bought Molly and himself sarsaparillas, then led the way to a spot under a ponderosa pine. As they sat down in the shade Young figured it was as good a time as any to broach the subject of Walter Smythe. He cast a glance toward Sheriff Jim Naylor, who was stationed near the two outlaws, ready to call out for Young if they showed an inclination to leave.

Molly was sipping her drink. Not knowing how to ease into the subject, the marshal looked her in the eye and said, "Molly, I want to talk to you about Walter Smythe."

Her eyes widened slightly. "Ken Eastman told you about him too?"

"Yes."

"Why and what do you want to know?"

"Well, I want to know . . . because I'm your friend, and I care what happens to you. Sam is gone. Somebody has to look out for you."

"I appreciate that," she said softly. "Let's deal with the other question. What do you want to know?"

"How he got into your life in the first place, and where he fits in right now."

"Ken didn't tell you?"

"I want to hear it from you."

Molly Dunne explained how Walter Smythe had come to the Circle D shortly before Sam was killed, wanting to buy the ranch. His offer had been quite low, but Sam had told him that even a high price would not interest him. The ranch was not for sale. Smythe seemed to accept Sam's decision and went on his way.

A few days after Sam's funeral Smythe had shown up at the ranch, saying that he happened to be in the area and had heard about her husband's death. He offered his condolences and said that if there was anything he could do, she should tell him. He wanted to be of comfort to her in her sorrow.

Tight-lipped, Young asked, "Is comfort all he had in mind?"

Molly looked at him curiously. "What do you mean?"

"Ken told me Smythe came back several times."

"Well, yes. He did."

"Just to comfort you?"

"Well, no. If Ken told you this much, he also told you that Walter has asked me to marry him."

"Yes, and I'll be quick to tell you, Molly, I don't like it."

The widow's jaw slacked slightly. "What do you mean?"

"What I mean is . . . well, what I mean is . . . Mr. Smythe should have had the decency to let Sam get cold. Please forgive my bluntness, but that's how I feel."

Young was glad to hear her say, "I feel the same way."

"So what did you tell him?"

"I told him that I'm not going to consider another marriage for a long time."

"Did he accept it?"

"Not really. I expect him to be back, asking again."

Young was relieved to hear from Molly's own lips that she was not going to rush into marriage with this Walter Smythe. But he decided that with Smythe showing interest, he needed to tell Molly exactly how he felt about her. She needed to be aware of her options. This was not the time nor the place, however. Thinking of Butch Cassidy and the chore at hand, he said, "Molly, I'll be tied up for a few days when I leave here, but I'd like to know if I can come to the ranch and talk to you sometime soon. There are some things I need to discuss with you."

Setting her deep-blue eyes on him, the lovely brunette said, "Since when does Mark Young have to ask to visit me? We've been friends since we were kids. You're welcome at the Circle D anytime."

A day earlier, on July 3, Tom McCarty and his eight men approached the outskirts of Osage, Wyoming, thirty miles south of Sundance. The town lay hot and lazy in the early afternoon sun.

Just outside of town they stopped to water their horses. As they gathered around their leader, McCarty said, "Now, boys, we're going to ride nice and easy—one or two at a time—up the street to the Blue Parrot Saloon. The town is four blocks long. At the main intersection you'll see the Weston County Bank on your right. Diagonally across the street is the Wyoming State Bank. Take a good look, 'cause we're going to hit them both at the same time."

Speaking in a slow and casual manner, McCarty divided the gang into two groups. He would lead the group that would take the Weston County Bank, and Elzy Lay would lead the other one. Bob McCarty would go with his uncle.

Before mounting up, McCarty said, "Now, boys, here's what comes after we've emptied the banks. We'll ride northeast just over the border to Deadwood, South Dakota, where Bob and Elzy will buy themselves some new business suits. From there we'll cut back to Sundance. You boys can stay in town at one of the hotels, and I'll take Bob and Elzy with me to the Circle D. With the two of them dressed fancy like myself—and don't forget that my name will be Walter Smythe—they should pass as my two business partners from Denver. It'll take a day or so to get my plan rolling. I'll send Elzy for you when it's time for your part."

McCarty went on to explain that at a specific time, which Elzy would give them, the gang would wait along the road between the ranch and Sundance. About five miles from the ranch, on the east edge of the Circle D property, was a patch of dense forest that covered about twenty acres. The road ran right through the forest. The gang would load their guns with blanks, and so would Elzy and the McCartys.

McCarty would ask Molly to have dinner with him at the Black Hills Hotel in town. Bob and Elzy would ride along in the wagon. When they reached the wooded area the gang would come charging out of the trees, wearing their masks, as if they were going to rob the occupants of the Circle D wagon. McCarty and his two "business partners" would open fire on the attackers, seeming to wound some of them. McCarty would heroically throw his body over Molly, shielding her from the gunfire.

With several members of the gang being shot by the expert marksmanship of the three brave men, the gang would turn tail and ride away. Of course, after this harrowing experience Molly would not want dinner in town, and they would return to the ranch house. McCarty's brave act would make him a hero to Molly, and she would not be able to refuse his wedding proposal. Soon Molly Dunne would become Mrs. Walter Smythe, and the ranch would be legally placed into joint ownership. Mrs. Smythe would shortly thereafter meet with her "accident," and Tom McCarty would be the sole owner of the biggest spread in Crook County.

McCarty promised his gang that they would reap benefits for their efforts in helping him achieve his goal, then concluded by saying, "But first we take the banks."

McCarty and his men mounted their horses. Then McCarty signaled for the first two men to head into town. Every few minutes thereafter, another pair of riders followed. When all eight gang members were gone, McCarty set his horse into a slow walk toward the main street of the town.

People along the dusty street paid no attention to either McCarty or the eight riders that preceded him. Osage saw drifters, travelers, and settlers pass through almost daily, and the number had increased dramatically due to the Fourth of July celebration at Devil's Tower to the north.

While moving through the second block Tom McCarty scrutinized the marshal's office from the corner of his eye. He could see the lawman sitting at his desk inside. He continued along the street and nonchalantly sized up the banks, then pulled up his horse in front of the Blue Parrot Saloon. Elzy Lay and Bob McCarty were standing beside their horses, while the other outlaws were inside having a drink.

Without looking at them, McCarty quietly said, "Go on in, Elzy, and have a drink with the others. I'm going to put that marshal out of commission so we don't have him to contend with." Setting his dark gaze on his nephew, he said, "Bob, you're coming along with me. You're going to kill your first lawman."

Bob McCarty's eyes gleamed. "Let's go," he replied eagerly.

As Elzy headed into the saloon McCarty said to his nephew, "Get your hunting knife out of your saddlebag. Strap it on your belt so it looks natural."

Within a minute the two McCartys were walking down Osage's main street in the brilliant Wyoming sunlight. As they drew near the marshal's office Tom McCarty whispered, "I'll get him to talking. You slip around back of him and put that knife where it will kill him instantly."

"With pleasure." Bob grinned, his eyes gleaming.

Marshal Art Sailors looked up from his desk as Tom McCarty came through the door with Bob behind him. Without rising, he said in a friendly manner, "Good afternoon, gentlemen. Is there something I can do for you?"

"I'm Tom, and his name's Bob," McCarty said, gesturing toward his nephew. "We've come to report a crime."

"A crime? What kind?" asked Sailors, leaning forward on his elbows.

"*Bad* one," McCarty said, with emphasis on the first word. "People dead and everything."

The marshal picked up a pencil, pulled a clean sheet of paper from the top drawer, and prepared to write down the forthcoming information. "All right," he said, looking down at the paper, "where did the crime take place?"

With his eyes McCarty signaled for Bob to move around behind the man. Slowly the younger man began to inch in that direction.

"Right here in Osage," McCarty answered. "Down at the main intersection."

"In the street? When did this happen? I didn't hear anything."

"Not in the street, Marshal," McCarty said, fixing him with his dark eyes. "In the banks."

"The banks? Which one? Do you mean a holdup?"

Bob was directly behind the marshal now, and totally unnoticed.

"Two holdups," corrected McCarty, keeping his voice level.

Bob quietly lifted the long-bladed hunting knife from the sheath on his belt and watched his uncle for the signal.

"Is this a joke?" Sailors asked. "There have been no bank holdups in this town since I've been marshal."

"Who said anything about them already having taken place?" McCarty said, growing excited with what was about to happen. "I merely said we came to report a crime. You assumed it had already been committed, when actually it is going to take place in just a few minutes."

Instantly Art Sailors went rigid. Standing up, he said, "Listen, mister, who are you?"

"I told you," McCarty replied, "my name's Tom." With a wicked smirk curling his upper lip, he added, "Tom McCarty."

The name hit the marshal like a bucket of ice water. He winced, turning gray with fear. Instinctively his hand went for his gun, but even as it flashed downward, Bob plunged the knife into the small of the man's back. Sailors sucked air through his teeth, bowing his back. His hand stopped short of the gun butt. Quickly Bob pulled the knife free. As the marshal was folding backward toward the floor Bob swung the bloody weapon over his head and drove it full hilt into Sailor's chest, the blade piercing the marshal's heart. Bob pulled it out with a grunt, wiped the blood on Sailor's shirt, and placed it in the sheath.

Moving swiftly, Tom McCarty went to the door and closed it. Near the window lay a small sign that read MARSHAL IS OUT. McCarty placed it in the window and pulled down the shade. Turning to Bob, he said, "Let's move him to the back. We'll put him in a cell."

When the deed was done the two outlaws headed for the door. But as McCarty swung it open a woman stepped into the doorway. Eyeing both men with suspicion, she said, "Where is my husband?"

"Your husband, ma'am?" Tom McCarty said, his voice a bit unsteady.

"I'm Mrs. Sailors," she said, looking him square in the eye. "My husband is expecting me. Where is he?"

Bob was wondering what his uncle would do if the marshal's wife insisted on entering the office, especially if she did a quick search and found the body.

"I don't know, ma'am," McCarty lied. "We were looking for him too. The sign in the window says he's out."

"Then what are you doing in the office?" she demanded.

McCarty could see that the woman would have to be reckoned with. Quickly he stepped forward and seized her, yanking her inside and covering her mouth. Mrs. Sailors was a stout woman, and she fought him with tenacity. Seeing this, Bob hurriedly closed the door and waited for word to move in and help. As the woman struggled she worked her mouth free from McCarty's hand and let out a yell. When McCarty covered her mouth again, she bit his hand. He grimaced and tried again to silence her, swinging her around, but she stiffened and caught him off balance. The two of them landed on the floor, rolling.

Suddenly her mouth was free again, and she screamed

loudly, fighting the outlaw with all her might. Acting on impulse, Bob whipped out the hunting knife, moved close to the struggling pair, and plunged the knife through her throat. She slumped in Tom McCarty's arms, dead.

McCarty was furious. Suppressing his voice, he lashed at Bob vehemently. "You *fool*! What did you do that for? I've told you, we don't kill women!"

"She was screaming!" Bob retorted defensively. "You couldn't keep her quiet! I had to stop her from screaming before somebody heard her!"

Bob hurried to the window and peered past the side of the drawn shade. Everything seemed normal on the street.

Tom McCarty rose to his feet, breathing with a furious rasp, his eyes bulging. "You could have just hit her on the head and stunned her. You didn't have to kill her."

Bob jutted his jaw. "You were trying too hard not to hurt her, which is why she kept getting her mouth loose. I had to kill her to shut her up . . . one of those necessary situations—like what you are setting up for Mrs. Dunne."

Without warning, Tom McCarty slapped his nephew hard, following it up with a second blow. For an instant Bob raised the knife, but his uncle instantly brought a fist to the hollow of his nephew's jaw. Bob's knees buckled and he dropped to the floor, shaking his head.

While Bob cleared his muddy brain McCarty dragged Mrs. Sailors's body to the rear, tossing it in the cell with her husband. When he returned he helped his nephew to his feet and said, "Bobby boy, when I talk, I don't do it to hear my head rattle. Didn't I tell you to never again mention my plans to kill Molly Dunne? Huh? Didn't I?"

"Yeah," gasped Bob, "but—"

"But nothing! I say what I mean, and I mean what I say!" McCarty forced his voice to be calm. "Okay, I'll let it pass this time. But never again, do you hear?"

Still somewhat dazed, the younger man nodded his head.

"As for your killing that wildcat a moment ago, we'll let that pass too. I'd rather fight ten men at once than try to handle a woman."

"You shouldn't be so afraid of hurting them," Bob said.

Bolting his nephew with piercing eyes, McCarty said, "I hold women in a sacred place. They shouldn't be treated like us men. Don't you *ever* molest another woman while you're working for me, and don't you ever kill another one."

Bob followed his uncle out of the marshal's office. Both men were thankful that the woman's screams had not brought the town down on top of them. They made a casual walk to the Blue Parrot Saloon, where they joined the gang.

Several patrons were in the saloon, and so the gang members did not ask about the marshal when the two McCartys returned. Knowing the others were curious, however, Tom McCarty nodded his head and winked. He and Bob belted down a couple of shots of whiskey, and the gang then left the dark coolness of the saloon.

The nine men led their horses down the sun-bleached street. They separated a half block from the banks, moving to opposite sides of the intersection. Tying their horses loosely at the hitch rails, they sauntered toward the doors of the two banks. Each man held his stocking-cap mask in his hand, waiting for a signal from Tom McCarty.

The outlaw leader's dark eyes surveyed the street, but he saw few people moving about in the harsh sunlight. The gang members' nerves sharpened, and their muscles strained as they waited. Then the signal came. Each man slipped the mask over his face and moved toward his assigned target.

At the Weston County Bank, Tom McCarty bolted through the door, waving his gun and shouting, "This is a holdup! Everybody reach for the ceiling! I'm Tom McCarty!"

The bank had three employees: a teller, a bookkeeper, and the bank president. An elderly man and his wife were seated in front of the president's desk, and a middle-aged man, apparently a merchant from the looks of the money bag he was holding, was at the teller's window. A man in his early twenties was standing at a waist-high table, making out a deposit slip.

When Tom McCarty gave his name, a shock of fear came over the employees and customers alike.

Gus Waymore moved to the president's desk and ordered him to open the safe. Mike Landy held his gun on the man who was making the deposit, while Bob McCarty went to the teller's window. The merchant eyed him with disdain as Bob snatched the small bag of money from his hand and snapped orders at the teller to produce a bag and empty the money from his drawer into it.

"One of these days they'll catch you dirty skunks," the merchant said with scorn.

Bob's black eyes filled with anger. In a cool, smooth move, he brought the muzzle of his revolver around, leveled it in line with the man's belt buckle, and dropped the hammer. The gun belched fire. The elderly woman at the president's desk began to scream as the merchant fell to the floor. Quickly the woman's husband quieted her.

Tom McCarty joined Waymore at the big safe, helping him load the money into a cloth sack with the bank's name printed on it. The bookkeeper, a woman in her fifties, sat at her desk behind the teller's cage, frozen with fear.

From his spot by the safe Tom McCarty called out, "Bob! You about ready over there?"

"Got all the money here, Tom," responded his nephew.

Just then McCarty became aware that the bank president, a man in his early sixties, had returned to his desk and sat down. He was attempting to slide open the top drawer of his desk without being noticed. Dashing to the desk, McCarty brought his gun barrel down savagely on the man's wrist. The bone cracked under the blow, and the man grabbed the wrist with his other hand, wincing from the pain.

McCarty pulled open the drawer and saw a .32 caliber revolver lying in plain view. McCarty swore and said, "So you were going to shoot me, huh?" He picked up the gun and shoved it in a hip pocket.

McCarty noticed that behind the president's desk on a shelf was a kerosene lantern. While the elderly woman clutched her husband and whimpered in fear, the outlaw leader smashed the top off the lantern and poured kerosene over the president's head.

"Please don't!" begged the president, knowing what the masked man had in mind. He blinked against the stinging kerosene that was dripping in his eyes.

"What's your name, mister?" McCarty asked.

"Ralph Terrell," he said timorously.

"Well, Mr. Terrell," rasped McCarty, "they'll tell your story all over these parts. Ralph Terrell had the brains to be a bank president, but he didn't have the brains to outsmart Tom McCarty!" With that he lifted a match from Terrell's desk and thumbed it into flame, then cruelly ignited Terrell's thick head of silver hair.

While the president howled in pain, attempting to beat out the flame with his hands, the robbers headed for the door. As Bob McCarty passed the young man who was standing at the waist-high table, he stopped and eyed him coldly. "I don't like the way you look," he said, thumbing back the hammer of his revolver. The young man, who was unarmed, knew what was coming. In self-defense he reached for the bottle in the inkwell. His fingers were closing around it when Bob shot him through the heart.

Shots were ringing out from the bank across the street as Tom McCarty and his group plunged through the doorway. The five gang members assigned to the other bank emerged in single file, and McCarty hollered for them to get on their horses. In less than half a minute the McCarty gang was galloping northward out of Osage in a cloud of dust.

Citizens of the town came running to the banks. Two men were dead in the Wyoming State Bank. At the Weston County Bank two men had been shot and killed, an elderly woman had died of a heart attack, and Ralph Terrell was in critical condition with bad burns on his head, neck, shoulders, and hands.

Clyde Terrell, Ralph's brother—the owner of the Osage Gun and Hardware store—was seething with fury. It took him but a few minutes to round up the men of the town and form a posse. From his store's shelves he took weapons to arm to the teeth himself and twenty men. The posse thundered out of town, vengeance burning in their breasts.

McCarty and his men had been riding hard for a solid hour when he slowed his horse and pointed to a deep ravine off to the right. The horses were slick with lather and breathing hard. The men swung in and dismounted, pulling whiskey bottles from their saddlebags. They sat down in the shade of a cluster of scrub oaks, congratulating each other.

McCarty, laying a hand on his nephew's shoulder, said, "Hey, boy! You did all right today. You've enhanced the fear of the McCarty gang a thousand percent!"

Not to be ignored, Elzy Lay piped up, "I did in two at the other bank. One was a teller and the other a smart-mouthed customer."

"Good, Elzy!" McCarty grinned. Running his eyes over the group, he said, "All you boys did okay. Let's see how much we got."

"Shouldn't we keep movin', Tom?" asked Gus Waymore. "With all that blood and you settin' that old guy on fire, they'll sure enough put a posse on our tails."

"We have time, Gus," McCarty assured him. "The horses need a breather. It'll take the folks in Osage a little while to throw a posse together."

Twenty minutes later the gang was rejoicing over a haul of more than eighty-three thousand dollars. Tom McCarty laughed heartily as he gave each of his eight men an equal share, retaining a larger amount for himself, as usual. Then he gave Bob and Elzy bonuses for killing people during the holdups.

"Now, boys, you know what comes next. We ride for Deadwood to buy some new clothes." McCarty went on to review his scheme to win Molly Dunne's hand in marriage.

"We're with you, Tom," spoke up Gus Waymore, "but I think right now we'd best be hot-footin' it out of here."

"Okay," said the dark-haired leader. "Let's ride."

The gang mounted up and began to pull out of the ravine. As they reached the crest Ernie Derks caught sight of movement due south and hollered, "Posse!"

Riding hard toward them, Clyde Terrell and the posse spread out and began shooting. Returning fire, the McCarty gang spurred their mounts and galloped fast, heading straight north. They were leaving the relatively flat land behind, entering rugged country with rock-strewn hills, gullies, and boulders.

The posse had not stopped to rest their horses since leaving Osage, and McCarty's bunch was soon pulling away from them. Shortly the nine men were weaving their way among giant boulders, out of a steep ravine.

Bob McCarty looked back over his shoulder. The posse was not yet in sight at the crest of the huge ravine behind them. Pulling close to his uncle, he said, "Maybe I could stop those vultures behind us if I lay back and toss a couple dynamite sticks on them when they start the climb we're making right now."

McCarty regarded his nephew with a wicked smile. "Now that's right smart thinking, Bob. How many sticks have you got left?"

"Five."

"Okay, toss them a couple. Save the other three though. We might need them later."

"Will do," Bob said, a demented look in his eyes.

Tom McCarty had never seen anyone enjoy killing quite as much as Bob. He explained to the men what his nephew was going to do, telling the rest of them to push on. After Bob had dropped the dynamite on the posse he would catch up.

With murderous glee Bob McCarty pulled rein while the rest of the gang continued their ascent out of the ravine. After riding up after them a short way he slid from the saddle and hid his horse behind some brush-covered boulders. Quickly he slipped two dynamite sticks from his saddlebag and headed back down about fifty yards, where a clump of bushes around a huge boulder would provide him adequate cover. He wanted to catch the posse while they were beginning their ascent and would find it difficult to turn and run when the hissing sticks were sailing down upon them.

It was just a few minutes later when Bob heard a couple

of horses blow, then saw the hats of the men in the lead as the determined riders approached. Soon the whole posse was descending into the ravine.

Clyde Terrell leaned from his saddle as the posse followed him downward, studying the horse droppings on the path. "They're not more than ten minutes ahead of us, men," he said. "Even their animals have got to be getting tired."

"I'll follow them till doomsday if I have to, Clyde," spoke up one of them. "Those dirty skunks are gonna swing from a tree if I have to hang every one of them myself."

Other voices joined in, echoing the same sentiment.

From his hiding place Bob McCarty smirked, thinking, *Ha! You'll have to climb out of your graves to do it!*

The youthful killer breathed faster as the posse bottomed out and began their ascent up the steep side of the ravine. He leaned against the huge boulder, his eyes dilated and wild. Mumbling to himself, he waited until the band of twenty-one riders was about thirty yards up from the bottom. Placing the two dynamite sticks in his left hand, he fished in his shirt pocket for a match.

The men's voices became more distinguishable as he flared the match. Snickering gleefully, he touched the flame to both fuses and studied them as they gave off a soft hissing sound, sending up a thin trail of smoke. When the fuses were half gone he raised up and shouted, "Hey, possemen! Here's a little present from the McCarty gang!"

Clyde Terrell was in the lead and therefore the first to catch sight of the black-haired youth as he appeared from behind the boulder. Terror struck the posse leader as he saw the hissing, smoking sticks arch skyward then drop speedily toward him.

"Dynamite!" Terrell shrieked, attempting to turn his horse.

Suddenly there was a mad scramble to backtrack, but it all happened too fast. The first stick exploded thirty feet behind Terrell, and the other stick farther yet. In his excitement Bob had thrown them too hard. The last six men in the column were blown from their saddles, dying instantly in the double explosion. A seventh was down under his horse, crying for help. The animal had been hit in the eyes with flying pieces of rock and had blindly fallen on top of its rider and could not get up.

Some of the other fourteen men had been pelted with flying rock fragments but were not seriously injured. One posse member volunteered to stay behind and help the man who was pinned under his horse. The remaining thirteen jammed spurs to their horses' sides, bolting forward. Anger burned within them. These vile killers must be punished.

Bob caught up with the rest of his gang as they were climbing up a long, rocky incline—much like the one at which he had just dynamited the posse. This one, however, was steeper. Large rocks and huge boulders dotted the area. Bob reported that he had taken out about a third of the possemen but that the others would soon be on their tails.

As the gang wound toward the top of the steep incline they could hear the posse coming. Tom McCarty looked around the area and had an idea. As they reached the crest he said, "Out of your saddles, boys. Give the animals a breather. I've got an idea how we can take care of the rest of that posse."

"What you gonna do, boss?" asked Ernie Derks.

"Bury them in a rockslide," McCarty answered with a cold smile. Turning to his nephew, he said, "Bob, give me those other three sticks of dynamite."

McCarty pointed out a huge boulder nearby, almost teetering on the lip of the steep ravine. Just below were numerous large rocks. If the boulder could be dislodged, it would tumble downward, tearing the rocks loose as it went, creating a massive rockslide. Somewhat beyond the boulder were more sizable rocks in a jumbled pile. A single stick of dynamite would set them rolling down the grade.

The outlaws could hear the posse shouting as Tom McCarty placed two sticks of dynamite under the huge boulder. He swung his gaze beyond the boulder, studying the position of the other pile of rocks. Handing the remaining stick to Bob, he said, "Put this one over there under those rocks at the edge. I'll tell you when to light the fuse."

McCarty's men scattered from sight as he and Bob hunkered down in their places. The posse came into view, with Clyde Terrell again in the lead. They filed slowly down the path into the deep ravine and soon were beginning their climb. They were in a vulnerable spot now, with no avenue of escape. McCarty struck a match and nodded to Bob. They touched flame to the fuses simultaneously and darted for cover over the crest of the ravine.

When the explosions shook the area Clyde Terrell's head came up. He heard his men crying out in terror and the horses screaming as hundreds of tons of dirt and rock cascaded toward them with a deafening roar. Frantically he wheeled his horse in a futile attempt to escape.

McCarty and his gang ran to the rim of the draw to watch. Within seconds the posse was buried in a permanent common grave. The brutal outlaws laughed while the dust settled, and then they mounted up and headed for Deadwood.

Chapter Five

It was high noon on July 4 when Bill Rogers reached the five-hundred-foot point on his climb up Devil's Tower. The blazing Wyoming sun lanced him from above, as well as reflecting its heat on him from the sheer rock wall. He finished driving a stake in the crack and hooked an arm around it. His feet were resting on a stake he had pounded in only moments before.

An experienced climber, Rogers knew the danger of looking down. Even as he pulled up the rope bearing a fresh supply of stakes he was careful not to set his eyes on the dizzying distance between himself and the bottom of the vast, vertical wall. From time to time sounds filtered up from the crowd below, and his natural tendency was to look down, but he fought the temptation and continued to inch his way upward. While resting for a moment, he took a swig of water from the canteen strapped over his shoulder. He capped the canteen, sleeved the sweat from his brow, and began driving another stake.

Far below, among the scattered boulders and trees, the crowd watched Rogers's progress. The wind was picking up, sending its hot blast across the tumbled rocks at the base of Devil's Tower. Butch Cassidy looked past Etta Place to his outlaw friend. The Sundance Kid was searching the multitude of faces with his unblinking stare.

"What are you looking for, Kid?" asked Cassidy.

"Just trying to see where Young is," Sundance replied in an even tone.

"Don't let him bother you."

"I don't trust him," said Sundance. "I don't trust any man who wears a badge. He's here for a reason, and I doubt that it's the festivities."

"I tell you, Kid," protested Cassidy, "Young ain't got nothing on us."

Pulling his hat down tighter against the rising wind, Sundance said, "Butch, I think it would be best if we'd—"

His words were cut short by a fearful gasp that swept over the crowd. People leaped to their feet, eyes glued to the place on Devil's Tower where Bill Rogers was climbing.

High up on the face of the monolith, while Rogers was driving in a stake after pausing for a drink of water, a fierce gust of wind had caught him off balance. The mallet slipped from his hand as he reached for the half-sunk peg to steady himself. The mallet, secured by a thin cord to his belt, dangled freely as Rogers's weight loosened the stake. Suddenly the stake came out, and he plummeted downward. He grasped at the next peg, but it also came loose. He fell farther to the next one and seized it with a death grip. This one was well anchored and held firm as he struggled to get his footing on one of the lower stakes.

Below him the two loose stakes were falling toward the three assistants at the base of the tower, who scattered to get out of the way. With the wind in his ears, Rogers could not hear the gasps and screams from below.

At the Circle D wagon Anna Laura Leslie gripped Cory Bell's arm, digging her fingernails into the flesh as she screamed, her eyes riveted on the dangling figure high above. For the moment Cory forgot his jealousy over Anna Laura's attention to Rogers; the man was in danger of falling, and Cory felt for him too. Molly Dunne and Mark Young stood inches away, mesmerized by the climber's plight.

Far above the crowd Rogers managed to get his footing and tenaciously held on to the stake above while the wind gusted at him. He waited until it died down to lift his eyes upward. The lofty summit of the tower seemed to mock him, saying he never would set foot on it. Gripped by dogged determination, he said, "Oh, yes, I will. You've been poking your head up into the sky for centuries. It's time you were conquered, and I'm going to do it!"

By chance the peg at Rogers's waist was the one to which the rope bearing more stakes was tied. Five more were in the cloth sack at the end of the rope. Taking a few moments to catch his breath and sleeve away sweat, he took another swig from the canteen. Capping it once again, he drew a stake from the sack, took the mallet in hand, and began driving the stake. He could barely hear the throng far below, cheering his courage and determination.

Once U.S. Marshal Mark Young saw that Bill Rogers was again on a steady climb, he excused himself to Molly Dunne and moved through the crowd toward the brightly colored stagecoach that had been converted to a medicine wagon. He had a feeling that Doc Witherspoon might be selling colored water in the bottles labeled Indian River Elixir.

Witherspoon was giving two Cheyenne Indians a glowing testimonial of his product when he saw the man wearing the U.S. marshal's badge picking his way toward him through the crowd. One Indian had swollen knuckles in his right hand, and the sincere "doctor" was guaranteeing the miraculous liquid in the dark brown bottles would ease the pain immediately and take away the swelling within a day or two.

The suffering Indian paid the three-dollar price for the bottle in coins and left with his partner. As the marshal came near, Witherspoon pocketed the coins and turned on a wide smile for the lawman.

"Well, good afternoon, Marshal!" he said in a jovial manner. "Could I interest you in a bottle of my magical Indian River Elixir?"

Young ran his gaze over the brightly painted stagecoach, then looked at the round-faced, paunchy little man. Witherspoon's face was so fleshy that when he smiled, it nearly closed his eyes.

Several bottles of the elixir were sitting on a shelf that had been built onto the side of the stagecoach. Young picked up a bottle and read the wording on the red and white label. "So this is really magical stuff, huh?"

"Oh, yes," the peddler assured him. "It's a special

formula I learned from the Habaskas Indians years ago. It's been handed down through the centuries by their ancestors."

Young eyed him warily. Puckering his brow, he said, "Habaskas Indians?"

"Uh . . . yes, sir." Witherspoon nodded.

"Where are these Habaskas Indians located?"

"Well . . . uh . . . they're, uh, *extinct* now," stammered the hustler. "I happened to stumble onto the last two Habaskas Indians left. They gave me the formula."

"I asked you where." Mark Young's piercing eyes rattled Witherspoon, who ran a finger around the inside of his collar.

"They, uh . . . up in . . . uh . . . Canada, Marshal. Northern Canada. Way up in the woods. North."

Eyeing the bottle in his hand, then fixing his gaze on Witherspoon again, he said, "Special formula, huh?"

"Oh, yes, sir."

"Three dollars?"

"Well, that's to the average customer, you see. But to a lawman, especially a United States marshal, I could make it a dollar."

Young pulled a silver dollar from his pocket and laid it in Witherspoon's sweaty palm. Uncorking the bottle, he put it to his lips and took a small swig. His face pinched as he swallowed it. Coughing, he said, "Mercy, that's powerful!"

"Well, it does have a little alcohol in it, Marshal. It . . . uh . . . helps preserve the formula."

The hustler felt relief when he saw the marshal grin. He relaxed slightly and grinned back.

"What percent is alcohol?" asked Young.

"Oh . . . uh . . . only about twenty-five percent," replied Witherspoon, pulling out a handkerchief to wipe his sweaty brow. Cocking his head sideways and regarding the marshal carefully, he said, "Say, aren't you Mark Young?"

"That's me," responded Young.

Witherspoon extended his hand. As they shook he said exuberantly, "I've always wanted to meet the famous Mark Young! I've heard and read about you for years!"

Reaching in his pocket, Witherspoon retrieved Young's silver dollar and handed it back. "Here, Marshal. Let me just give the bottle of elixir to you. It's my pleasure, I assure you!" Shaking his head and looking at the ground, he said in wonderment, "Marshal Mark Young! Who would've believed it? I finally got to meet Marshal Mark Young!"

"Well, now," Young said with a smile, "I appreciate your kindness, Mr. Witherspoon. But I can tell that the alcohol content is more than my system can handle, so I'll give the bottle back to you. Maybe it'll settle your nerves. You seem to have a problem along that line."

"Uh . . . sure, Marshal. Maybe it'll help. Thanks."

The marshal handed Witherspoon the bottle and turned away, heading back toward the Circle D wagon.

As Young threaded his way among the various clusters of people, he suddenly noticed two men in a heated argument. Their faces were beet red, and they were standing nose to nose, hurling angry words. One was thin, with a freckled face and a thick shock of red hair. The other was heavyset and bald, with huge jowls. The marshal was only a few steps away. Just as he turned toward them, the bald one produced a .25 caliber derringer, pointing it directly in the other man's face. The thin man took two steps back, his complexion going from red to white.

Instantly Young moved in close as people were scattering. "Put down the gun, mister!" he bellowed.

Not far away Sheriff Jim Naylor turned at the sound of Young's voice. Pivoting, he headed in that direction.

The angry bald-headed man did not take his eyes off the other to see who was talking to him. From the side of his mouth he snarled, "You butt out, whoever you are! This slimy welcher owes me money and he's gonna pay up, or else!"

Squaring his jaw and straightening his back, the slate-eyed lawman said in a gritty manner, "I am United States Marshal Mark Young, and I am ordering you to drop that gun. Immediately."

Shifting his bulky weight from one foot to the other but holding the gun steady, the man said through his teeth, "I'll drop the gun when this filthy welcher produces the money he owes me."

"I don't owe you a red cent!" exclaimed the thin man.

Mark Young knew that a gunshot could startle Bill Rogers and might even cause him to fall. Not only that, but a .25 caliber slug in the face would no doubt kill the smaller man. The big man appeared to be the hot-headed type, and at this point his temper was so hot that he was not thinking clearly at all. One wrong move by the marshal could cause the man to fire the derringer.

Jim Naylor drew up about ten feet from Young and planted his feet. Young moved a few inches closer, so that he stood only five feet from the bald man. Speaking calmly, he said, "Just what is the problem here? Who are you men?"

A woman stepped up beside Young and said, "Marshal, this man holding the gun is my husband. Don't try to step in and take it from him."

"She's right, Marshal!" blurted the fat man. "You try it and Nelms will die!"

"Now, just take it easy, mister," said Young. "I'm not going to try it. Just tell me what the problem is."

"Ask Nelms!" blared the man with the gun.

Nervously the other man set his frightened eyes on Young and said, "I'm Carl Nelms, Marshal, from Pinedale, Wyoming. This man's name is Johnson. I . . . I don't know his first name. We—"

"His name is Cullen Johnson, Marshal," cut in the woman. "We're from Greeley, Colorado. Cullen's always getting in trouble because of his gambling. He's always got to be betting on something. Keeps us dirt poor, he does." Her burning eyes were fixed on her husband.

"Why don't you just shut up, Mabel?" rasped Johnson, still holding the derringer aimed at Nelms's nose.

Young motioned for Mabel to step away. As she obeyed he said, "Now, Mr. Johnson, I want you to take the gun off Mr. Nelms. Then we can quietly talk this thing over."

Ignoring Young, Johnson said angrily, "Cough up the hundred dollars, Nelms, and this whole thing will be over."

Carl Nelms answered shakily, "If I owed it to you, I would pay you, Johnson. I don't welch on my bets."

"Mr. Nelms," said the marshal, turning to the smaller man, "suppose you tell me what this whole thing is about."

Nelms slowly raised a hand and wiped sweat from his face. The muzzle of the derringer seemed to stare at him like a single menacing eye. Holding his gaze on Johnson, he said, "We had a bet going, Marshal. I bet that Rogers would not make it to a certain dark spot on the wall of the tower. We both described the same spot and agreed on our bet. We shook hands on it. Rogers hasn't reached the spot yet."

"Oh, yes he has!" roared Johnson. "He passed it just before he almost fell a few minutes ago. You just want to welch on your bet, so now you say it's another dark spot farther up! Well, you ain't welching on me, mister. Pay up or die!"

"I tell you Rogers has not reached the spot we agreed on!" Nelms retorted.

"You're a dirty liar!" blared Johnson, spewing saliva. His gun hand tensed.

Mark Young, trying hard to hold his own voice steady, said, "Mr. Johnson, this has gone on long enough. Now, I want you to lower the gun and give it to me."

Cullen Johnson's moon-shaped face was still florid. "You get the gun when I get my hundred dollars, Marshal!"

Coolly Young said, "If you shoot Mr. Nelms, you'll go to prison. If he dies, you'll hang. You can't spend the money behind bars, and you certainly can't spend it in the grave. Is it going to be worth a measly hundred dollars?"

"It's not the amount involved," argued Johnson. "It's the principle. There's nothing lower than a welcher."

"Principle or not," said Young, "you won't find shooting this man worth it when you go to prison or hang."

Young saw a change come into Cullen Johnson's eyes. He finally seemed to be getting through. Keeping his voice on an even keel, he continued to reason with him.

Not far from the scene of the confrontation Butch Cassidy turned to the Sundance Kid and said, "Maybe it would be smart if we sort of fade out of here while Young's busy."

Etta Place eyed Cassidy with scorn and said, "Come on, Butch. You're the one who's been telling Harry not to worry. Now all of a sudden you get ants in your pants. Go on and leave if you want to. Harry and I are staying. I want to see if that fool climber makes it to the top."

"Look, honey," said Sundance, standing up, "this Mark Young is no dude to mess with. I agree with Butch. It'd be better if we disappear while Young's occupied with those two guys. Let's go."

Etta swore under her breath and began to rise to her feet. When Sundance took hold of her arm to help she scowled and jerked it from his grasp. "I can do it myself," she said in a tone of disgust.

While Mark Young was still talking to Cullen Johnson, who was slowly weakening, he saw the two outlaws and the woman heading toward their horses. Panic gripped him. He must not let Butch Cassidy get away, but he could not make a sudden move without endangering Carl Nelms.

Young noted that Cullen Johnson's face muscles were beginning to relax. Already he had lowered the muzzle of the derringer from Carl's nose, and it was now on a level with his chest. Young was sure he would have the small gun in his own hands within seconds. There would still be time to stop Cassidy and arrest him.

While Young talked sense to the irate man he did not notice the two Pinkerton detectives ride up and dismount. They both threw a glance at Bill Rogers, high up on the face of Devil's Tower, then turned their attention to the drama taking place on the ground. Slowly they moved closer to the scene, listening as the U.S. marshal attempted to talk the fat man out of shooting the thin one.

Detective Durwood Peters stood beside his partner and thought about the situation before him. Marshal Young had voiced his opinion of the Pinkertons, and it had not been flattering. Here was Peters's opportunity to show the marshal that Pinkerton men knew their stuff. He would personally throw a tackle on the fat man holding the gun and help Young subdue him.

Peters took a deep breath and darted toward Johnson, coming at him from the side in an attempt to throw the muzzle of the gun away from Nelms. Even if it fired, Peters was confident it would do no damage.

Cullen Johnson tensed as he heard someone come rushing at him. He thought it was the marshal, and just as the man came barreling into him, his hand jerked reflexively, causing the hammer of the derringer to drop.

From his lofty position high above, Bill Rogers heard the crack of a gunshot and a series of sharp echoes. He heard women scream and men shout, but he did not look down.

Carl Nelms dropped to the ground with a bullet in his chest. Sheriff Jim Naylor quickly dashed to Nelms and kneeled beside him, while Mark Young rushed over to Durwood Peters and hoisted him to his feet.

"I thought I told you to go back where you came from!" growled Young, stabbing Peters with blazing eyes.

"I was just trying to help," gasped the detective. "You ought to appreciate it."

Young's lips came together in a severe, thin line. "Your help just got a man shot!" He unleashed a violent blow that caught the detective flush on the jaw.

Peters went down hard and lay still, crumpled like a broken doll.

Cullen Johnson scrambled to his feet and hurried over to Carl Nelms, looking down as if he could not believe what had happened. The crowd was pressing close. Molly Dunne elbowed her way through and knelt beside the bleeding man. When the sheriff saw Molly he stood up and said, "Do what you can for him."

Mark Young turned to the sheriff and said, "Jim, put Johnson in handcuffs."

Naylor nodded as Young wheeled and hurried toward the place Cassidy and Sundance had tied their horses. The outlaws and the woman were moving quickly now and had almost reached the spot. Young moved steadily but did not run full speed. He wanted Butch Cassidy to be in the saddle of the stolen horse before he gave the command to stop.

Cassidy played right into Young's hands, mounting the stolen horse even before Sundance could help Etta Place onto her sidesaddle. It was all the marshal needed.

Bellowing at the top of his voice, Young shouted, "Cassidy! Hold it right there!"

Robert LeRoy Parker—alias Butch Cassidy—felt his insides draw in like drying rawhide. Carrying an outlaw's constant feeling of guilt, he spurred the stolen horse and headed for the river. As the startled animal lunged forward, the loosened saddle rolled sideways, dumping the surprised outlaw on the ground.

Young was running at full speed by now. Seeing that the Sundance Kid's attention was on Cassidy, he came whisking by him from the rear and snatched the gun from his holster. He charged on toward Cassidy, thumbing back the hammer of Sundance's revolver.

Cassidy, recovering from his awkward sprawl, drew his revolver. He was rising to his knees, shaking his head as Young skidded to a halt. Lining Sundance's gun between Cassidy's eyes, he rasped, "Where you going, Butch?"

The outlaw froze in a crouch with the muzzle of his gun still pointed downward. He held it there, lifting his gaze to the lawman. The look of the gambler was in his eyes. It would take only a split second to raise the gun and fire.

Young read what Cassidy was thinking and warned, "Don't do it, Cassidy, or July fourth, 1893, will be the second date on your tombstone."

The outlaw held his position for a long moment.

"Besides," chided the marshal, "even if you did manage to kill me, you would mar your shining record. You wouldn't want to do that, now would you? Butch Cassidy, who has never killed a man? Wouldn't that be awful? The first man he ever killed would be a federal marshal. What a blot on such a clean record! So why not just get up on your feet."

With a sigh, Cassidy dropped his gun in the dust and straightened up on his knees. Standing, he glared hard at the marshal and said thickly, "You ain't got nothing on me, Young."

"Then why were you running?"

Cassidy hunched his shoulders. "Just habit, I guess."

"Bad habit to get into," replied the marshal dryly. "Could get you shot. However, for your information I do have something on you. Why do you think I loosened the cinch on your saddle?"

Cassidy eyed him warily without answering.

From his shirt pocket Young produced the sketch that matched the brand on the horse Cassidy had been riding. Thrusting it in the outlaw's face, he asked, "Where did you get the horse, Butch? A man in Kaycee drew this. Told me the horse that wears this brand was stolen from him."

A cynical smile worked its way across the outlaw's face. "So what does that prove? I bought the animal three days ago from a drifter about forty miles west of Sundance. Stupid drifter must have stolen it." Shaking his head, he added, "Man must really be short on brains to steal a horse around here. Everyone knows what happens to horse thieves."

"Why don't you tell me what happens to horse thieves, Butch," said Young, regarding him with narrowed eyes.

"Why, they get hung, Marshal," said Cassidy, "unless the law gets to 'em before the ranchers do."

"And what does the law do with them?"

"Well, the law's a little more lenient. They just slap the horse thieves in jail."

"Then you've got something to be thankful for."

"Like what?"

"That I caught you before that angry rancher did."

"Now look, Young," Cassidy said nervously. "I didn't steal that horse. I told you. I bought it from a drifter."

"You have a bill of sale, of course."

"A what?"

"A bill of sale."

Cassidy's face lost color. "Well, no. I don't. Like I told you, the fella was a drifter. He couldn't even read or write. He couldn't have written out a bill of sale if his life depended on it. Like I say, he really was stupid. He showed it by stealing that horse."

Mark Young's face seemed to turn to granite. Whipping out his handcuffs, he said, "Turn around and put your hands behind you, Butch. You're under arrest for horse theft."

The outlaw looked at the marshal with innocence written all over his face. "Young, I told you—"

"Yeah, I know what you told me. You're a liar, Butch. Now turn around and place your hands behind your back." While Young closed the cuffs over the outlaw's wrists he added with gravel in his voice, "Like you said, Butch, the man who stole that horse really was stupid."

When Young spun him around, Butch Cassidy's features settled into morose, hopeless lines.

"Let's go," said Young, pushing him toward the spot where Sheriff Jim Naylor stood with Etta Place and the Sundance Kid. The stolen horse had drifted in that same direction, the saddle dangling from its side.

Sundance put on a shocked look as the two men approached. "What's going on, Marshal?" he asked. "You ain't got nothing on Butch."

"I've been through that already with Cassidy," Young said with disgust. "There's no need to go over it with you. Your friend stole that horse. He's going to jail."

The Sundance Kid bristled. Etta Place, who knew him well, saw the storm signals in his eyes. She knew he was extremely dangerous when he was like this.

Sundance spoke to Young in a voice that was thin and reedy. "Butch didn't steal that horse, Marshal. The man he bought it from must have stolen it."

Annoyance clouded Mark Young's gray eyes. In a cold, deep tone, he said, "You're as big a liar as your friend."

Sundance flinched at the words. Beside him, Etta touched his arm. "Come on, honey," she said softly. "There's nothing we can do. The marshal is going to take Butch. Let's go."

"That's sound advice, Sundance," Young said through tight lips.

"Butch is my friend," Sundance retorted heatedly. "I can't just ride off and leave him."

"I'll be glad to arrange a cell for you too."

"You ain't got no reason to lock me up!"

"I will if you try anything like you're thinking."

Again Etta placed a steady hand on Sundance's arm. "Come on, Harry. It's best we go."

The two men were still locked in a hard gaze. It was Sundance who broke it. He looked over at Etta, then back at the marshal. Gratingly he said, "I want my gun back."

Spacing his words deliberately so as to give them precise emphasis, the marshal replied, "Write me when you've crossed the Wyoming border, Sundance, and I'll mail your gun to you. Now get on your horse and ride."

A brilliant flame flared in Sundance's eyes, but he saw

that the fire burning in Mark Young's was hotter. At thirty years of age Young was a legend in this raw country, and Sundance knew it was for good reason. Men foolish enough to buck him were always sorry for it—if they lived. Resignedly he drew in a deep breath and let it out slowly through his nose.

"Let's go, honey," Etta Place interjected again.

The Sundance Kid looked wistfully at Butch Cassidy, who knew his friend had no choice. Forcing a tight smile, he said, "Go on, Sundance. I'll take care of myself. It's a long way to Kaycee."

Mark Young spun around and glared at his prisoner. "If you want to die young, you just try to make a break for it."

Cassidy gave him an insolent grin but said nothing.

Looking back at Sundance, Young said, "Good-bye, Kid."

As Sundance and his girlfriend started to turn away Young said, "Miss Place . . ."

Etta paused, then turned slightly, giving him a bland look.

"If you know what's good for you, young lady, you'll quit running with the likes of Sundance, here, and go back to teaching school. At least that's respectable."

With a look of disdain Etta turned away and accompanied Sundance to their horses. As she mounted up she shot a last malignant look at Mark Young. Beside her Sundance reined his horse around and started to say something to Cassidy.

"Good-bye, Sundance!" the marshal lashed at him.

The Sundance Kid pressed his lips together, wheeled his horse around, and spurred away, Etta following close behind.

Butch Cassidy shouted after Sundance, "See you later, Kid!"

"Yeah," breathed Mark Young. "A lot later."

Chapter Six

When the Sundance Kid and Etta Place had crossed the Belle Fourche River and disappeared from sight, Marshal Mark Young pivoted and walked to where Sheriff Jim Naylor stood beside Butch Cassidy, who stood looking at the last spot where he'd seen his friend vanish into the trees on the other side of the river.

Molly Dunne came over, and Young said to her, "How's Nelms doing?"

"He's still alive," she responded, "but I think he'll die if the bullet isn't taken out soon."

"Has someone gone for Doc Breslin?"

"One man started to go, Mark," Molly said advisedly, "but some of the ladies told him that the doctor had been called to Oliver Hamblin's ranch early this morning. Mrs. Hamblin is giving birth to her seventh child, and she always has a terrible time. Doctor Breslin is probably still there with her. I'm sure that in your years as a lawman, you've dug bullets out before. It looks like you—"

Throwing up his palms, Young cut in, "Surely there's someone else in this crowd who's more qualified to do it. I'm a U.S. marshal, not a physician."

"I've been asking around, Mark," Molly said, looking worried, "but no one's come forward. I'm no physician either, but I think Mr. Nelms will die if that bullet doesn't come out soon."

The marshal sighed, raised his gray Stetson, ran a sleeve

across his brow, and sighed again. "Okay, but Nelms will have to give his permission first. Is he conscious?"

"Yes, come on."

"Just a minute," Young said, turning toward his prisoner. Taking Cassidy by the arm, he grunted, "Over here, Butch."

Quickly the marshal led Butch Cassidy to the Circle D wagon. He unlocked the handcuffs long enough to make the outlaw put his wrists between the spokes of the left front wheel, then cuffed them together again. "That will hold you until we're ready to ride, Butch," he breathed. As he stepped to Molly he said to the sheriff, "Keep an eye on him, will you, Jim?"

Naylor nodded.

Anna Laura Leslie was kneeling beside the wounded man when her sister and Marshal Young came over. She had torn a patch of petticoat from under her dress and was using it to stay the flow of blood. Nearby, Cory Bell stood looking on, with a large crowd of people gathered around in a circle. Cullen Johnson sat on a large rock just outside the circle, his wrists still in handcuffs. His wife sat next to him, trying to comfort him.

Carl Nelms tried to smile as the marshal dropped to his knees beside him.

"Pain pretty bad, Mr. Nelms?" asked Young.

Nelms swallowed hard, nodding slowly.

"I need to look at the wound," Young told him. "I'll try not to hurt you."

The wounded man's shirt had been torn away before Anna Laura had placed the petticoat compress on the wound. Young took hold of the blood-soaked cloth and carefully peeled it back. Nelms winced, sucking air through his teeth.

Studying the wound for a moment, the marshal saw that the .25 caliber bullet had lodged in the upper right side of the man's chest, apparently barely missing the lung. He knew if the lung had been punctured, Nelms would be coughing up blood, and there was no trace of it at the corners of his mouth. The wound, however, was bleeding profusely, and one did not need to be a physician to see that the flow of blood was going to have to be stopped soon or Nelms would bleed to death. This meant the bullet would have to come out first. Then the wound would have to be cauterized.

His features grim, the U.S. marshal set his eyes on Nelms and said, "I guess they've told you that reaching Sundance's doctor is out of the question?"

Nelms nodded. "Yes."

"I'd try to get you into town, Mr. Nelms, on the chance Doc Breslin would be back by the time we got there. But I'm afraid the wagon ride would be too much for you."

"I understand," Nelms said weakly.

"Molly, here, has checked through the crowd, sir. It seems that I'm the one with the most experience at this sort of thing. You're bleeding pretty bad. The bullet must be taken out immediately."

Nelms nodded again, his face pallid.

"Now, Mr. Nelms," said Young, "I'm no expert. As a lawman I've dug out a few slugs. I'll be perfectly honest with you. If memory serves me correctly, I've done it eight times. Five of the men lived. Three died."

Molly laid a hand on Mark Young's arm. He looked at her briefly, then set his gaze back on the bleary eyes of Carl Nelms. "I'm not much of a doctor, but it looks like I'm all you've got. I'll go after the bullet if you want me to, Mr. Nelms, but you'll have to give your consent."

The bleeding man worked his tongue inside his bone-dry mouth. "Please do, Marshal. I know you'll do your best."

Young licked his own lips. "You must understand, sir, that the slug is very close to your lung. If I should puncture it, you could die. I'll do my very best not to, but there are no guarantees."

"I understand," gasped Nelms. "You best get started."

The marshal nodded and stood. Molly's hand remained on his arm, which she firmly squeezed, looking deep into his eyes. "You're the kind of man who can do anything he sets his mind to, Mark," she said. "I know you can get that bullet and save his life. Anna Laura and I will help you."

As Molly's deep blue eyes held his own, Young felt his love for her warm his heart. He wanted to tell her then and there how he felt, but it would have to wait. He patted her hand and said, "Molly, would you go over to the stagecoach and ask Doc Witherspoon to bring a couple bottles of his elixir?"

As Molly hurried off, the marshal turned to the crowd and said, "Folks, it would help a lot if you'd go on back to where you were and watch Bill Rogers. I'm going to be very busy here, and I can do my job better without spectators."

As the crowd dispersed, Young asked two Circle D men to carry Nelms to the wagon where Butch Cassidy was shackled. They were to lay the wounded man on the wagon bed and drop one sideboard, making it easier to work on him.

While Nelms was being carried toward the wagon, Doc Witherspoon came with Molly, bearing two bottles of the Indian River Elixir. Looking the hustler straight in the eye, the marshal said, "Doc, I want an honest answer. What is the alcohol content of your magic juice?"

Witherspoon shifted his eyes uncomfortably up and down. "Well, sir," he said. "It's . . . uh . . ."

"I want the truth. I won't hold it against you . . . this time."

Clearing his throat, Witherspoon said sheepishly, "Well, Marshal, it's ninety proof."

"That's what I thought," mumbled Young. "Come on."

The marshal led the peddler to the wagon. Molly and Anna Laura followed, with Cory Bell hovering close to the strawberry blonde. Taking one of the bottles from Witherspoon, Young uncorked it and moved up to the side of the wagon where Carl Nelms lay. "I want you to get some of this in you, Mr. Nelms," he said, displaying the bottle. "Anna Laura, here, will help you."

Young passed the bottle to Anna Laura, who supported the wounded man's head with one hand and put the bottle to his lips with the other. Young turned to Witherspoon and took the other bottle from his hand. While twisting the cork out he said to the Circle D foreman, "Cory, you've got a jackknife, don't you?"

"Sure do," he replied, pulling a knife from his pocket.

"Light a match and sterilize the blade while I'm washing my hands."

While Cory followed the order, Young handed the bottle of elixir to Molly. Cupping his hands, he said, "All right, Molly. Pour it over my hands slowly."

Molly poured, and Young rubbed his hands together, allowing the alcohol to cleanse them. While so doing he lifted his eyes toward Devil's Tower. Bill Rogers, totally unaware of the drama taking place on the ground, was making steady progress toward the top.

The marshal turned to Cullen Johnson, who sat nearby, next to his wife. Johnson's face was colorless, worry and fear filling his eyes. His cuffed hands lay weakly in his lap. Young gave him a baleful look and spoke with words that snapped like dry twigs. "You better pray he lives, mister." Johnson's features went whiter still.

Young caught sight of Durwood Peters, who was standing within earshot next to his partner, Jack Clancy. "You too," he said ominously.

Peters ran a nervous palm over his face. "I was only trying to help, Marshal," he retorted defensively.

A red tide flooded Young's features as he rasped, "You hotshot city detectives don't belong out here. You're nothing but nuisances. Do like I told you and vamoose."

Peters blinked, looking injured. Jack Clancy eyed the lawman stolidly.

While Young was shaking his hands dry Molly searched about the area for a short stick. Finding one about six inches in length and as big around as her thumb, she doused it several times with elixir. Moving to Carl Nelms, she said, "We'll put this between your teeth in a moment. You will need it to bite on."

The wounded man thanked her with a faint smile. Then Anna Laura appeared, carrying a pan of water and a bundle of petticoat strips donated by women in the crowd. Setting them on the wagon bed, she looked at Carl Nelms and said, "Think you can take some more elixir now?"

Nodding, Nelms replied, "I'll try. It's pretty strong stuff."

"Just what you need." The blond woman smiled, lifting the bottle from the wagon bed where she had left it. She slipped the cork out and placed the bottle to his lips.

Mark Young took the knife from Cory Bell after Molly

poured elixir on the handle. "Now, Cory," he said, "ask among the people and find a hunting knife. The wider the blade, the better. Borrow a kerosene lantern from one of the families that camped here last night. Put the knife blade in the lantern flame and get it red hot. I'll need it to cauterize the wound after the bullet is out."

The young foreman nodded and hastened away.

Stepping up to the wagon, Young cast a dry look at Butch Cassidy, then set his eyes on Nelms. Anna Laura stood to his left, Molly to his right.

"Mr. Nelms," Young said calmly, "I will go as easy as I can, but this is going to hurt. Once I start I'll have to keep digging till I get the bullet out. The worst pain will come afterward. I'll have to cauterize the wound to stop the bleeding, and then I'll have to pour elixir in it to make sure the entire area of the wound is sterilized."

Nelms's brow was already beaded with perspiration. Solemnly he said, "I understand, Marshal."

Bracing his feet, Young said, "Molly, put the stick in his mouth."

As Molly did so, Nelms clamped it tight between his teeth and Anna Laura mopped the moisture from his brow.

Young took a deep breath. "You ready?" he asked Nelms.

Nelms nodded with short, jerky movements. The marshal took another deep breath, leaned over, and began probing through blood and flesh for the .25 caliber slug.

The sun was dropping toward the earth's western rim, lengthening the shadows along Sundance's main street. The shaggy-haired rider pulled his hat lower, shading his eyes against the harsh sunlight. Guiding his horse down the dusty street, he let his gaze rake the boardwalks on both sides. Except for a lone bay mare standing at the Wagon Wheel Saloon hitch rail, the street was deserted.

Duke Dixon had the look and the cut of the gunfighter. Attempting to emanate a fearsome aura of death, he dressed completely in black. His flat-crowned hat, shirt, vest, pants, belt, boots, gun belt, and holster were solid black. Even the grips on his Colt .44 were black. His thick mane of black hair protruded from under his hat in an unkempt manner and dangled over his shirt collar. He walked with an arrogant swagger, as if daring anyone to challenge him.

Dixon was a mixture of many things, with evil prominent in the mixture. He was a dark-complected, rawboned man who acted as death's business partner—and loved the job. Duke and his younger brother Rex were known to be two of the deadliest gunmen west of the Missouri River. When the Dixon brothers rode into town, men gave them a wide berth. If a man was foolish enough to think he could outdraw either one, he died a fool's death in a cloud of gun smoke.

Pulling his horse up beside the lone bay mare at the hitch rail, Duke Dixon eased down from his saddle. Wrapping the reins around the rail, he ducked underneath and planted his black boots on the boardwalk. Pausing momentarily, he ran his cold gaze up and down the dusty street, taking in the stark, seemingly deserted buildings, then shouldered his way through the swinging doors.

Nat Randolph, the bartender, looked up from his place behind the bar as the gunfighter came in. He instantly recognized him. Randolph had lived in this raw country all his life and had seen gunslicks come and go. Even though he knew the reputation of the Dixon brothers, the presence of Duke Dixon at this moment did not fill him with awe.

Dixon allowed his eyes to adjust to the gloomy interior of the saloon, then he moved slowly toward the bar. There was one customer in the whole place, a small man who stood leaning on the bar with one foot resting on the brass footrail. He was nursing a glass of beer.

The gunman bellied up to the bar, expecting to see some recognition in the eyes of the bartender. When it did not appear, he said in a gravelly tone, "You know who I am?"

Randolph slipped a towel from where it was draped on his shoulder and began wiping the surface of the bar. "Yep," he said blandly.

"What's my name?"

Randolph gave an insolent look and said, "You oughta know your name by now. You've had the same one for at least thirty years, haven't you?"

Duke Dixon was not used to this type of reaction. He straightened, and growled at the bartender, "You like livin', mister?"

Meeting the gunman with unflinching steadiness, Randolph grunted, "As much as anybody."

"Then don't smart-mouth me!"

The small man nursing the beer at the bar began to inch away. Dixon turned to him and said, "Stay where you are, little man."

The man obeyed, obviously out of fright.

Turning back to Randolph, Dixon said, "Give me a double shot of rye."

Randolph took a bottle from the shelf behind him and set a glass on the bar in front of the gunman. Dixon was nettled because Randolph didn't appear intimidated. While the bartender poured the double shot from the bottle, Dixon said, "I still want you to tell me my name."

Nat Randolph was a beefy, thick-necked man of fifty. He had a shiny bald pate and thick, bushy eyebrows. Tilting his head down so as to eye the gunfighter through the bushy brows, he grunted, "If it really means that much to you, your name is Duke Dixon."

"That's better." Dixon grinned, lifting the glass to his lips. He took a gulp, then turned to the little man next to him. "What's your name?" he demanded.

"W-Willie Chance," replied the intimidated man.

"Where you from?"

"I was born in Missouri," said Chance, trying to press a smile on his lips. "Been living in Wyoming for the last twenty years or so."

Enjoying Chance's uneasiness at his presence, Dixon looked back at Randolph and asked, "Somebody die around here? Where is everybody?"

"Out at Devil's Tower," the bartender replied evenly.

"What're they doin' out there?"

"Big Fourth of July celebration."

Dixon shook his head and thumbed back his hat. "Oh, yeah. I guess this is July Fourth, isn't it?" He sipped more rye, then said, "The whole town always go out there for the Fourth?"

"Not like this," replied Randolph. "Today is something

special. Cowboy named Bill Rogers from one of the ranches around here is climbing the tower."

Dixon's eyes widened. "You mean climbin' to the top?"

"That's the plan."

"He won't make it. That tower's straight up and down."

"Lot of folks have those same sentiments," said Randolph, unconsciously wiping the bar by habit. "That's why they're out there. They want to see him take a plunge."

Dixon laughed. "Be funny if he got almost to the top before he fell. They'd have to mop him up with a sponge!"

Willie Chance laughed nervously, attempting to please the gunfighter.

Dixon finished his glass of rye and set it on the bar. To Randolph he said, "You know Marshal Mark Young?"

"Sure do."

"Seen him around here lately?"

"Why?"

"Because I'm lookin' for him!" snapped the gunman, irritated.

Still unimpressed with Dixon's crusty behavior, he asked, "What you want with him?"

A frigid, wintry look settled in Duke Dixon's eyes. "I'm on his trail. Gonna find him and kill him."

"What's the problem?" asked Randolph, his voice steady.

Jutting his craggy jaw, the gunman hissed through his teeth, "The dirty skunk murdered my brother three weeks ago over at Casper."

Randolph arched his eyebrows. "Rex?"

"Yeah, Rex."

"Murdered him?"

"That's what I said."

Randolph flipped the towel over his shoulder. Shaking his head, he said, "Mark Young ain't no murderer."

Jaw still jutted, Dixon said, "Well, he murdered Rex."

"You see it?"

"No. I was over in Utah at the time."

"Are you telling me that Young shot him in the back?"

Dixon ran a hand over his mouth. "No. It was a quick draw."

"So Young outdrew him. Why do you call it murder?"

Duke's face pinched. "Listen to me, mister," he growled.

"The only man faster'n Rex is me. I don't know how he did it, but somehow Young pulled a dirty trick on Rex. Otherwise he never would have beat him to the draw."

"Were there witnesses to the shoot-out?"

"Yeah. A whole street full of 'em."

"Anybody say it wasn't a fair fight?"

"No," retorted Dixon, "but they'd be afraid to tell it if they did see it. Young would probably murder them too."

A cynical grin spread across Nat Randolph's broad face. "Seems to me you're afraid to admit your little brother just went up against the wrong man. I'll tell you right now—there ain't a man alive that's as fast as Young."

Dixon's face crimsoned. Lifting the empty glass a few inches off the bar, he slammed it down hard. "I trained Rex myself!" he roared. "I saw him work. I saw him take out plenty of gunslicks who were at the top of the ladder!"

"Too bad you didn't see him when he went up against Mark Young," said Randolph caustically. "Then you wouldn't have to make up a story to convince yourself that your little brother was tricked."

Angered, Duke Dixon reached across the bar and sank his fingers into Randolph's shirt. Spewing saliva, he hissed, "I don't need your smart mouth, barkeep! You keep it up and you're a dead man!"

Randolph held his eyes on Dixon's and lifted a meaty hand to the wrist that held his shirt. Closing his fingers over it, he squeezed down savagely in a viselike grip. Dixon winced, trying to pull loose. The thick-bodied bartender held him firmly and said in a grating tone, "The only way you could kill me, Duke, would be in a shoot-out. But I don't wear a gun. You could shoot me down in cold blood, but it would mar your image if word got out that you gunned down an unarmed man. You know it, and I know it. So let's cut the tough talk, or I'll break your wrist."

Dixon looked at the powerful hand that gripped him. He was clutching Randolph's shirt with his gun hand. If the wrist were broken, he could not draw his gun. Slowly he relaxed his hold on the shirt. "Okay, okay," he said, trying to back away.

Randolph clenched the wrist tightly, holding the gunman close. Looking him square in the eye, he said, "Don't ever lay a hand on me again. Understand? Next time I'll tear your arm off and beat you with it. Understand?"

"Yeah, I understand," responded Dixon.

Randolph let go of him. The gunfighter briskly rubbed his wrist, trying to restore the circulation in his hand.

"Let me give you a little friendly advice, Duke," said the bartender. "Don't go up against Mark Young. The man is death on two legs."

Ignoring the advice, Dixon continued to rub his wrist and said, "You didn't answer my question. I asked if you'd seen him around lately."

"Yeah. He was here this morning. Word is that he's hunting Tom McCarty. When Mark Young's on the hunt he's doubly dangerous. I'd steer clear of him if I were you."

The mention of McCarty's name brought Willie Chance's head up. "I hear Tom McCarty is one mean hombre," he said to the bartender. "You really think this Marshal Young can track him down and bring him in?"

Speaking with confidence, Randolph said, "One of these days Young will ride McCarty down and bring him in ready for the noose or draped over his saddle. You can bet on it."

Willie Chance was thrilled with the prospect of seeing Tom McCarty hang. It would be just as fine with him if McCarty was brought in draped dead over his saddle. All Chance wanted was revenge for what the outlaw leader had done to him.

"Which way did Young go from Sundance?" Dixon asked Randolph.

"I heard he went out to Devil's Tower," answered the bartender. "Maybe he expected McCarty to show up out there. I don't know. He has a lot of friends around Sundance. I expect he might come back this way to spend the night."

"Good!" exclaimed the dark-skinned gunfighter. "I'll just wait around and find out. Gimme another double shot."

Randolph poured Dixon another glass of rye, then corked the bottle and set it back on the shelf behind the bar.

When Dixon picked up the glass and headed for a table, Randolph called after him, "You owe me a dollar, Dixon."

Dixon stopped, wheeled, and stepped back to the bar. Lifting a silver dollar from his vest pocket, he said laconically, "Wouldn't want the place to go broke."

"I'm warning you again, Duke," Randolph said as the black-clad man made his way to a table, "you'd best stay clear of Mark Young. You tangle with him, you'll join your little brother. Young makes chain lightning look slow."

Dixon laughed derisively. "You haven't seen speed with a handgun until you've seen me in action! Don't get an ulcer over it, barkeep. My draw will make Young's look slow. The man who murdered my brother is gonna die!"

"We're all gonna die, Duke," clipped Randolph deftly. "Mark Young will too. But not by your hand."

The gunfighter slacked onto a chair and gave Randolph a cold, malevolent stare.

At Devil's Tower the lowering sun was stretching the shadows eastward. Mark Young had successfully removed the bullet from Carl Nelms's chest, cauterized the wound, and sterilized it with Doc Witherspoon's Indian River Elixir. During the operation Nelms had passed out.

The excitement of the crowd was reaching a fever pitch as Bill Rogers neared the top of the formidable monolith. Devil's Tower was a brilliant red-orange, reflecting the great ball of fire in the western sky. Every eye in the throng was fastened on Rogers, while members of the brass band held their instruments ready.

High above the crowd, with the wind whipping around him, the daring climber drove the final peg that would lift him over the crest. When the peg was secure Rogers let the mallet dangle on the cord at his side. He hoisted his lean frame up and over the edge. Immediately he could hear the band strike up the "Battle Hymn of the Republic."

Rolling from his belly to his knees, Rogers took a deep breath and stood. The people below were cheering and waving. He waved in return, then pulled the folded flag from where it was strapped to his back. In dramatic fashion he unfurled it, holding it by the edge. When the wind caught in Old Glory, making it wave gracefully, the band broke into "The Star-Spangled Banner."

On the ground amid the cheering crowd, Anna Laura Leslie, with great admiration in her eyes, applauded the climber. Cory Bell felt the gnawing of a green monster in his belly as he witnessed how much attention and admiration the woman he loved was giving Bill Rogers.

While Rogers descended from his lofty perch, Carl Nelms, still lying in the bed of the wagon to which Butch Cassidy was handcuffed, regained consciousness. Sheriff Naylor and Marshal Young stood over the wounded man, while Molly Dunne was at the ready to wipe his face and give him more elixir to drink. Cullen Johnson and his wife sullenly watched from a few feet away.

As his vision came clear Nelms thanked Molly for her kindness, and then looked at Young. "Marshal," he said weakly, "thank you for saving my life."

"My pleasure, Mr. Nelms," Young assured him. "I'm glad you're all right."

Turning to Naylor, Nelms said, "Sheriff, I want this incident to die right here. Please . . . let Mr. Johnson go."

"As you wish," replied Naylor. Pivoting, he walked over to Johnson and said, "You're free to go since Mr. Nelms doesn't want to press charges."

Tears filled Cullen Johnson's eyes as the sheriff removed the cuffs from his wrists. Immediately he rushed to the wagon where Carl Nelms lay and said, "Nelms, I—I'm sorry for all of this. I've struggled with my bad temper for years, but I think I learned my lesson today. Will you forgive me?"

Carl Nelms managed a smile and said, "I forgive you, Johnson. And it looks like I owe you a hundred dollars."

Shaking his head vigorously, Johnson said, "Oh, no, you don't. After what I did to you, the bet is off."

"I'm no welcher," came Nelms's weak voice. "Rogers made it all the way to the top, so he had to pass the dark spot I had in mind. I owe you a hundred dollars." To Young he said, "Marshal, will you reach in my hip pocket and pull out my wallet?"

Young quickly produced the wallet.

"Take out five twenty-dollar bills, please," said Nelms. "Give them to Mr. Johnson."

Cullen Johnson wanted to refuse the money, but to honor Carl Nelms's integrity, he accepted it. In turn he said to Jim Naylor, "Sheriff, is there an unfortunate family in this county that could use some help?"

Naylor grinned. "Yes, I know a family living on a little tract of land a few miles south of Sundance. Eleven children, and the mother has just come down with tuberculosis."

Placing the five twenty-dollar bills in Naylor's hand, Johnson said, "Give this to them."

The sheriff folded the bills and stuffed them in a shirt pocket. "Will do," he said. "I can guarantee you they will appreciate it."

The two Pinkerton agents, Durwood Peters and Jack Clancy, stood nearby and watched as Nelms was transferred to another wagon. With interest they observed Mark Young step back to the Circle D wagon, where Butch Cassidy was shackled, and say, "I'm taking you to the Sundance jail for the night. Tomorrow morning we'll head for Kaycee, and you can stand trial there for stealing the horse."

The outlaw's countenance was heavy. He was in the hands of the most proficient lawman in the territory. There was no doubt about it: Butch Cassidy was going to jail.

Looking his prisoner straight in the eye, Young said, "Tell you what, Mr. Robert LeRoy Parker. I'll see that the judge goes easy on you, if you'll give me some information."

Cassidy looked at him warily. "What kind of information?"

"I want to know where Tom McCarty is hiding out."

The Pinkerton detectives' ears perked up, and Cassidy bristled, his jaw tightening.

"I know you've recently been working with McCarty, Butch," Young said. "And you know where he is right now."

The outlaw curled his upper lip into an insidious sneer. "I'm not telling you a thing about Tom McCarty."

"Is he at the Hole-in-the-Wall?" Young pressed.

Holding the sneer, Cassidy said, "Tell you what, Mr.

U.S. Marshal. Why don't you go to the Hole-in-the-Wall and look for yourself?"

Mark Young knew the implications of Butch Cassidy's challenge. No lawman could hope to ride into the Hole-in-the-Wall and come out alive. The barren, red-walled canyon was a stopover haven for outlaws who traveled the so-called Outlaw Trail, which ran south from the Canadian border through Montana, Wyoming, Utah, and Arizona, and curved into the southwestern tip of New Mexico.

The Outlaw Trail had a communications system all its own. Men on the dodge could count on shelter and meals at particular stops along the way. At any given time several outlaws would be hiding at the Hole-in-the-Wall.

Young shook his head in wonder. Butch Cassidy would rather do prison time than break the outlaw code of honor.

The marshal released Cassidy from the wagon wheel and shackled his hands behind his back. Taking him by the arm, he said, "Okay, let's go."

Cassidy put on a stoical look as Young led him to the stolen horse. Young shoved the outlaw up into the saddle, then mounted his own animal. Taking the reins of Cassidy's horse, he rode to the Circle D wagon, where Molly Dunne, her sister, and Cory Bell were standing together. To Molly Young said, "Butch and I will be leaving for Kaycee at sunup tomorrow. I'll head back as soon as he's behind bars there. If it's all right with you, I'll come out to the ranch. There's an important matter I want to discuss."

Molly stepped to him, reached up, and laid her hand on his, then said, "Like I told you, you don't need an invitation to the Circle D. You be careful."

Young squeezed her hand. Looking down at Anna Laura and Cory Bell, he said, "I'll see you two at the ranch."

Anna Laura smiled. "We'll look forward to it."

"Sure will," added Cory.

With Young still holding her hand, Molly looked up at him, admiring how he sat so tall in the saddle. She told herself that Mark Young was truly a handsome and considerate man, and she wondered why he'd never married.

Giving her hand another squeeze, he said, "See you in a couple of days."

As they released hands Molly smiled pleasantly. "See

you then." She watched the marshal and his prisoner ride away among the trees toward the river.

Suddenly a shout went up from the crowd. Bill Rogers had touched ground and was making his way to the make-shift bandstand, where he was rapidly surrounded by ad-mirers. Many young ladies planted kisses on his cheek, including Anna Laura Leslie. Cory Bell was eaten up with jealousy but kept it to himself. After the mayor made a short congratulatory speech the band played a final rous-ing number as Rogers signed autographs.

A few minutes later the Circle D cowboys mounted up and followed the wagon carrying Molly Dunne, Anna Laura Leslie, Cory Bell, and Bill Rogers. As they started off the slope that led to the river Molly caught a glimpse of two riders in the distance and recognized them as the marshal and his prisoner. She wondered what important matter Mark Young had to discuss with her. Straining her eyes, she looked through the trees to follow their movement. For a moment she lost sight of them as the wagon bobbed and rocked toward the Belle Fourche River. Then there they were again, the tall man leading the outlaw's horse toward Sundance in the golden hue of the sunset.

Chapter Seven

Darkness was blanketing the town as U.S. Marshal Mark Young and his prisoner rode in. The huge form of Sundance Mountain loomed against the southern sky. Above its dark peak tiny stars were winking like lights in a fairy palace.

Many of Sundance's citizens, not waiting for Bill Rogers to climb down off Devil's Tower, had made the long journey back to town ahead of Young and Butch Cassidy. Main Street, dimly lit by kerosene lanterns, was already crowded, and the saloons were rapidly filling up. Everywhere people were talking with excitement about Rogers's heroic deed.

Cassidy had not spoken during the long ride. Now, as they neared the sheriff's office, Young said to him, "Butch, you can still change your mind. Tell me where to find McCarty and I'll see that the judge goes easy on you."

Cassidy regarded the lawman with malicious eyes. "Even if I did, you couldn't bring him in. He's as ruthless as they come and as sly as a fox. Besides, you don't even know what he looks like. There ain't no pictures of him around."

"I have his description," Young said tonelessly. "I'll know him when I see him."

Cassidy grunted. "You'll rot before I tell you where to find him."

Willie Chance waited in the shadows along Main Street,

watching for two riders to appear. He had heard from the people returning from Devil's Tower that the marshal was bringing in Butch Cassidy. Chance wanted Mark Young alive to go after Tom McCarty. He did not know how Duke Dixon was planning to do his dirty work, but the marshal would be better prepared if he knew Dixon was gunning for him.

His heart quickened when he saw them pull up at the jail. He did not want to be seen by Cassidy, who could identify him as one of McCarty's gang. He would wait until Young had locked Cassidy up, then approach the marshal.

As the two riders dismounted in front of the sheriff's office Chance heard Young say, "I may rot before you tell me where to find McCarty, Butch, but at least I'll do my rotting in the free air, while you'll do yours in a cold, damp cell."

Cassidy did not reply.

From his hiding place Chance saw Deputy Ken Eastman emerge from the office door, a smile splitting his lips. "Folks been telling me you got him, Marshal. I've got a cell all fixed up and waiting."

Cassidy eyed the deputy malevolently, his cheeks reddening. It was plain that he hated lawmen. Every one of them.

Chance watched as Eastman led the way into the office, from where he would take his prisoner back to the cellblock. A few minutes later Young pushed on through the door to the street, saying over his shoulder, "Feed him breakfast before dawn, will you, Ken? I'll be here to get him at sunup."

After that Young headed for the nearest café. He had taken no more than a dozen steps when Chance emerged from the shadows and said, "Psst! Marshal Young! Can I talk to you?"

The tall, broad-shouldered lawman halted and looked down at the small, wiry man. "What is it?"

"My name's Willie Vance," said the former member of Tom McCarty's nefarious gang, taking care not to give his real last name. "You don't know me. I just happened to drift into town today. I was having a beer at the Wagon

Wheel when a gun-toting dude dressed in black came in and asked the bartender if he'd seen you. His name's—"

"Duke Dixon," cut in Young.

"Yeah, that's it! Says he's gonna kill you for murdering his brother. I just thought you'd want to know."

Laying a hand on the man's bony shoulder, Young said, "I appreciate this, Mr. Vance. Thanks."

"Not at all." Willie Chance grinned. "I'm just a law-abiding citizen trying to do his duty."

The marshal wheeled and headed in the direction of the saloon. He decided he might just as well get this Dixon situation over with before eating supper. As he walked he lifted the Colt .45 from its holster, flipped open the cylinder, and checked the loads. Snapping it shut, he eased it carefully back into the holster, then tested it to make sure it was sliding freely.

Young was forty feet from the saloon when he saw an elderly man come through the swinging doors. At the same instant the old man spotted the marshal, and rushing up to him, he said breathlessly, "Marshal! A feller named Duke Dixon, inside the saloon there, sent me to fetch you. He's mean-lookin', Marshal. Said to tell you he wants to do a little gun talkin' with you."

"I understand, old-timer," Young said softly. "Thanks. You go on home now."

The old man nodded, but stood and watched the broad back of Mark Young as he moved to the saloon, where light spilled out over the swinging doors and onto the street. Two men were coming along the boardwalk. The oldster stopped them and said excitedly, "You better go get the sheriff. There's gonna be a gunfight at the Wagon Wheel!"

Both men hastened toward the sheriff's office.

With his jaw set in determination, Marshal Mark Young pushed through the squeaky doors and entered the crowded, smoke-filled saloon. Faces turned to the tall figure silhouetted against the pale light of the street. The normal laughter and hubbub of the saloon faded, then died.

Duke Dixon stood at the bar, a shot glass in his hand. The patrons near Dixon began to scatter, but Nat Randolph stayed at his place behind the bar, a towel draped over his shoulder. The black-clad gunslinger eyed the marshal in the big mirror behind the bar, then slowly turned around.

Grinning wickedly, Dixon held up the shot glass. "Here he is, everybody! Let's drink a toast to the dead marshal! That's what he's gonna be very shortly!"

Young's cold voice lanced across the room like an arctic wind. "Get out of Sundance, Dixon! Right now!"

The swarthy gunman laughed. "That's pretty tough talk from the murderer behind the badge! I wonder if the brave federal marshal can back up his talk!"

Holding his forceful eyes on Dixon, Young said, "If the word *murder* refers to your dead brother, I gave him the same chance I'm offering you. He could've walked out of Casper alive, but he chose to see if I could back up my words."

"You murdered Rex!" shouted Dixon. "He was too fast for the likes of you. I don't know what you did, but you had an accomplice distract him or somethin'. You could never have outdrawn him. I trained him myself. Naw, you tricked him somehow. You murdered my little brother, Young, and I'm gonna kill you!"

Looking like an immovable statue, Mark Young said through half-clenched teeth, "I am only going to say this once, Duke. If you want to live, you set down that shot glass and walk out of this saloon. Get your dirty carcass on your horse and ride. Don't come back. Don't even look back."

With a bold, impudent toss of his head, Duke Dixon said, "Now, Markie boy, you know I can't do that."

The yellow light from the kerosene lanterns above accented Mark Young's bronzed features, making prominent the sharp angles of chin, cheekbones, and jaw. "No," he breathed. "I guess you can't at that. The savage beast inside you is clawing at your guts—just like it was with your thick-headed brother. You've just got to show yourself and the whole world that you're faster and deadlier than me. All right. Let's head for the street. No sense messing up Nat's place with your blood."

Dixon spit on the floor and hissed a profanity that only those close to him could distinguish. As he set the shot glass on the bar he noticed the smile on Nat Randolph's face. Scowling, he grated, "After I kill Young, Mr. Bartender, I'm comin' back for you. Whether it mars my reputation or not, I'm puttin' a bullet 'tween your eyes."

Randolph chuckled. "You won't be coming back, *Dukie boy*."

Regarding the bartender with eyes like the dead of winter, the gunman growled, "Like I said, I'm comin' back for you, Mr. Bartender. You just wait."

Blandly the bartender turned away and went back about his business.

At that moment heavy footsteps rumbled on the boardwalk, and the swinging doors squeaked open. Sheriff Jim Naylor moved through the doors, glanced quickly at Dixon, then at Young. Speaking to the marshal, he said, "Mark, I'll just throw this troublemaker into jail till his heels cool, and stop this nonsense."

Slowly shaking his head, Young said, "Wouldn't do any good, Jim. This piece of buzzard meat has got it in his craw. It'd be the same when you let him out. I've got to kill him sooner or later. Might as well be sooner."

Dixon breathed the same profane word half under his breath, then twisted his mouth into a sardonic smirk. Looking around at some of the wide-eyed onlookers, he said in a cocky manner, "Come on, folks. Watch the big man behind the badge breathe his last!"

Jim Naylor stayed close to Young as the marshal moved outside. Word was spreading along the street that a gunfight was pending. While the patrons of the Wagon Wheel filed out behind the two lawmen and the gunfighter, excited patrons spilled from Sundance's other two saloons. Soon people lined both sides of the street.

Naylor stayed with the younger lawman until he stopped in the middle of the street and faced his adversary. "Dixon is plenty fast, Mark," Naylor said, worry in his voice.

"I'm faster, Jim," the marshal replied confidently. "You'd best get out of the way now."

Jim Naylor backed toward the gathering swarm, his eyes on Duke Dixon, who was taking his stance forty feet from Mark Young. As the gunfighter made sure his gun was loose in the holster he could hear his name being whispered among the spectators, and he grinned with perverse pride.

In the dim light of the flickering lanterns Dixon bent into a catlike crouch and balanced on the balls of his feet. His black eyes seemed to turn blacker as all the evil of his soul filled them. "Okay, Markie boy," he called across the forty feet that separated them, "pick the second you want to die. It's your play."

The marshal splayed his hand over the .45 on his hip and retorted, "You're the one who came to town looking for this little party, Duke. It's your play."

Dixon's hand plunged downward.

No one saw Mark Young move. It seemed that the Colt .45 leaped from the holster into his hand. In the thunder of Young's shot Duke Dixon quivered like a lightning-struck tree and seconds later toppled backward into the dust of the street. His own gun, which was out of the holster, slipped harmlessly from his fingers.

The crowd stood rooted in place as Young walked slowly through the haze of smoke and stood over the dying gunman. Dixon lay breathing with short gasps as a ring of blood gathered around the hole in the center of his chest. A look of frozen surprise was etched on his face. He gave the man who had outdrawn him a brief, incredulous stare, then his eyes fluttered. He knew in that last fateful, fleeting second of life that someone was faster with a gun than himself.

When Dixon's heaving breast went still and his eyes ceased to flutter, Mark Young holstered his gun and headed for the café.

Under the black canopy pierced with stars, Tom McCarty, his nephew Bob, and Elzy Lay sat on the edge of the porch at the Circle D ranch house. The cowboys who had stayed behind instead of going to Devil's Tower had told them to wait there for Molly's return. Three red cigarette tips glowed in the dark as the outlaw trio watched the bunkhouse and saw the cowboys milling about in the yellow light that shone from the windows.

Tom McCarty was dressed in one of the expensive suits he always wore when he visited the Circle D as Walter Smythe. Bob and Elzy were a bit uncomfortable in their stiff new suits, and both detested having to wear shirts with buttoned collars and string ties.

"Hope this masquerade doesn't have to last too long," complained Bob. "I'd rather be in my regular clothes."

"You'll wear that suit and like it," McCarty said in a cold monotone. "Anything that's worth having has its little sacrifices."

"Isn't me that's going to own this place," grunted Bob.

"You'll benefit from my owning it," said McCarty. "Now why don't you—"

McCarty's words were interrupted as Elzy Lay stood and said, "Hey! Here they come!"

The jangling sound of wagon harness and the rumble of hooves filtered through the gloom of night and slowly grew louder. Within minutes the wagon and accompanying riders came into view in the light from the bunkhouse windows. The ranch hands at the bunkhouse came rushing out excitedly and cheered Bill Rogers upon learning that he'd conquered Devil's Tower. Rogers hopped out of the wagon and entered the bunkhouse with his friends, while Cory Bell clucked to the team and swung the wagon toward the house.

The outlaws stood as the wagon pulled to a halt. Molly eyed them in the dim light and said, "Is that you, Walter?"

"Yes," replied McCarty.

Molly asked Cory if he would dash into the main house and light a couple of lanterns. As the foreman hurried across the porch and into the darkened house Molly gave a brief description of Rogers's daring feat to the man she knew as Walter Smythe.

Cory returned quickly, carrying a lighted lantern, and hung it on a nail near the door. Another burned just inside. As the faces came alive in the ring of light Molly asked, "Now, Walter, who are these gentlemen?"

The outlaw impostor introduced the younger man as his nephew Bob Smythe and Elzy Lay as Ed Jones, explaining that they were his business partners from Denver. Molly, in turn, introduced them to her sister and foreman. Cory, who did not like Smythe, decided at once that he was no more fond of the others—particularly Bob, who immediately had eyes for Anna Laura. Cory's temper was rubbed raw even more when he saw that Anna Laura enjoyed the obvious attention.

Molly looked the three men over and said, "Have you been here long?"

"Not too long," spoke up McCarty.

"And what brings you here this time?" she asked, looking the handsome, dark-haired man in the eye.

"Business." The outlaw leader smiled. "My associates and I have an offer to make to you on the ranch."

Cory silently ground his teeth as Molly said, "I am really not interested in selling the Circle D, Walter. I'm afraid it's been a long ride for nothing. But at least I can rustle up something for you to eat before you go."

McCarty furtively eyed his cohorts, then said to Molly, "That would be nice of you. And while we eat I can tell you about the proposal."

Molly led the three men through the door and into the parlor. Anna Laura turned to follow, but Cory grasped her arm gently and said in a low voice, "Anna, I don't like the way that Bob fellow looked at you."

Regarding the curly-headed cowboy, Anna Laura said, "Cory Bell, what are you talking about?"

"He eyes you like a hungry wolf at a limping rabbit."

Anna Laura drew a gusty breath. "Cory! Now, that isn't so! Bob seems like a warm and friendly person."

"I'm a man," Cory said stiffly. "I know what I'm talking about. You be careful of him."

"Well, I do declare," she said with a snicker. "It sounds to me like you're jealous, Cory!"

Cory stared at her with a mixture of anger and frustration. He had kept his feelings inside long enough. This was as good a time as any to tell the beautiful strawberry blonde exactly how he felt. "All right," he said, jaw protruding. "I am jealous."

Anna Laura raised her eyebrows. "What on earth for? You and I are friends, but we aren't courting."

"I wish we were," he blurted quickly. "If it was left up to me, we would be."

For a few seconds Anna Laura was without words. She looked at him strangely, as if she'd been unaware that he felt this way. Slowly a tender look came into her eyes.

Before she could speak the young cowboy added, "Anna, I might as well say it all right here and now. I—"

"Anna! Are you coming in?" It was Molly's voice from the parlor door.

"Uh . . . yes, Molly," replied the younger sister. "In just a moment. Cory and I are talking something over. I'll be in shortly."

Molly nodded and disappeared. When she was gone Cory quickly said, "I love you, Anna. I was infatuated with you the first time I ever saw you, even though you were just a young teenager. But it's love now. Real genuine love. I mean it, Anna, with all my heart. I love you."

Anna Laura was deeply touched by Cory's confession. She dropped a hand to one of his forearms and said, "Cory, I didn't realize you felt this way. I . . . I am flattered. I do like you a whole lot. I mean that."

A grin touched Cory's lips.

"I like being with you," continued Anna Laura. "As much as I like being with any man on this ranch."

"Even Bill Rogers?" asked Cory.

"Bill Rogers?"

"Yes. You like Bill better than me, don't you?"

"Why do you say that?"

"Because he climbed the tower and I didn't. You've said several times how brave he is."

"I have?"

"Yes."

Still touching his arm, she said, "What Bill did today was certainly a brave and manly thing to do, but that does not mean I like him any more than you. Why, I admire you very much."

"You do?"

"Of course. I am very proud that you're the foreman of this big ranch, yet you're only twenty-four years old. I think that is some accomplishment."

Cory Bell grasped at the straws Anna Laura was giving him, but he was all too aware that they were just straws. "You admire me and you like me, huh?" he asked, looking deep into her eyes.

"Yes, I do."

"If you give me a chance, I could make you love me."

Eyeing him with compassion, Anna Laura said tenderly,

"Cory, I am not ready to fall in love yet. That day will come, but not now. Do you understand?"

Feeling the keen edge of disappointment, he said quietly, "Yes."

Patting his arm, she said, "I must go help Molly with her guests. I'll see you tomorrow."

At that moment Molly appeared at the door again. "Cory," she said, "why don't you eat with us tonight?"

"What a nice idea!" exclaimed Anna Laura. "Will you?"

Cory Bell followed the two women into the house, vowing within himself not to give up. He would have Anna Laura for his wife one day or die in the attempt.

At the dinner table Cory watched the young man named Bob Smythe warm up to Anna Laura, dominating her attention. To ease the pain of his jealousy, Cory imagined driving his fists into each of Bob's wicked black eyes.

During dinner Walter Smythe made a generous offer for the Circle D—which he knew full well Molly would refuse. She did just that, very graciously, explaining that this ranch was her life. She would never sell it.

The conversation turned to Bill Rogers's heroic climb. Cory watched Anna Laura's eyes light up as Molly explained to the three guests how Rogers had driven the oak stakes in the vertical crack of the sheer stone wall, alongside one of the fluted columns. Walter Smythe showed interest in Rogers's accomplishment, asking questions as she gave the whole story in detail.

When the meal was finished Smythe asked Molly if he could take her to dinner at the Black Hills Hotel in Sundance the next evening. He and his partners would be leaving for Denver the next day, and he would like to spend a little time with her if he could. She accepted on the condition that Smythe understand that further marriage proposals were useless. She would not be considering remarrying for a long time. The handsome man threw his hands up, saying that he understood. He wanted her, but he would not press the issue.

Molly asked the three men to remain as overnight guests, offering them a vacant room in the bunkhouse, right next to Cory Bell's quarters. Then she and Anna Laura bid the men good night and began clearing the table. Meanwhile

Cory led the outlaws to the bunkhouse and showed them to their room.

As Cory prepared to leave he grew even more aware of the queasy feeling in his stomach regarding the three men. He especially did not like or trust Bob. On his way out he made a point of casually commenting that he needed to go to the barn for a while and would see them in the morning.

Moments later Cory crept through the darkness and moved up near the window where the three businessmen were quartered. It was his hope that they might talk freely if they thought he was not in the next room. When he drew near enough to hear what was being said he realized that their leader, Walter Smythe, had left the room. Just then he heard the door of the nearby privy shut, and he realized where Smythe had gone. The little building was on the same side of the bunkhouse and twenty yards away from where Cory was hunkering down. He was fortunate Smythe had not seen him; he could not be sure of being so lucky when Smythe came out.

Cory stayed only long enough to hear Bob Smythe tell Ed Jones that he was going to find a way to be alone with Anna Laura. Jones, in turn, was warning Bob about something when the door handle of the privy rattled. Cory dashed away from the window and melted into the night, promising himself that he would do all that he could to see that this unwelcome intruder did not get the chance to be alone with Anna Laura.

Inside the guest quarters Tom McCarty—alias Walter Smythe—put out the lantern and said, "Elzy, as soon as all the lights are out around here, I want you to go out the window and get your horse. Ride into Sundance and find the other men. They'll be at one of the two hotels. Tell them the big holdup is set for tomorrow. They should be in their places in the trees from about four o'clock on. We'll pass through there about five."

An hour later Elzy Lay was riding through the night on his way to Sundance.

United States Marshal Mark Young arose before dawn and lit the lantern in his room at Sundance's Black Hills

Hotel. As he shaved he thought of Molly Dunne. He was eager to see her alone and tell her how he felt. She must not be wooed by the wealthy land developer without knowing that someone else was in love with her. She needed to be aware that she had the choice of being Mrs. Mark Young. Maybe it would matter; maybe it wouldn't. At least she would know.

The eastern sky was turning pink as Young left the hotel and crossed the street to the Apple Blossom Café for breakfast. Thirty minutes later he emerged and headed toward the sheriff's office. As he approached he saw Jack Clancy and Durwood Peters waiting for him on the boardwalk.

He stepped up onto the boardwalk, raising his hand before either one had a chance to speak. "Seems I recollect telling you two sleuths to vacate these parts," he said.

"Now look, Marshal," spoke up Clancy. "We know you'll be going after Tom McCarty when you've delivered Cassidy to Kaycee. We want to go along."

"The answer is no," clipped Young, moving past them to the door. Placing his hand on the knob, he added, "I'll get McCarty on my own."

As he disappeared into the office the two Pinkerton men stared after him with sour expressions.

Moments later the marshal emerged, guiding a shackled Butch Cassidy in front of him, with Sheriff Jim Naylor and his deputy following. Young helped the outlaw up onto the horse he had stolen, then swung into his own saddle. Scowling down at the detectives, he said, "Are you two still here?"

There was no response from the two men. Then Sheriff Naylor stepped up and said, "My offer still holds, Mark. I'll be glad to ride along. Ken can watch things here."

Young turned to the sheriff and smiled. "Thanks, Jim. But the town needs you here. I can handle Cassidy by myself."

The sheriff, his deputy, and the two Pinkerton detectives watched Young and his prisoner ride west along the base of Sundance Mountain, then angle south and disappear among the rolling hills.

Chapter Eight

Willie Chance had decided to sleep in a rancher's barn about a mile west of Sundance, and he awakened at the sound of a rooster crowing in the barnyard outside. Sunlight filtered through the cracks and knotholes in the hayloft where he lay. Rolling over in the dry hay, he sat up, stretched, and yawned.

The same thoughts that he'd had before dropping off to sleep returned to his mind. Vividly Chance remembered the brutal beating that Tom McCarty had given him the day he expelled him from the gang. The outlaw's craggy face became a scowl as he thought of McCarty cheating him out of his share of the train loot. He felt pure hatred as McCarty's last words echoed through his brain: *Find your horse and get lost, Willie! If I ever see you again, I'll kill you!*

The little man could still feel the stinging blows that the outlaw leader had laid on his face . . . and the shame of being chastised in front of the gang. By this time Willie Chance was seething with hate. One way or another he was going to get even with Tom McCarty.

Chance climbed down from the hayloft and slipped out of the barn on the blind side from the ranch house. Rubbing his empty stomach, he made his way toward town. Minutes later he moved down the street in a bee-line for the Apple Blossom Café.

At the same time Sheriff Jim Naylor and Deputy Ken

Eastman were crossing the street, heading from the sheriff's office to the café. The wiry outlaw reached the door as the lawmen did, and he graciously opened it and allowed them to enter. Naylor and Eastman took a table in the far corner, and Chance sat down within earshot and picked up a menu.

Across the street the two Pinkerton detectives stood on the boardwalk and watched the local lawmen enter the café. Durwood Peters looked at Jack Clancy and smiled. "Jack, we can't let that federal man steal our thunder. He's gonna capture or kill Tom McCarty, and we need to be in on it. People need to think we had a part in it."

"You're right, pal," agreed Clancy. "If we just happen to be near the spot where Young captures or kills McCarty, we can make it look like we helped. Even that much would net us a bonus from the agency."

Peters rubbed his chin. "Of course, that shifty snake McCarty could show up here in Sundance while Young is delivering Butch Cassidy to Kaycee."

"That's a possibility," Clancy said with a nod. "Maybe it'd be best if one of us stays here in town while the other one follows Young. That doubles the chance of at least one of us being in on McCarty's capture or demise."

"I was thinking the same thing," remarked Peters. "Which would you rather do?"

"Six of one, half a dozen of the other," Clancy said dryly.

They flipped a coin to settle the matter, and fate sent Jack Clancy on the trail after Mark Young and Butch Cassidy. He walked to the livery stable and soon rode out. Durwood Peters was left standing on the boardwalk, rubbing his hands with nervous excitement. He felt certain that Tom McCarty was going to ride into Sundance—and that was just fine. He could handle the clever outlaw by himself.

Peters had already eaten breakfast, but he decided to go over to the café and have coffee. It would give him the chance to spend a little more time with Naylor and Eastman. It never hurt a detective to rub elbows with the local law.

Entering the Apple Blossom, the Pinkerton man threaded

his way past several tables to where the sheriff and deputy sat. The waitress had just set their breakfast before them. Approaching the table with a smile, he said, "Would you gentlemen mind some company?"

Both men gave him a bland look but did not answer. Acting as if they had welcomed him, he sat down and motioned for the waitress to bring him coffee.

The two lawmen tried to ignore him, but soon Peters was dominating the conversation. He began by telling of his escapades in the detective business, all of which he thought very exciting. Barely pausing for breath, he told one story after another. Though the two lawmen were not at all enraptured with Peters's litany of accomplishments, the little man with the craggy face sitting a few tables away was.

Willie Chance listened intently as the Pinkertons' most valuable detective described his heroic exploits. Chance was deeply impressed to learn of the infamous and dastardly criminals Peters had arrested and brought to justice singlehandedly. At one point, when the detective made one of his rare pauses, Naylor and Eastman—bored by Peters's stories—mentioned Marshal Young's trip to Kaycee with Butch Cassidy. Chance was disappointed to learn that Young and Cassidy were already on their way. He had planned to go to the marshal and give him all the information he could about Tom McCarty.

Chance's disappointment faded as he realized he could give his information to the proficient Pinkerton detective. Durwood Peters, with all his experience and success, was certainly qualified to bring in McCarty. The bruises on Chance's body—and in his soul—were crying for vengeance. He decided to get Peters alone and give him everything he needed to find the man who had cheated, beaten, and threatened to kill Willie Chance on sight.

Suddenly the door of the café burst open and a Western Union operator hurried in with a telegram for the sheriff. Weaving among the tables, he said, "Big news from Osage, Sheriff. Sorry to interrupt your breakfast, but I thought you'd want to know about it right away."

"That's all right, Webster," Naylor said, extending his hand. "Let's have it."

Anyone watching the sheriff's eyes as he read the message could tell that the news was bad. When he finished reading, Naylor swore and muttered Tom McCarty's name. Hearing this, Willie Chance listened even more closely.

"What's he done now?" asked Eastman.

"Held up a train north of Buffalo four days ago," replied the irate sheriff. "Dynamited the express car and the engine, murdered the crew, and escaped with at least forty thousand dollars."

Eastman shook his head.

"That isn't all," breathed Naylor hotly. "Two days ago McCarty and his bunch rode into Osage and held up both of the town's banks. Got away with more than eighty-three thousand. Killed four people and set the president of Weston County Bank on fire after dousing him with kerosene."

This time the deputy swore.

"There's more," grunted Naylor. "A posse chased them into the hills north of Osage, and McCarty's gang wiped out all but a couple of them with dynamite."

"Vicious bunch, aren't they?" said Durwood Peters.

"That's putting it mildly," replied Naylor. "They're mad-dog killers!"

Willie Chance swallowed hard, feeling a measure of guilt for having run with the nefarious gang—and realizing what would happen to him if anyone discovered that fact.

The sheriff glanced back at the paper in his hand. "Says they headed north out of Osage and are possibly coming here. We should be on the lookout for them."

Willie Chance's heart skipped a beat. One thing he did not want was to run into Tom McCarty. He knew he must talk to Durwood Peters as quickly as possible. If McCarty came to the area, he was certain to go to the Circle D ranch disguised as Walter Smythe. Since he always went there alone, it would be the perfect place for Peters to capture him.

For his part Durwood Peters felt a renewed tingle of excitement. If McCarty came to Sundance, it would give him a chance to capture the outlaw all by himself. Even if he had to call on Naylor and Eastman for help, he would get credit for the arrest. But he had to act fast and prepare himself. The gang could ride in at any time. Quickly he excused himself and disappeared through the door.

Willie Chance scooted his chair back, anxious to follow the Pinkerton man. He quickly paid his bill and hurried outside, but by the time he reached the street, Peters was nowhere in sight. The little outlaw swore under his breath as he gazed up and down the street. His eyes settled on the Black Hills Hotel across the street. He would try there first.

A few moments later six rough-looking men shouldered their way into the café and settled at two adjacent tables. From a table nearby they heard Sheriff Naylor say to his deputy, "Ken, we'd better spread the news around town. If McCarty's coming, we've got to brace ourselves."

The young deputy nodded in agreement, downed the last of his coffee, and followed the sheriff outside.

When the two lawmen had gone the six newcomers eyed one another steadily. One of them whispered, "Wouldn't those two gents have a heart attack if they knew they'd just walked past more than half the McCarty gang?"

It was midmorning when Cory Bell strode toward the ranch house carrying a bucket of white paint and a brush. He was concerned for Anna Laura's safety after hearing what Bob Smythe had said about wanting to get her alone. And, of course, he was extremely jealous. Anna Laura and Bob had been sitting on the porch steps for nearly an hour, talking and laughing. Cory had observed the upsetting situation since it began, just after breakfast. He decided it was time to crash the party.

Bob Smythe had just said something Anna found particularly funny as Cory drew near. Her laughter faded away when Cory's eyes found hers. "Good morning, Cory," she chirped warmly. "What are you doing?"

"I've been meaning to repaint the porch for Molly," he replied with a smile. "Thought I'd do it today."

Bob Smythe stood up quickly, dusting off his expensive business suit. As Anna was rising to her feet Bob said, "We can go somewhere else to talk."

"Oh, no!" exclaimed Cory, furtively eyeing the shiny

new black boots on Bob's feet. "No need for that! I'll just work around you. Please don't let me interfere." With that he made a clumsy move toward the porch, stumbled, and dumped half the bucket of paint on Bob's boots.

Anna screamed, leaping back to avoid getting paint on herself. Bob jumped instinctively, but his quick move only served to dislodge him from the top step where he stood. He slipped in the paint and fell down the steps, picking up the milky white liquid on his suit as he went.

Still holding the bucket with the paint sloshing, Cory Bell looked down at Smythe and said, "Oh, Mr. Smythe, I really am terribly sorry! How clumsy of me!"

Anna Laura was mortified. She stood on the porch, eyes bulging, mouth agape.

Bob's eyes flashed with fiery rage, taking on an insane look. The feverish heat of his anger instantly greased his face with sweat. Bounding to his feet, he blustered, "You impudent dog! You did that on purpose!"

Cory shot an innocent look at Anna Laura, then looked back to Bob. "Anybody can stumble, Mr. Smythe," he said defensively. "I really am sorry."

"Not as sorry as you're going to be!" snarled the outlaw, heading for him.

"Bob, no!" cried Anna.

Cory set down the bucket and tossed his hat aside. He welcomed the opportunity to pound his knuckles into Bob Smythe's finely chiseled face. He was so eager, he barged in and drove a piston-style punch square on Bob's nose.

Bob reeled backward from the blow, landing flat on his back. He did not notice his revolver come loose, slip from the holster, and land in the dirt. He shook his head and leaped to his feet. Wiping a hand across his nostrils, he brought it away and saw a shiny smear of blood. His eyes went wild, and with an animallike cry he lowered his head to charge.

Cory closed the gap first, chopping the outlaw with a violent right, followed by a smashing left. Bob wobbled momentarily, and Cory took advantage of it, belting him solidly on the mouth.

Bob's lips split and spurted blood. He gave another beastly cry and thundered forward like a mad bull. Cory sidestepped and let him pass. As Bob was wheeling around, Cory closed in and hit him repeatedly in the face, forcing him to raise his hands for protection.

Seeing an opening, Cory drove an ax blow to Bob's stomach, doubling the man over. Cory followed with a savage uppercut to the chin. Bob staggered, his legs going rubbery, and then fell.

At this point several ranch hands came running over, Elzy Lay among them. Molly Dunne came out of the house, followed by Walter Smythe, and they stared in amazement at wide-eyed Anna, the splattered paint on the porch steps, Bob rolling in the dirt, and Cory standing over him.

"Cory!" exclaimed Molly. "What's going on?"

"I stumbled and spilled some paint on Mr. Smythe, and he decided to make a fight of it," explained Cory.

Bob clambered to his feet, fury running like liquid fire through his veins as he set his murderous gaze on Cory Bell and clawed for his gun. It was not until then that he realized it had fallen from his holster. Cursing under his breath, he looked around for the gun and spotted it in the hand of a Circle D cowboy. Still a little woozy from Cory's last punch, he staggered toward the cowboy and demanded, "Give me my gun!"

The cowboy took a step back, clutching the gun. "I think you better cool off first, Mr. Smythe," he suggested.

"Now look here!" snorted Bob. "I want my gun!"

His uncle stepped in and laid a hand on Bob's shoulder. "Take it easy," he told him. "I'm sure Mr. Cory didn't purposely spill the paint on you."

Crimson rushed to Bob's dark eyes. "Oh, yes, he did! Plain as day, he did! And I'm going to settle the score!"

Molly moved up to Bob and said in a calm, soothing voice, "Bob, I'm sure it was an accident, but let's not allow it to ruin our whole day. I'll give you money to buy a new suit and a new pair of boots. In the meantime you can wear some of my late husband's clothes. You're close to his size. Maybe Cory can use some turpentine to clean the paint off your boots for now." Molly's smooth voice had its effect on Bob McCarty, and his temper cooled.

"I'll buy his new outfit, Molly," spoke up Cory. "It was my clumsiness that caused all of this."

For an instant Cory's face was turned away from Bob and his uncle, but Molly had a full view of it. There was a strange light in his eyes, and she saw a wolfish grin twist his lips. Immediately she knew the spilled paint had been no accident. She could also see that Anna Laura had seen the same thing and had probably come to the same conclusion.

Keeping a straight face, she said, "Cory, go get some turpentine and see what you can do about Bob's boots. I'll go in and lay out some fresh clothes."

The incident was over, and the ranch hands dispersed to go about their duties. The cowboy who had picked up Bob's gun approached him and handed it back. Young McCarty eyed him coldly, taking it with a jerk. The cowboy shrugged his shoulders and walked away, shaking his head.

Tom McCarty followed Molly inside the house. While she was in a back bedroom digging through her late husband's clothing McCarty sat in the parlor, thinking about the attempted robbery planned for that afternoon. He was eager to move ahead with his plan to take over the ranch, and he hoped that his act of heroism would break down Molly's defenses.

Suddenly McCarty became aware of the bulges in the left and right inside pockets of his coat. It was a pair of envelopes containing his share of the last two robberies—nearly thirty thousand dollars. He did not want to carry the money on him, nor did he wish to leave it at the bunkhouse. Making sure Molly was still at the back of the house, he tiptoed into the library. There he stashed the envelopes on a shelf behind a dusty old dictionary, then hastened back to the parlor.

In the bedroom Molly Dunne laid out a set of clothes for Bob. She found herself smiling as she envisioned the wolfish grin on Cory Bell's face. Her young foreman had his heart set on Anna Laura, and he was not about to let some other man muscle in. She was sure Cory would not let her sister out of his sight while Bob Smythe was at the ranch, so she decided she might as well invite him to join them in the house for lunch.

During lunch a cowboy named Dutch Wright knocked on the door and asked for Cory. Molly and the others listened as Wright told Cory that the cattle had broken down a fence in a north pasture and had scattered onto a neighboring ranch, where they'd trampled the neighbor's vegetable garden. The neighbor was upset and wanted to talk to someone in authority. Molly could almost hear Cory's heart sink, for he knew that it was his job as the Circle D foreman to tend to such matters and that he'd have to leave Anna Laura with his chief rival for her attentions.

Moments later Bob and Anna Laura headed out onto the front porch and watched Cory Bell ride away. With his uncle, Elzy Lay, and Molly still inside, Bob knew this would be his one and only chance.

Looking around to make sure no one was in earshot, he said warmly, "Anna, how would you like to take a little ride with me? I'd like to see the southern part of the ranch, and it would be more enjoyable if you rode along."

Anna Laura found herself charmed by Bob's good looks and gentlemanly manners. "All right," she said. "I'll tell Molly we're going."

Touching her arm, he said, "No need to do that. She's busy with my uncle and Ed. We won't be gone long."

Cory's words of warning ran through Anna Laura's head, but she shook them off. *Cory's jealous*, she thought. *That's why he distrusts Bob.*

Anna Laura had begun to feel different toward Cory from the moment he'd confessed his love for her. She realized that she had warm feelings toward him too. Maybe their relationship would develop into something serious— perhaps even marriage someday. *But that's for later*, she told herself. *I'm not ready to settle down yet. Besides, Bob will be leaving tomorrow. What harm can come from a simple ride around the ranch?*

The afternoon sun had dropped below the midway point in the western sky when Molly and her two visitors stepped outside for some fresh air. Molly looked around for Anna

Laura and Bob, but they were nowhere to be seen. With the two men trailing along, Molly scoured the area. Finally she went to the barn to see if her sister's horse was in the corral. When she saw that it was missing and that Bob's horse was gone, too, she said to the two men, "It's not like Anna Laura to go off without letting me know."

Molly had noticed more than mere casual attraction in Bob's eyes when he looked at Anna Laura. She'd tried to tell herself that it was nothing to be worried about, but now she found it weighing on her mind. Turning to Tom McCarty, she said, "Walter, I . . . I . . ."

"What is it, Molly?" the outlaw asked tenderly.

"Well . . . Bob is your nephew, and I hate to . . ."

Moving close to her, he laid his hands on her shoulders and said, "What's wrong?"

"I . . . I've noticed a certain look in Bob's eyes when he's with Anna Laura. Is he . . . is he trustworthy? I mean . . . is she safe with him?"

McCarty felt a flush of heat wash through him, and he silently cursed his nephew's insatiable lust. With all his plans at stake, there was only one answer he could give Molly Dunne. Forcing a smile, he said, "Bob was born with hungry-looking eyes, Molly. There's no need to worry. Your sister is in no danger with him."

Molly sighed. Her fears abated, she said, "Why don't you and Ed sit down, and I'll fix us some lemonade."

The two outlaws took chairs on the front porch, while Molly passed through the door and headed for the kitchen. As soon as she was gone McCarty frowned bitterly and said, "Elzy, if he kills that girl, this whole scheme could blow up in my face."

"Maybe we'd better go find him," Elzy suggested.

"We don't dare," responded McCarty. "If we go chasing after them now, Molly will know I was lying about that girl being safe with Bob."

Elzy checked his pocket watch. "We have to head for Sundance in an hour to stage our robbery. Bob knows it. Maybe he'll control himself and not touch the girl."

Tom McCarty's dark features grew even darker. In a gruff voice, he said, "He'd better."

* * *

Willie Chance climbed the stairs of Sundance's Black Hills Hotel and knocked on the door of the Pinkerton detective's room. He was relieved to hear footsteps. A moment later the lock rattled and the door came open a few inches.

Through the crack Peters eyed the little outlaw up and down and then said, "What is it?"

"My name is Willie Chance, Mr. Peters," he replied with a nervous grin. "I overheard your conversation with the sheriff and his deputy at the café. I also heard the sheriff tell what was in the telegram."

"And?" came Peters's dry reply.

"You're after Tom McCarty, right?"

Peters's dull expression brightened. "Yes, I am."

Looking around to see that no one was near, Chance whispered, "I have some information for you."

Peters swung the door wide. "Come in, Mr. Chance."

As the wiry man stepped in Peters closed the door and ushered him to a small table with two chairs. Peters waved him into one of the chairs, then sat down in the other and said, "Now, what is this information?"

"First," Chance said, wiping a hand across his brow, "you gotta make me a promise."

"And that is . . . ?"

"You gotta promise that what I tell you will stay between you and me—that you won't sic the law on me after I tell you."

Durwood Peters would do anything to nail Tom McCarty. Whatever this man had to tell him would be worth plenty if it resulted in Peters capturing or killing McCarty. To promise what Chance was asking required little thought. Smiling broadly, he raised his right hand and said, "I promise. This conversation will remain forever between the two of us."

Chance grinned, settled more comfortably on his chair, and began. He told Durwood Peters of how he'd been part of the McCarty gang until just a few days before. With hatred burning in his eyes, he recounted the beating McCarty had given him and explained why he'd been thrown out of the gang. Then he detailed all of McCarty's activities and plans, from McCarty's bushwhacking murder of Sam Dunne, his assuming the identity of Walter Smythe, his scheme to get his hands on the Circle D ranch by marrying Molly Dunne, and his intention to murder her afterward.

"Since McCarty was in Osage two days ago," concluded Chance, "I can guarantee you he'll show up at the ranch. If you want to get him, that's where you need to be. He always goes there alone. It shouldn't be too hard for a man of your caliber to take him."

Peters fished in his shirt pocket and produced two printed posters. Unfolding them, he handed one to Chance and said, "Is this an accurate description of McCarty?"

Chance read the wanted poster on Tom McCarty and commented, "Yeah. That's pretty close. Too bad there ain't no picture of him, but the description is good enough. You'll know him when you see him."

The detective took back the poster, then handed Chance the other one. "You know this fellow named Elzy Lay?"

Chance looked at the face of Elzy Lay. In the last poster he'd seen, Elzy was worth two thousand dollars dead or alive. Now he was worth five thousand. Nodding, he said, "Yep. That's Elzy, all right."

"He still running with McCarty?"

"Sure is. Sometimes he'll take off alone for a while, maybe hide out at the Hole-in-the-Wall, but when he's working, he rides with McCarty."

Peters folded the posters and placed them back in his pocket. Smiling at the little man, he said, "Mr. Chance, you've done the smart thing here. I guarantee you, you've come to the right man. I will capture Tom McCarty. He's going to stand trial for murder, and he's going to hang."

"I hope so," came Chance's nervous reply. "Because McCarty said if he ever saw me again, he'd kill me. If he ever found out that I gave you all this information, he'd probably torture me good before he did it."

The Pinkerton detective stood up and walked to where his suit coat was hanging on a clothes tree. He reached inside and pulled out his wallet. Walking over to Chance, he said, "You needn't worry about Tom McCarty, my friend. He's as good as on the gallows right now." Pulling fifty dollars from his wallet, he added, "You've done me a good turn. I want you to take this money and have yourself a good time."

Chance's eyes bulged. A smile broke across his craggy face. "That's mighty nice of you, Mr. Pinkerton—I mean, Mr. Peters," he said, accepting the bills.

Peters moved around him and opened the door. "You just enjoy yourself," he said congenially.

Chance stuffed the bills in his pocket and headed out the door. At the same instant heavy footsteps were heard on the stairs. The little outlaw looked down and saw a group of familiar faces moving up the steps. Speedily he wheeled and darted back through the door, his face pale.

"What's the matter?" asked Peters, closing the door.

"It's them!" exclaimed Chance. "The McCarty gang!"

"Did they see you?"

"I don't think so."

"Did you see McCarty?"

"No. He's out at the Circle D for sure."

"Then I've got to get out there," breathed Peters. "You can stay here in my room till you feel it's safe to leave." He checked the load in his revolver, slipped into his suit coat, and plunged into the hallway.

Closing the door behind the detective, Chance turned around, leaned against the doorjamb, and smiled. He was elated. He would have his revenge on Tom McCarty. As the realization struck home he felt a sudden cold chill course through him, as if Tom McCarty were in that very room with him and had heard everything Willie Chance had divulged.

Chapter Nine

At the Circle D ranch house Tom McCarty pulled the wagon to a halt at the porch. He was boiling inside but fighting to keep a cool facade as he stepped to the ground. It was five o'clock, and Bob still had not returned. McCarty dare not show his concern to Molly Dunne.

McCarty and Elzy Lay were standing on the porch when Molly came out the door dressed for dinner in town. Looking around, she said, "Anna Laura and Bob aren't back yet?"

"Looks like they decided to make a day of it." McCarty chuckled hollowly. "Guess we'll have to go on without them."

Calmly, Molly said, "I'll tell the cook to have something prepared for Bob and Anna Laura when they return."

As she walked toward the cook shack, which was near the bunkhouse, McCarty turned to Elzy and said, "Looks like she isn't worried. I guess she took my word that the girl is safe with Bob."

Elzy lifted his hat, ran a sleeve across his brow, and remarked, "This whole picture is going to change, though, if that sister of hers turns up dead."

McCarty's eyes became dark and moody. "If Bob messes up my plan, I'll kill him."

Elzy Lay saw the dangerous look in McCarty's eyes. He had no doubt that McCarty would kill his nephew if his plans for the Circle D were ruined.

Molly entered the cook shack where Bo Heflin was preparing the evening meal for the ranch hands. Bo was a big
thick-bodied man, with heavy shoulders and muscular arms.
To him Molly Dunne was the queen of the Circle D.
Whatever she desired, he would break his neck or anyone
else's to provide.

Bo gave her a wide smile as she entered. "Evenin', Miss
Molly," he said warmly. "I hear you're goin' into town to
have dinner with them wealthy gents from Denver."

"Yes, Bo," she replied. "Anna Laura and Bob Smythe
were to go with us, but they went riding and haven't
returned yet. It's time for us to be on our way, so we'll be
going without them. They'll have to eat with you and the
boys here in the mess hall. I'll leave a note on the door of
the house and tell them to see you, okay?"

"Sure, Miss Molly." The big man nodded. "The boys
will love to have Miss Anna eat with them. I'll make sure
both them kids get plenty to eat. You just have yourself a
nice time in town."

"Thank you, Bo." Molly smiled and headed back outside.

When she reached the wagon the man who called
himself Walter Smythe helped her aboard. She took time
to write a note, which Smythe left on the front door of the
ranch house. Then they were on their way, with Molly
Dunne sitting between the two impostors—Smythe on her
right, and the man named Ed Jones handling the reins on
her left.

As the wagon rolled eastward Tom McCarty picked his
time just right and said, "Molly, I've been here a whole
day and I want you to know that I've thoroughly enjoyed
being here. We really do seem to get along well. I wouldn't
doubt that if—"

"Please, Walter, don't," Molly cut in. "I appreciate
what you're saying, but I need some time to put my life
together. Do you understand?"

"Sure," he said, putting an arm around her shoulder.
"It's just that I'm so crazy about you, and I know you need
someone to look after you. I want to be that someone."

While he spoke McCarty was watching the dense wooded
area that was now in full view up ahead. The lowering sun
was casting long shadows where his men were hiding.

"Thank you, Walter," Molly said softly. "But I need time to get over Sam's death. Maybe I'll fall in love again; maybe not. For now let's just be friends. Okay?"

"Whatever you say, my dear." The outlaw leader nodded, shifting his eyes toward the deep shadows as they entered the wooded area.

Molly jumped with fright as seven riders suddenly came thundering out of the trees. Their faces were masked and they were waving guns. Pulling alongside, one of them shouted for them to stop, but Tom McCarty, playing his role of Walter Smythe to the hilt, whipped out his revolver and blasted him from the saddle. Molly screamed.

Elzy Lay—as Ed Jones—snapped the reins and shouted at the horses, and the wagon picked up speed. McCarty fired a blank at another one of his men, who toppled from his horse and hit the dust. Then McCarty shouted to Elzy, "Turn it around, Ed, and head back to the house!"

Elzy wheeled the vehicle around, spraying dust. As Molly gripped the seat and held on, the masked gunmen opened fire. As planned, McCarty threw his body in front of Molly, shielding her from the bullets. As the wagon bounded across the uneven land McCarty fired twice more, dropping another robber. Abruptly the robbers that remained pulled rein and were quickly left in the dust.

Molly looked back and cried, "Walter! You've driven them off! They're giving it up!"

"Looks like your deadly accuracy with that revolver was too much for them, Walt!" Elzy laughed excitedly. Looking at the widow, he asked, "Are you all right, Mrs. Dunne?"

"Yes!" answered Molly. "Thanks to Walter!"

Tom McCarty grinned to himself. His plan was working perfectly. When Molly Dunne had time to settle down and think this incident over she would realize that she needed someone to take care of her. Certainly her choice would be the man who had sheltered her body with his own.

Not long after Molly and the outlaws had first left the ranch for town, Pinkerton detective Durwood Peters guided his horse among the hills and gullies of the Circle D and approached the ranch house from the back side. He had obtained directions to the ranch at the livery stable in Sundance when he had picked up his horse.

Before leaving town Peters had debated whether he should inform Sheriff Jim Naylor about the situation. Though it would have been safer to have the lawman along, he had dismissed the idea. Peters took pride in his accomplishments, and though he had stretched the truth a bit when telling of his exploits in the café that morning, he knew he was good at his job. With his vast experience and keen intelligence, he could use the element of surprise and apprehend Tom McCarty. If McCarty decided to resist, Peters could handle that too.

As he approached the quiet ranch house he thought of how careful he'd been and smiled. Not far from town he had veered off the road and cut across the open land, making a wide circle to the west so that he would come in from the back side of the ranch, thus avoiding traffic on the road. He chuckled to himself. The infamous Tom McCarty was practically in his grasp. U.S. Marshal Mark Young would soon realize how wrong he was about Pinkerton's men.

Peters pulled up in front of the porch and dismounted, then stepped up to the door and knocked. When there was no answer he led the horse toward the bunkhouse. Thin wisps of smoke were curling skyward from the chimney of the cook shack, and the aroma of hot food filled the air.

The door was slightly ajar, and Peters pushed it open and stepped inside. As Bo Heflin looked up, Peters smiled and said, "Good afternoon, sir. I assume you're the cook."

"That's right." Bo grinned, wiping his hands on a towel. Extending the right one, he said, "I'm Bo Heflin."

Shaking hands, Peters said, "My name is Durwood Peters. I'm a detective with the Pinkertons."

Heflin's bushy eyebrows arched. "Oh? What can I do for you?"

"I'm looking for a man named Walter Smythe," replied Peters. "I was told he might be here."

"You just missed him," said Bo. "He and his partner, Mr. Jones, have taken Mrs. Dunne to town."

"When will they be back?"

"Not till sometime late this evenin'."

Peters pulled the wanted posters out of his shirt pocket, unfolded them, and handed Heflin the one describing Tom McCarty. "I would like you to read this and tell me if it reminds you of anyone."

When Bo saw the name of Tom McCarty in bold print he said, "McCarty, huh? Everybody around here's heard of him."

"Read the description, sir," said Peters.

Bo's eyes ran rapidly across the lines, then came up to meet those of the detective. Licking his thick lips, he said, "Well, it *could* be describin' Walter Smythe, but then I guess there are lots of dark-haired men that height who are built like that and tip the scales at that weight."

Holding his gaze steadily on the big man, Peters said, "Did you say Smythe had a partner with him?"

"Yeah. Fellow about medium height. Sandy hair. Name's Ed Jones."

"Is his nose bent a little to the left?" asked Peters, hoping that the man might be McCarty's cohort, Elzy Lay.

"Yeah." Bo nodded.

"Like this?" The detective handed him a poster with Lay's picture on it.

Heflin's eyes widened. His ponderous jaw sagged. "Why, th-that's . . . Ed Jones!"

"As you can plainly see," Peters continued, "Ed Jones is an impostor. He is the wanted killer Elzy Lay."

A cold chill shuddered through Bo Heflin. "Then . . . then Walter Smythe is—"

"Tom McCarty."

Bo swung his meaty fist through the air and swore. "Everyone knows that McCarty and his gang are cold-blooded degenerates who kill people like they were insects." A sudden look of fear clouded his eyes, and he gasped, "Molly! She's alone with the two of 'em!"

Peters quickly told Bo that he had learned from a former gang member that McCarty planned to trick Molly into marrying him and then arrange an accident for her so that he would become sole owner of the Circle D.

Bo sleeved sweat from his face and said, "If McCarty sticks to his plan, Molly isn't in danger yet, but I don't want her with those two killers any longer than she has to be. All the hands are at the north end roundin' up stray cattle and repairin' a break in the fence. I'm gonna ride out, get a bunch of 'em, and go after Molly."

"I'll go with you," said Peters, pleased he would have a posse of gunhands and wouldn't have to face the outlaws alone.

"All right," said Bo, heading toward the door. Suddenly he stopped in his tracks. "Wait a minute! I just remembered somethin'!"

"What is it?" asked the detective.

"There's another member of McCarty's gang here on the ranch!"

"What?"

"Yeah! A slick-lookin' dude McCarty said was his nephew. They look a lot alike too. Called him Bob. Miss Molly's sister, Anna Laura Leslie, went ridin' with him. If he's a killer like the rest of 'em, that girl could be in real danger. I saw them head south when they rode out earlier this afternoon. You'll have to ride out and find them, while I round up the boys and go after Miss Molly!"

Durwood Peters started to object and say that he would find the men and go after Molly. Then it struck him that if he brought in this other member of the gang plus Tom McCarty and Elzy Lay, he would be the Pinkertons' all-time hero. And it couldn't be too dangerous to take the lone, unsuspecting outlaw named Bob. Taking hold of Bo Heflin's arm, he said, "Look, Bo, it will mean a great deal to me if I can deliver Tom McCarty and Elzy Lay to the law in Sundance. When you and the boys catch them, will you bring them back here so I can take all three in at the same time?"

"Don't see why not," Bo said. "You go on now, and find Miss Leslie. Can't miss her. She's got a headful of reddish-blond hair and is pretty as a picture. Watch that Bob. He might be as mean and dangerous as his uncle."

"I will," said Peters, dashing toward his horse. Swinging into his saddle, he asked, "You said south?"

"Yeah!" blurted Bo. "Get goin'!"

As the detective galloped away Bo ran toward the corral. Nearing the gate, he saw Bill Rogers riding in from the range. Bo waved for Rogers to hurry, and the cowboy spurred his mount, thundered in hard, and skidded to a halt.

After learning that Rogers was riding in to tell him that the crew would be late for supper Bo quickly explained the situation. Then he told Rogers to ride like the wind and bring back the rest of the men so that they could go after Molly Dunne. Since the cowhands would have to come past the ranch house to head for town, Bo would stay behind, saddle up, and be ready to ride when they arrived.

Bill Rogers nodded, then wheeled his horse and galloped away.

In early afternoon Bob McCarty allowed Anna Laura Leslie to lead him slowly across the rolling hills of the Circle D ranch. He played the role of the young gentleman perfectly as they worked their way southward, wanting to get a safe distance from the ranch buildings before he attacked the beautiful strawberry blonde. When he'd satisfied his lust he would bludgeon her to death and make it appear that she had been thrown from her horse and trampled.

The lecherous nephew of Tom McCarty grew impatient as Anna Laura stopped to pick flowers, then rode on slowly, pointing out landmarks and telling stories of incidents that had taken place during her numerous visits to the Circle D over the years. He wanted to hurry her farther away from the ranch buildings, but forced himself to bide his time and remain outwardly calm. The time slipped by, and Bob realized he was not going to make it back before his uncle and Molly left for town. Tom McCarty would be furious.

But as Bob thought about it, he decided it was best this way. His uncle and the others would be gone before he returned bearing Anna Laura's battered body. This way McCarty would already have displayed his heroism to Molly in the fake robbery, and she would naturally turn to him for comfort when she learned her sister had been accidentally killed. The whole episode could seal their relationship and result in the marriage McCarty desired.

Bob laughed to himself. McCarty would never know how much he owed his nephew!

Anna Laura interrupted young Bob's thoughts by saying, "Here's a beautiful spot, Bob. What do you think?"

The couple had ridden up to the bank of a small creek lined with tall cottonwood trees. The immediate area was surrounded with thick brush.

"Beautiful," agreed Bob, realizing that Anna Laura had unwittingly led him to the perfect spot.

She smiled as Bob dismounted and helped her down. As he removed his gun belt and looped it over the saddle horn of his horse, the pearl handle of the gun caught her eye and she said, "That's a beautiful revolver, Bob."

Bob McCarty was proud of the fancy Colt .45 he wore. He had stabbed a man to death in Cheyenne to get it. Slipping it from the holster, he held it up for her to see. "I bought it in Cheyenne," he lied. "Has a hair trigger. When you cock the hammer all the way back you can trip the trigger with a feather."

"Isn't that dangerous?" she asked.

He laughed. "Only for the guy you're pointing it at."

Bob replaced the gun in its holster, then took the reins of both horses and tied them to a branch. Anna Laura walked to the creek bank and sighed, taking in the beauty of the land. As she stood gazing into the water Bob moved up behind her, a wild look building in his eyes. But for the rippling of the water, Anna Laura would have heard his heavy breathing.

Bob's hands trembled as he reached for the lovely young woman. He licked his lips as a burning hunger surged through his veins. Suddenly a sharp cry pierced the warm afternoon air. *"Hold it right there!"*

Bob McCarty jerked with shock and whirled to see Durwood Peters holding a gun on him from the bushes. Startled, Anna Laura pivoted, her face frozen with fear.

Peters stepped from the bushes, holding the muzzle steady on McCarty. Halting with some twenty feet between them, he kept his eyes on the man but spoke to the terrified young woman. "You are Miss Anna Laura Leslie, right?"

"Yes," she gulped.

Bob tensed, preparing to leap toward him. Peters snapped back the hammer, gripping the revolver with both hands. "Try it and you're dead, McCarty!" he blared.

As Bob froze in his tracks Anna Laura shifted her frightened gaze to Bob, then back at the man with the gun. "His name is Bob Smythe!" she said with trembling voice.

"So he says," hissed Peters. "But his real name's McCarty."

"That's not true!" Anna Laura objected.

"Allow me to introduce myself, Miss Leslie," said Peters, keeping his eyes trained on the outlaw. "My name is Durwood Peters. I am an agent of the Pinkerton Detective Agency. You've heard of it?"

"Yes."

"I've been hired by the Union Pacific Railroad to hunt down and capture outlaw Tom McCarty. This impostor here is McCarty's nephew. The man who passed himself off to your sister as Walter Smythe is Tom McCarty, himself. And the man you know as Ed Jones—"

"Don't listen to him, Anna!" cut in Bob, turning to where she stood, a few feet away. "The real impostor is this man holding the gun! He's no Pinkerton detective. He's a hired killer! He's been after my uncle Walter for months. He's after me too!"

Anna Laura stood numb with fear and confusion.

Keeping the black muzzle of his gun pointed at McCarty's chest, Peters said, "Miss Leslie, I'm telling you the truth. The reason I was able to trail the McCartys to this ranch was because I was given information from a former gang member, who told me what Tom McCarty was up to."

"Don't stand there and lie to her, Williams!" bellowed Bob, his eyes shifting wickedly. "I tell you, Anna, he's a hired killer. His name is George Williams. If you don't do something to help me, he's going to kill me!"

Anna Laura's shaky hand went to her mouth. Her mind was spinning. Bob's uncle, Walter Smythe, had shown himself to be a perfect gentleman—not a dangerous cutthroat the likes of the infamous Tom McCarty. Bob himself was a trustworthy young man and was certainly telling the truth. This stranger was going to gun him down if she didn't find a way to stop him. She needed time to think. For the moment she would keep him talking.

"Mr. Peters," she said, trying to force the tremor from her voice, "please tell me what Tom McCarty is up to."

Thinking Anna Laura was accepting the truth, the detective said, "To begin with, he murdered your sister's husband. It's all part of a diabolical plan. McCarty wants this ranch, and when Sam Dunne wouldn't sell it to him dirt cheap, he just decided to take it. He bushwhacked Mr. Dunne, then showed up at the Circle D to give your sister his condolences. In the process he has been trying to win her hand in marriage."

Anna Laura was not really listening as her mind frantically searched for a way to save Bob's life. To keep him talking, she said, "Why would he do that, Mr. Peters?"

"Because he wants to be joint owner of the ranch, Miss Leslie," came the detective's reply. "My informant said McCarty is planning to arrange a fatal accident for your sister after they're married. Then the place will be his."

Still trying to gain time, Anna Laura asked, "And just who is this informant you keep telling me about?"

Eager to convince Anna Laura, Durwood Peters ignored his promise to the vengeful outlaw who had given him the information. "His name's Willie Chance," he said flatly.

Bob McCarty's eyes widened. *So that's how this man knows so much!* he thought. *Tom will kill Chance an inch at a time!*

"Since you're part of the family, Miss Leslie," Peters continued, "McCarty may be planning to kill you too."

Still unsure what to do, Anna Laura stalled further by asking, "How did you know to look for Bob out here?"

"The cook told me."

Anna Laura had no way of knowing what this hired killer had told Bo Heflin or anyone else on the ranch, but she was about to despair of any solution for the present problem when Peters solved it for her.

Still holding McCarty with steady eyes and hand, the detective said, "Now, Miss Leslie, I want you to go over there and get on your horse. Ride on back to the house and go inside. You'll be safe there."

The eyes of the strawberry blonde flicked to the horses. They were tied together at a bush that was behind Peters and to his left. With his gaze fixed on Bob, he could not see them. Anna Laura focused on the gun belt looped over Bob's saddle horn. Calmly she obeyed Peters and walked toward the horses.

"Anna! No!" pleaded Bob. "Don't leave! Once you're out of sight he'll kill me! Please, Anna!"

The young woman did not break her stride. She had to convince the man with the gun that she believed him. She would get the drop on him with Bob's gun, then let Bob take over. They would take this evil hired killer to the house, then let some of the men haul him off to jail in Sundance.

Bob's eyes followed Anna Laura as she moved between the horses. He was still pleading with her not to leave when he saw her lift his revolver from its holster. Suddenly he realized what she was doing.

With his gaze still riveted to the outlaw's face, Durwood Peters called, "Hurry, Miss Leslie! This man has a demon in his eyes. If he puts up a fight, I may have to wing him in order to bring him in alive. I don't want you around if any bullets are flying."

Anna Laura came around the back of Bob's horse holding the cocked revolver in both hands, with a trembling finger on the trigger. Her entire body shook. The tip of the gun barrel was quivering. Forcing strength into her voice, she lined the hair-trigger Colt on the detective and barked, "Drop the gun!"

Holding his own muzzle on McCarty, Peters looked over his shoulder at the determined young woman. Instantly Bob shouted, "Shoot him, Anna! He's a professional gunman! If you don't shoot him right now, he'll trick his way out of this! He'll kill both of us!"

Pulling his line of sight back to Bob McCarty, the detective shouted to Anna Laura, "Listen to me, young lady! This man is a vicious outlaw! You've got to believe me! Take the gun with you and ride out of here!"

Again Bob begged her to shoot Peters before he tricked

her and ended up killing them both. While Bob was shouting the detective reached for his shirt pocket and called out, "Miss Leslie, let me show you something!"

In the same split second Anna Laura heard Bob's burning words, "Watch out, Anna! It's a trick!"

The frightened young woman tensed when she saw the stranger's hand reaching for his pocket, and her trembling finger inadvertently pressed the hair trigger. The Colt .45 belched fire, bucking in her hand before she knew what she'd done. The bullet ripped through Durwood Peters's head, killing him instantly.

Molly Dunne had calmed herself by the time the wagon swerved to a halt in front of the ranch house. She sat waiting while Walter Smythe—the man who had saved her life—jumped out of the wagon and helped her down. Her knees were a bit weak, and she leaned against him, then embraced him, thanking him for what he'd done.

For his part Tom McCarty was more than a bit proud of himself and the rest of the gang. The robbery ruse had gone off without a hitch, and now, he told himself as Molly embraced him, the whole thing was in the bag. Soon Molly Dunne would be Mrs. Walter Smythe. And not long thereafter she would be dead and the ranch would be his.

Looking down into her ink-blue eyes, McCarty said softly, "Would you still like to go into town for dinner?"

"No, thank you, Walter," she sighed. "I seem to have lost my appetite. If you don't mind, I'll have Bo feed you and your partners at the mess hall tonight. I need to go in the house and sit down."

"Of course," he replied, ushering her toward the porch.

Molly's knees buckled after taking two steps. McCarty tightened his grip on her arm, holding her up, while Elzy Lay bounded out of the wagon, saying, "Here, Walter, let me help you. We'll get her inside."

As the two outlaws walked Molly Dunne slowly up the porch steps she said, "You know, Walter, I can't help but wonder if those masked men that came after us are in some way connected with whoever murdered Sam. Maybe they're after me, too, for some reason."

"You could be right, dear," said McCarty. "It might be best if I stick around here until we clear the matter up."

When they reached the door McCarty let go of Molly's arm and let her enter first, since the doorway was too narrow for all three to pass through abreast. Just as he and Elzy Lay were stepping through into the front parlor a hand reached out and jerked Molly off to the side. Before either of the men could react, they found themselves looking down the black muzzle of Bo Heflin's revolver.

"You two freeze right where you are!" demanded Bo as he eased Molly down on a chair to one side. The wild look in his eyes told both outlaws that he meant business. They stood like statues.

Molly looked up at her cook and said, "Bo, what's the matter with you?"

"These two skunks are impostors, Miss Molly," Bo breathed hotly.

The stunned woman shifted on the chair. "Impostors? What are you talking about?"

While McCarty and Elzy Lay stood helpless under Bo's ominous gaze the big man told Molly of Durwood Peters riding in just after her wagon had pulled out. He filled her in on what the detective had told him, including the fact that Peters had shown him the wanted poster describing Tom McCarty and the one bearing Elzy Lay's picture.

At this point McCarty saw Molly's eyes widen and her face blanch. She stared incredulously at him for several moments. He knew the ruse was over. No matter what he did, the Circle D would never be his. The incredulous look on Molly's face was replaced with a cold stare, and her mouth drew into a grim line.

She was about to speak when Bo said, "There's more."

Keeping her cold eyes on McCarty, she said, "You mean there's more than the fact that this reptile crawled out from under a rock somewhere and decided to take advantage of a bereaved widow by marrying her, then murdering her so that he could sink his claws into her ranch?"

Tom McCarty's mind was racing. Who could have told the Pinkerton detective all these details? Only his men knew the plan. Had one of them turned traitor? He felt his stomach tightening.

The muscles tightened in Bo's huge jaws as he replied, "Yes, Miss Molly, I'm afraid there's more. McCarty, alias Walter Smythe, is the sneakin' coward who murdered Sam."

As Bo's words sank in, a burning hatred welled up in Molly Dunne. Standing, she glared at the man who had murdered her husband. "You're lucky I'm not a man," she hissed. "Because if I were, I'd tear the life out of you with my bare hands."

An evil grin formed on Tom McCarty's mouth. "I might like that," he sneered.

Bo waved the muzzle of his revolver. "Shut up, McCarty!" he growled. To Molly he said, "I sent the detective to find Anna Laura and Bob. Bill Rogers rode in early from the north range, so I told him what was goin' on and he went back to bring the men. When they get here they can take these two and Bob into town and turn them over to Sheriff Naylor. When Mark Young gets back from Kaycee he can do with them what he wants."

When Tom McCarty heard the U.S. marshal's name he felt a cold shudder. He and Elzy were going to have to get out of this somehow, and fast. Once the ranch hands arrived they would be hopelessly outnumbered.

While Bo Heflin was speaking Elzy Lay's eyes were taking in the area around him. There was a heavy alabaster lamp within a foot of his right hand. He watched the big man's eyes, waiting for his attention to be drawn away, just for an instant.

Chapter Ten

The roar of Bob McCarty's revolver thundered across the hills of the Circle D ranch. Anna Laura Leslie had acted by reflex in squeezing the hair trigger, never really intending to shoot the man she thought was a hired killer. When the gun discharged, the sudden loud concussion threw her back on her heels, as if she had checked herself at the edge of a high cliff. She could not believe her eyes when she saw the black hole appear so quickly in Durwood Peters's head and the spray of blood that shot out the other side.

When the detective toppled soundlessly to the ground, already dead, Anna Laura gasped and dropped the gun. Seeing Bob McCarty moving slowly toward her, she felt a dizzy coldness sweep through her and her stomach grow nauseated. Her face lost its color as intense pressure began to build behind her eyes. When Bob reached her she breathed tremulously, "Oh, Bob!" and buried her head against his chest.

Bob held Anna Laura close to him and smiled. His lie had worked, and his warning that Peters would try to trick them had set her up for the simple move the detective made when he reached toward his shirt pocket. When Bob had shouted at the same time, her reflexes did the rest.

Anna Laura pressed herself hard against him, attempting to gain control of her reeling emotions. For an instant she lifted her head and looked around at the dead man, then bit her lower lip and drew a shaking hand across her sweat-beaded forehead. Once again burying her head on his chest, she was thinking of that awful split second when she squeezed the trigger—and what had made her do it.

Suddenly Anna Laura remembered that the man had been reaching toward his shirt pocket. It struck her, then, that he was already holding a gun. What dangerous thing could he have pulled from his pocket? Pushing herself away from Bob, she walked toward the crumpled form of Durwood Peters.

Bob tried to grasp her, but she'd surprised him by moving away so quickly. Hurrying to where she was kneeling beside the body, he said, "Anna, what are you doing?"

Over her shoulder she replied, "I want to see what's in his pocket."

"Maybe you'd better not," he said, gripping her arm as she knelt down.

"Let go, Bob." She whipped her arm from his grasp.

Intent on opening the detective's pocket, Anna Laura did not look at Bob's face and was unaware of the wild look in his eyes. She was equally unaware of the heavy, uneven way he was breathing.

Bob McCarty stood over the beautiful young woman as she unbuttoned Durwood Peters's shirt pocket and produced two folded pieces of paper. While still on her knees she opened them and spread them out. The awful truth came home quickly as she recognized the face of the man who called himself Ed Jones and realized he was the killer Elzy Lay.

The words of the dead man, spoken only moments before, echoed through Anna Laura's mind: *I've been hired by the Union Pacific Railroad to hunt down and capture outlaw Tom McCarty. This imposter here is McCarty's nephew. The man who passed himself off to your sister as Walter Smythe is Tom McCarty, himself. And the man you know as Ed Jones—*

Bob's response rang clear in her mind, also: *Don't listen to him, Anna!*

A cold sensation washed over Anna Laura as she quickly scanned and recognized the description of Tom McCarty on the wanted poster. Without looking, she was aware that Bob was standing directly behind her, and now she could hear his hungry breathing. Panic gripped her. The detective had been telling the truth, and now she was alone with a killer. If Elzy Lay and Tom McCarty were killers, so was Bob.

With terror in her eyes Anna Laura turned and looked up at the leering face of Bob McCarty. She sat transfixed with fear as the wild-eyed young man leaned over and picked up the dead man's gun. Standing up straight, he heaved it into the creek. She felt her heart pound as his lips parted in a mocking sneer. With a tiny cry, she suddenly sprang to her feet and ran toward the gun she had dropped.

Bob was instantly on her heels, and with a desperate leap, he grabbed one of her ankles and knocked her to the ground. Like a wild, ravenous beast he pulled himself over her and began tearing at her blouse. Anna Laura screamed, twisted loose, and staggered to her feet.

The gun was only a few yards away, but as she ran toward it, Bob crashed into her, and she tumbled to her knees. A second later Bob's fingers closed around the revolver. But as he came up with it and spun around, she threw a handful of dirt in his face. Bob roared like a wild animal, swearing and thumbing at his eyes. As he blinked against the stinging particles he saw Anna Laura running toward her horse.

Clutching the gun, he barreled after her, tackling her again. Anna Laura screamed, kicked, and clawed at him, fighting for all she was worth. Dropping the gun, Bob pinned her down by the throat with one hand and ripped at her blouse with the other.

Anna Laura had never before been in such danger, and the instinct to survive gave her a wild strength. Bob was on his knees straddling her, and so she savagely brought up her own knee into his groin. He howled and doubled over, and she immediately sank her fingernails into his eyes, then raked them down across his face. Releasing the hold on her throat and clutching at his eyes, Bob fell sideways to the ground, enabling Anna Laura to roll free and leap to her feet. She looked for the gun, then realized Bob had fallen on top of it.

Pivoting, Anna Laura ran toward her horse, brushing the tousled hair from her face. Bob seized the gun while wiping the dirt and blood from his eyes. Rising, he thumbed back the hammer, swore at her, and fired. The bullet whizzed past her right ear, causing her to fall. Because of his impaired vision, Bob thought he'd hit her. He wheeled and dashed to the creek. Dropping to his knees, he laid the gun on the bank and began splashing water into his eyes.

Bob heard a faint whimpering behind him, and he spun around to see Anna Laura clamber to her feet and race over to her horse. Realizing she hadn't been hit, he swore again and picked up his gun. "I'll kill you!" he bellowed, snapping the hammer back.

Anna Laura struggled to get her foot in the stirrup, mumbling tearfully, "Please, God! Please let me get away!"

Just as Bob was taking aim a sharp voice thundered across the clearing: "Drop it, McCarty, or I'll kill you!"

Bob's head snapped around. Anna Laura, recognizing the voice, let go of the saddle horn and whirled about. At the edge of the heavy brush Cory Bell stood with his revolver pointed straight at Bob McCarty.

Bob's fingers tightened on the gun in his hand. His body was tense. Blinking against the water and blood in his eyes, he glared at Cory. Slowly he turned to face him.

Raising his gun and sighting down the barrel, Cory repeated his command. "I said drop it, McCarty! Or so help me, I'll kill you!"

The muzzle of Bob's weapon was still aimed toward the ground. A wicked grin curled his lips. "You're just a bum cowboy. It isn't in you to gun a man down. You aren't going to kill me. You don't have the guts to do it."

Cory Bell could hear Anna Laura weeping at the spot where she stood by her horse. He had caught a brief glimpse of her tattered blouse just as he broke from the bushes. His temper was already rubbed raw. Gritting his teeth, he shouted, "Nothing would please me more than to send you to hell right now! Go ahead! You're thinking about raising that gun. Go ahead!"

Suddenly Bob McCarty did just that. He lifted the revolver, bringing it to bear on the young cowboy. Cory's weapon roared. The impact of the bullet drove Bob backward into the creek. He kept his footing, but the gun slipped from his fingers and sank out of sight in the rushing current. He screamed with pain, thrashing about in the water as blood pumped from the hole in his left shoulder. Managing to reach the shallows, he dropped to his knees and tried to crawl onto dry ground.

Cory holstered his gun and raced over to the creek. "You tried to rape her, didn't you?" he demanded in cold, clipped tones.

Bob's right hand gripped his wounded shoulder. With his scratched, bleeding face twisted in agony, he staggered to his feet and whined, "Help me, Bell! I'm hurt!"

Cory stepped forward and brought a violent roundhouse punch against Bob's jaw. Bob fell backward into the creek, and Cory waded in after him, his eyes burning with hatred. Sinking his fingers into the dazed outlaw's hair, he plunged his head under the water. Bob started to struggle against the powerful hands that held him under, but Cory grasped him in a viselike grip, all the while cursing at him for what he'd tried to do to Anna Laura.

Suddenly, amid the splashing and his own shouting, Cory heard a voice crying, "Cory! Don't kill him! You'll go to prison! Don't kill him! He isn't worth it!"

Cory lifted his eyes to see beautiful Anna Laura standing on the bank, holding her torn blouse closed, a pleading look in her eyes. Coming to his senses, he lifted the sagging form of Bob McCarty out of the water. Bob coughed, drew a sharp breath, and went into a spasm of coughing. Cory dragged him ashore, dropped him, and took Anna Laura in his arms.

With tears streaming down her cheeks, Anna Laura wrapped her arms around Cory, digging her fingers into his back, her head resting on his chest. "Oh, Cory!" she sobbed. "I killed that detective! He told me who he was, but Bob swore he was a hired killer, out to get him and his uncle. Bob tricked me, Cory, and I killed that man!" She broke into sobs, her body shaking.

Cory eyed the lifeless form of Durwood Peters lying

nearby. Cupping Anna Laura's tear-stained face in his hands, he gently asked, "Are you saying that you shot him without giving him a chance to surrender his gun?"

Shaking her head vigorously, she replied, "No! I was holding Bob's gun on him with the hammer cocked. Bob shouted for me to kill the man, saying if I didn't, he would kill us both. The detective . . . he . . . he reached for his pocket, saying there was something he wanted to show me. I was scared, Cory! Just then Bob shouted that Peters was pulling a trick. I . . . I panicked and jumped. The gun went off in my hand, and Mr. Peters fell down dead!"

Looking deep into her dark-brown eyes, Cory said with conviction, "Anna, you didn't kill Peters. Bob McCarty did by making you believe you were being confronted by a hired killer. He tricked you into putting the gun on Peters in the first place and then made sure that your hand would jerk and the gun would go off."

Biting her lip, Anna Laura nodded. "Yes, that's true."

"Then, honey, you didn't kill Mr. Peters." Turning, Cory pointed toward Bob, who was crumpled on the creek bank, holding his bleeding shoulder. "That lying snake is the one who killed him." Cupping Anna Laura's face in his hands again, he said, "It was not your fault."

Turning away, Anna Laura nodded weakly.

"Look at me, Anna!" he insisted.

Slowly she brought her eyes up to meet his, looking at him through a veil of tears.

"Anna, darling, you're not the killer," Cory said softly. "Bob McCarty is the killer."

Suddenly Cory found Anna Laura's lips with his own. She responded slowly at first, then with increased passion, as if she were drawing strength from the kiss. When their lips finally parted she took a deep breath and said, "Oh, Cory, I should have listened! You warned me about Bob!"

"It's all right now, honey," he soothed. "Everything's going to be okay. Let's get you back to the house."

"Cory . . ." she said, looking at him timidly.

"Yes?"

"How did you know we were out here? Why did you come?"

"I sent Bill Rogers to the ranch house to tell Bo that

we'd be late for supper. When Bill returned he told us that a Pinkerton detective named Peters had shown up with proof that Walter Smythe is really Tom McCarty. He explained that you and Bob had come riding this way and that Molly and the other two outlaws had already headed off for Sundance. I sent the rest of the men to rescue Molly while I took off to find you."

Embracing him tightly, Anna Laura said, "Cory, if you hadn't come, he would have . . ." Her face twisted with anguish. "He would have . . ."

Core placed a forefinger on her lips. "He *didn't*, honey. That's all that matters. Now, come on. Let's go."

Moments later they left the creek behind, with Durwood Peters draped over his horse's back and Bob McCarty sitting astride his mount, his mouth in a sullen frown.

At the house Bo Heflin trained his gun steadily between the two outlaws as he explained to Molly Dunne that the ranch hands were on their way in from the range and would be there soon. He did not notice Elzy Lay eyeing the alabaster lamp within inches of his grasp.

When Bo mentioned the name of Mark Young, Molly smiled confidently and said, "When Mark learns that McCarty, here, bushwhacked Sam, he'll make sure that he hangs."

Bo chuckled, glancing momentarily at Molly. It was in that unguarded moment that Elzy Lay made his move. With the speed of a rattler his hand flicked to the alabaster lamp and hurled it at the big cook. The heavy base struck Bo on the temple, and he buckled to his knees. His gun fired, sending a bullet into the door casing, and then slipped from his fingers as he fell to the floor.

Reacting quickly, Molly made a dive for the gun, but Tom McCarty stepped in and kicked her savagely in the ribs. The impact sent her careening against the wall, the breath knocked out of her.

As McCarty picked up the gun Elzy Lay shouted, "Let's get out of here, Tom!"

McCarty spun around. "There's something I've got to do," he told Elzy, thinking of the money he had stashed in the library.

Elzy saw that Molly was pulling herself up to her knees, gasping for air. Impatient, he growled, "We ain't got time for you to do nothing! Those cowboys will be here any minute! Come on!"

Elzy turned toward the door. McCarty started in the direction of the library, then checked himself as he heard the thunder of hooves coming from outside.

"Come on, Tom!" Elzy shouted again, then raced through the door.

McCarty realized that the Circle D ranch hands were closing in. It was too late to retrieve his money. He moved toward the open doorway, but suddenly Molly leaped at him from behind, sinking her fingers into his face.

"You murdered Sam!" she screamed, clawing him savagely.

McCarty swore, throwing her down, but before he could make it to the open doorway, she had rolled to her knees and was on him again, clawing and scratching as before. Spinning around, he slammed her against the doorjamb, then brought up his elbow full force against her jaw.

Molly dropped to her knees, head spinning. She made a feeble attempt to grab McCarty's legs, but then fell forward onto her face as he leaped over her and dashed out into the yard, where his partner was already in the wagon. Even as McCarty was clambering up onto the seat the wagon was starting out across the yard toward the open road.

The Circle D hands were coming in from the north, riding hard, and were only a few hundred yards away. Bill Rogers, riding in the lead, saw the wagon bounding eastward, leaving a cloud of dust. Rogers was just veering his horse in that direction when he saw Molly Dunne stagger out onto the porch of the ranch house. Pulling rein, he raised his hand to signal the men behind him. They followed suit, and within seconds the whole bunch skidded to a halt at the porch. Rogers leaped from his saddle and bolted to Molly, who was gripping one of the upright posts on the porch.

"Miss Dunne!" Rogers gasped, eyeing the red mark on her jaw. "What happened?"

Holding one hand to her throbbing jaw, Molly looked at him with hazy eyes and said, "Those two outlaws knocked Bo unconscious. He's in the house."

"Looks like they beat up on you, ma'am," Rogers said, reaching to steady her.

"I'll be all right," she gasped. "Leave one of the men to help me with Bo and go after those snakes!"

Rogers turned and called for one of the older cowboys to stay behind. Then he vaulted onto his saddle, called out, "Let's go get 'em, boys!" and took off at a gallop.

Tom McCarty had told his men to hide out in the wooded area after the staged attack in case he needed them. Now he was glad he'd done so. He glanced over at Elzy Lay, who was snapping the reins at the horses and yelling at the top of his voice, then looked behind them at the boiling cloud of dust and knew the Circle D riders would soon be upon them. If they could just make that thick stand of trees where his men were waiting, they would have a chance.

The next three minutes seemed like an hour, but finally the trees came into view. "Faster, Elzy!" McCarty shouted, catching a glimpse of the oncoming riders through the dust cloud behind the wagon. "They're coming!"

McCarty's five men peered through the trees and saw the wagon closing in. As soon as they recognized their boss and Elzy Lay, they knew something was wrong. Pulling their guns, they waited for the wagon to roll to a stop.

McCarty jumped from the wagon and shouted, "Things went sour, fellas! We've got a gunfight on our hands!"

No sooner had McCarty spoken than the thundering horde came into view. One of his men shouted, "There must be twenty or more! We can't hold out against that many!"

"We've got to!" blared the outlaw leader. "Our chances are better here among these trees than if we make a run for it and get caught in the open!"

The outlaws spread out, each man picking a tree to hide behind. As the Circle D riders drew near, the gang opened fire.

Immediately the cowboys fanned apart, leaping from their mounts, dropping to the ground, and returning fire. They did not know how many men McCarty had with him in the woods, but they had no intention of letting them get away.

While guns roared Bill Rogers raised up slightly and shouted for some of the men to work their way around the stand of trees and try to circle in from the sides. They nodded and began moving in both directions. Just then a bullet tore into Rogers's right thigh, and he fell backward to the ground. Keeping his head low, he tore his pants open and saw where the slug had gouged a half-inch-deep furrow. Quickly he pulled the bandanna from his neck and tied it tightly around his thigh, staying the flow of blood.

"Bill," came the voice of one of the men a few yards away, "you okay?"

"Yeah!" he called back. "Let's move in on 'em!"

Hiding behind one of the trees, Tom McCarty loaded his revolver with the remaining bullets on his belt. Nearby, one of his men lay dead in the brush. He glanced around the tree and saw that the Circle D hands were working their way closer from three sides.

McCarty pulled his head back sharply as a bullet chewed into the bark beside his head. Turning to where Elzy Lay was crouching behind a tree, he shouted, "Elzy! Our only chance is to make a run for it while the rest of these guys fight it out!"

Elzy nodded. "Let's go!"

The two outlaws bent low and ran toward where the gang's horses were tied. Grabbing the reins of the two nearest animals, they leaped into the saddle and galloped out of the thicket, heading straight toward the Circle D men. As they charged across the clearing one of the cowhands rose up on his knees and lifted a rifle to his shoulder. Before the man could take aim McCarty drew his revolver and shot him in the chest.

As the fleeing outlaws topped the first rise they looked back to see two more of the gang following. Slowing up, they allowed Mike Landy and Gus Waymore to catch up. Soon the four riders had passed over the ridge and were beyond sight of the Circle D hands.

At a full gallop Waymore drew his horse abreast of McCarty's and shouted, "We just gonna leave the others back there?"

"Every man for himself!" bellowed McCarty. "Let's go!"

The four riders dropped down into a gully, then passed over another rise. By the time they descended into another gully the gunfire was fading from their ears.

Above the thundering hooves McCarty shouted, "Let's head for the Hole-in-the-Wall! It's the only safe place!"

Back at the wooded area the two remaining gang members fought doggedly, unable to escape because McCarty and Elzy Lay had taken their horses. Meanwhile the Circle D hands, unaware of how many men they were facing, continued to fire a barrage of lead into the thicket, attempting to bring down what gang members were left.

A few minutes later one of the outlaws took a bullet to the head. The remaining one looked around and realized the hopelessness of his situation. Throwing down his gun, he raised his hands and ran toward the clearing, shouting, "Stop! I give up! I give up!"

The cowhands saw movement among the trees, but the noise of their own gunfire drowned out the outlaw's cries of surrender. Every revolver and rifle opened up at once, with the fire concentrated at the spot in the trees from which a figure was emerging. The outlaw stiffened as numerous slugs tore into his body. He clawed for the sky, then dropped lifeless to the ground.

Soon the firing stopped, and there was an eerie silence as the late afternoon breeze carried the gun smoke away. Bill Rogers stood and limped toward the trees, his pant leg soaked with blood. Calling to one of the men, he hollered, "Take some of the men and go after the rest of them!"

An even dozen men mounted in response and headed west at a full gallop.

Night fell over Sundance. Willie Chance had waited until he was sure all of the McCarty gang had left town before heading for the Wagon Wheel Saloon. With fifty dollars in his pocket he was going to make friends fast. By eight o'clock Chance's money was gone and he was dangerously drunk, along with six of his new friends. The seven of them leaned on the bar, eyes drooping listlessly as they demanded that Nat Randolph let them have more whiskey on credit.

The burly bartender was pouring drinks for two trail hands, who also stood at the bar. Giving the seven drunks a scowl, he said, "You boys have had enough for one day. Get on out of here and sleep it off."

One of them, a stout-bodied man himself, mumbled, "Now, l-look here, Randolph. My friend Willie's spent f-fifty dollars right here at this bar o' yours. I think you . . . you oughta feel some 'preciation for his p-patronage. And you oughta have some 'preciation for his friends here t-too. After all, we coulda gone down the st-street t'another saloon, you know."

"I said no credit!" barked Randolph. "Now, you guys may leave quietly."

The whiskey in Willie Chance's veins had fired up his courage and his temper. Slamming an open palm on the bar, he rasped loudly, "Look here, tarbender—uh, bartender. Maybe you don't know who you're dealin' with."

Nat Randolph moved directly in front of Chance and gave him a stiff glare. Chance's eyes were bloodshot, and his head lobbed lazily from the effects of the large amount of alcohol that he'd consumed in the past several hours. "If you're talkin' about yourself, mister," said Randolph, "I'm dealin' with a little man who is dead drunk and doesn't even know where he is. Go on and get out of here."

Chance's already florid face turned deeper red. All his bitterness toward Tom McCarty seemed to gather in the middle of his chest. "You're dealin' with a tough outlaw, you are!" he blared. "My name's Willie Chance!"

Before Randolph could respond Willie dragged out his revolver, eared back the hammer, and waved it in his face. Randolph ducked just as the gun discharged, shattering the mirror behind the bar. Randolph came up with a shotgun but found himself looking down the barrel of a gun in the hand of one of the other six drunks. The bartender froze, and the man yanked the shotgun from his hands.

By this time all of Chance's friends had produced guns.

Chance raised the muzzle of his revolver toward the wagon wheel chandeliers overhead and said, "Hey, fellas! Let's put out the lights!"

Immediately the whole bunch began shooting at the small kerosene lanterns that adorned the wagon wheels. Patrons were scattering, plunging through the doorway as the seven guns continued to blast away, with few of the lanterns being hit.

Suddenly the swinging doors flew open. Sheriff Jim Naylor and Deputy Ken Eastman barged in, bearing double-barreled shotguns. "Drop your guns, every one of you!" roared Naylor.

The sight of the deadly shotguns sobered the seven drunks enough for them to know that the party was over. Their weapons rattled to the floor, and they were immediately ushered out the door, with Naylor promising Nat Randolph that the damage would be covered by the guilty men.

Moments later the two lawmen and their prisoners made their way into the sheriff's office. While Naylor held his shotgun on the seven men, the deputy crossed the office and opened the door to the cellblock in back. There were four cells along the corridor, two on each side. Two prisoners each were placed in three of the cells, with Willie Chance being given the fourth cell alone.

"We'll make them pay up in the morning," Naylor told his deputy, "and the judge'll probably give them ten days in here besides."

As the lawmen returned to the office a man burst in from outside and said excitedly, "Sheriff! The Circle D bunch just rode in, packin' a passel of dead bodies!"

Naylor and Eastman shouldered past the man and stepped into the lantern-lit street. A Circle D wagon with Cory Bell at the reins led a procession of a dozen riders. Hunched over beside Cory was a dark-haired man clutching a bloody shoulder. Next to him Bill Rogers gingerly held a wounded leg. In the back of the wagon were several corpses.

The lawmen hurried to where Cory Bell was pulling the wagon to a halt in front of the doctor's office. Stepping close, Naylor pushed his hat to the back of his head and said, "Cory, what the—"

"I'll tell you the whole story, Sheriff," cut in Cory, "but right now I've got to get Bill to Doc Breslin. His leg's shot up. He's losing blood."

Setting his eyes on the dark-haired man in the middle, Naylor said, "Looks like you've got another one shot up pretty bad. Who's he?"

"He's part of the story, Sheriff," replied Cory. "His name's Bob McCarty."

"*McCarty!*"

"Yes, sir. Tom McCarty's nephew. Our men got into a gunfight with the McCarty gang and almost wiped them out!"

Running his eyes to the corpses in the bed of the wagon, Naylor said, "Tom?"

"He got away," Cory replied dejectedly. "He and three others. Some of our boys chased after them, but it got dark and they lost them."

"Well, get these wounded men inside," the sheriff said, swinging his arm. "Then come on back and fill me in."

"You got some handcuffs I can use, Sheriff?" asked Cory. "McCarty, here, will have to be handcuffed to one of the beds in Doc's office."

Bob McCarty glowered at Cory but said nothing.

"Right here," spoke up Ken Eastman, pulling a pair of handcuffs from his back pocket. "And here's the key."

"Thanks." Cory smiled, then signaled some of his men to help get the wounded men inside.

Twenty minutes later Cory Bell entered the sheriff's office and sat down in front of the desk. Naylor leaned forward on the desk, while Ken Eastman pulled up another chair. "My boys have hit the saloons," said Cory, "so I'll have plenty of time to tell you the story."

When Cory had finished telling of all the events that had happened out at the Circle D ranch Jim Naylor shook his head and said, "I was afraid one or both of those Pinkertons was going to end up dead. The other is probably following Mark Young. As for McCarty and the three who got away, you can bet your boots they're headed for the Hole-in-the-Wall."

"That's what I'd guess," put in Eastman. "We sure can't chase them in there."

"Wait a minute!" said Naylor, snapping his fingers. "Maybe they can be intercepted before they reach it!"

Naylor pointed out that Marshal Young had left early that morning to escort Butch Cassidy to Kaycee and that the Hole-in-the-Wall was just west of Kaycee. The only town between Sundance and Kaycee was Savageton, and Young and Cassidy would pass through Savageton sometime the next morning. It was quite possible Young would still be ahead of McCarty and his three men at that point.

Pulling a piece of paper out of a desk drawer, the sheriff said, "Ken, I'm going to write a message for Young. I want you to take this over to the Western Union office and have it sent tonight to Sheriff Eric Tubbs at Savageton. I want it waiting for Mark when he arrives."

Five minutes later Eastman stood in the Western Union office and watched the telegraph operator tap out Naylor's message:

SHERIFF ERIC TUBBS SAVAGETON WYOMING *STOP* GIVE MESSAGE TO MARSHAL MARK YOUNG WHO WILL PASS THROUGH MORNING OF JULY SIX *STOP* MCCARTY GANG SHOT UP BAD HERE *STOP* TOM MCCARTY BEAT UP MOLLY DUNNE *STOP* SHE WILL BE OKAY *STOP* MCCARTY AND THREE OTHERS THOUGHT TO BE RIDING TO HOLE IN WALL *STOP* INTERCEPT AND APPREHEND *STOP* SHERIFF JIM NAYLOR SUNDANCE WYOMING

Chapter Eleven

The sun rose over the rugged hills on the morning of July 6, following U.S. Marshal Mark Young and Butch Cassidy westward. As the outlaw rode in silence beside him Young's thoughts were on Molly Dunne. He would never have wished for Sam Dunne's death, but now that it had happened, he was not about to let Molly get away from him again. He hoped her affection toward him could be nurtured into real love.

With the prospect that Molly might one day be his, Mark Young felt a keen ray of hope. Up until now he'd been as unsettled and lonely as the Wyoming wind. His job took him back and forth across Montana and Wyoming, but with the beautiful brunette as his wife he would have roots and the loneliness would dissipate. With Molly to come home to . . .

The marshal's thoughts were pulled back to reality as the outline of Savageton's clustered rooftops came into view. It was just after nine o'clock when they pulled into town. The wind was picking up, sending swirls of dust along the single street that separated the bare, weathered buildings. The little town was only eighty miles from Sundance, but the area was far more barren, without the lush grass and green rolling hills that Sundance enjoyed.

Sheriff Eric Tubbs was sitting on the porch in front of his office. When he saw the two riders approach he stood up and smiled at Young. As they dismounted he gave

Butch Cassidy a sour look, then said to the marshal, "Hello, Mark. Been expectin' you."

Young's eyebrows arched. "You have?"

"Yep," came the reply as Tubbs pulled a piece of paper from his vest pocket. "Wire came last night from Jim Naylor. Pretty important. You'd better read it right now."

As Young took the paper he said, "I guess you know Robert LeRoy Parker here."

"Sure do." Tubbs gave the outlaw another sour look.

Young unfolded the paper and read Naylor's message. His expression grew dark as he absorbed the news. Looking back at Tubbs, he said, "I've got to get to Kaycee as fast as possible. I'll turn Cassidy over to the law there and then intercept McCarty. See you later."

Tubbs watched as Young and his prisoner galloped out of Savageton heading southwest for Kaycee. The distance was just shy of forty miles. Tubbs figured the two horses would be pushed to the limit.

It was early afternoon when the lathered horses brought Kaycee into view. As the riders drew near the edge of town Young said to the outlaw, "Well, Butch, here's where you get out of the hot sun and into a nice cool jail cell. Your next stop will be the state penitentiary at Rawlins." Seeing Cassidy's barely masked look of dread, he added, "Too bad you didn't cooperate earlier, Butch. Now it's too late. I hope the judge throws the book at you."

Cassidy did not reply.

They pulled up in front of the sheriff's office, and Young dismounted, then helped the handcuffed Cassidy down off his horse. As they entered the office Sheriff John Allinger looked up from his desk, smiling as he recognized the U.S. marshal. His smile broadened when he saw Butch Cassidy. Standing, he said, "Good work, Mark! I knew you'd do it! Did you bring Mr. Weyerhauser's horse back too?"

"It's at the hitch rail outside," said Young with a toss of his head. "I'm in a hurry, John. Got a lead on Tom McCarty. Take Cassidy, lock him up, and bring me back my cuffs. I have to get something from my saddlebag."

Two minutes later Young returned with an envelope which he handed to Allinger, who was just returning from

the cell area. "Give this to the judge, John," he said. "It's
my statement concerning the arrest of Cassidy, attesting
that I caught him red-handed with the stolen animal. Wire
me at Naylor's office in Sundance when the trial's over."

"Will do." Allinger nodded and handed Young his handcuffs, then added, "Mark, maybe you ought to let me
round up some men to go along and help you capture
McCarty."

Young's eyes flashed fire. "Thanks, John, but no thanks,"
he said crisply. "I'll handle McCarty myself."

"You're a good lawman, Mark," Allinger said cautiously,
"but I'm wondering if your decision isn't based on personal reasons."

"What do you mean?"

"I mean it's plain as daylight that you're eaten up with
anger. Is there something between you and McCarty?"

"Yeah," he breathed hotly. "Something personal." With
that, he turned and walked outside.

Allinger followed him. Stopping at the edge of the boardwalk, he said, "Are you sure you don't want me to send
some men along? They might keep you from doing something in anger that could cost you your badge."

As Young untied the reins of his horse he saw a rider
coming into town from the east. Instantly he recognized
the Pinkerton detective, Jack Clancy. Cursing under his
breath, he spat in the dust, then turned to Allinger and
said, "I won't shame my badge, John. But I assure you, it
will be a pleasure to get my hands on Tom McCarty."

Mark Young realized why Clancy was following him. He
would have to do something about the pesky detective
before leaving, and so he stood beside his horse and
waited until Clancy reined in.

"Good morning, Marshal." Clancy smiled and remained
seated on his horse.

Young nodded curtly but said nothing.

"Who is this?" asked Allinger.

"Pinkerton detective," replied Young caustically. "His
name's Jack Clancy. He figures I'm going on Tom McCarty's
trail after delivering Cassidy here."

"Well?" Clancy asked. "Isn't it so?"

"It's none of your business where I'm going when I

leave here, Clancy." Pointing a stiff finger, he added,
"And you'd better not follow me."

"Why not?" demanded Clancy, his face growing crimson.

"Because you would just get in my way, fancy pants,'
came the pungent reply. "Go play your game somewhere
else."

Clancy glared at the marshal. "I've been hired by the
railroad to track down McCarty and bring him in! And I
intend to do just that!"

"Then why are you following me? Go chase McCarty!"

"That's what I'm doing," Clancy replied with a sneer.

"When I find McCarty, he's mine!" Young snarled.

"I have as much right to apprehend him as you do!"

"I'm not going to stand here and argue with you, Clancy,"
Young said flatly. "I know your kind. The only reason
you're after McCarty is for what it'll bring you—a fat raise
a step up the ladder of success. That makes you a danger
ous man to have around in a crisis. So keep out of my way
understand?" With that the marshal swung into the saddle
and backed his horse from the hitch rail.

Seeing that Clancy was nudging his horse to follow
Young spun around and hissed, "If you follow me, Clancy
I'll break you in two!"

The detective smirked defiantly and retorted, "It's a
free country!"

Mark Young suddenly leaped from his saddle, charged
over to Clancy, and yanked him from his horse. The
detective tumbled down and went sprawling in the dust
Young leaned over, sank the fingers of his left hand in the
surprised detective's shirt, and pulled him to his feet
Cocking his right fist, Young let go of the shirt and sent
whistling punch to the man's jaw. There was the crack of
bone against bone, and Jack Clancy went down flat on his
back in the street. He was out cold.

Young rubbed his fist as he spoke to Sheriff Allinger
"Lock him up for forty-eight hours for obstructing justice
then let him out. See you later." With that the marsha
mounted his horse and rode to the livery stable, where he
changed to a fresh mount. Then he proceeded up the
street to the general store and purchased a sixty-foot lengt

of rope. Looping it over his saddle horn, he rode south out of town.

Young knew practically every square foot of Wyoming, including the trail that led to the Hole-in-the-Wall. The outlaws stuck to the trail so that if they ever ran into trouble, another of their kind would soon pass by and could offer assistance. Young was certain that McCarty and his three friends would use that trail to make a bee-line for the Hole, which would take them through a narrow pass nine miles south of Kaycee. The outlaws called it Knifeblade Pass.

The well-traveled pass was nearly a mile in length and ridged on both sides by ten-foot-high mounds covered with rocks and sagebrush. The west end of the pass was only forty feet wide and was partially obscured by a thick growth of scrub oak trees on both sides.

The sun was going down as the federal marshal completed his preparations at the west end of the pass. He hid his horse behind the north ridge, then brought the rope down to the thicket of scrub oak. Tying one end to the base of a tree, he ran it across the mouth of the pass to the thicket on the other side, then buried the rope in the dusty ground.

With the rope in place, Mark Young climbed the ridge and took up a position from where he could see any riders entering the pass from the east.

Tom McCarty rode west across the hills, sided by Elzy Lay, Mike Landy, and Gus Waymore. The horses were beginning to tire, but McCarty, eager to reach the safety of the Hole-in-the-Wall, had barely allowed them to rest since leaving their campsite at sunrise.

McCarty was in such a foul mood that none of the other men dared suggest that they stop and rest the animals. The outlaw leader had several things gnawing at him. He'd lost his chance to take over the Circle D ranch, shattering his dream of owning one of the largest spreads in eastern Wyoming. On top of that most of his gang had been killed. In addition he felt responsible for his nephew and had no way of knowing what had happened to him. By now Bob might be swinging from the gallows in Sundance.

The thing that bothered him most, however, was the loss of the thirty thousand dollars he'd left behind in Molly Dunne's library. He realized it would be next to impossible ever to get that money back, and he cursed under his breath as he thought of it sitting there beyond reach.

At that moment Tom McCarty's attention was drawn to Elzy Lay, who was pointing ahead. McCarty looked and saw Knifeblade Pass stretched out in front of them in the waning sunlight. He managed a crooked smile at the sight of the pass. Not far beyond lay the Hole-in-the-Wall, where he and his men would be safe from even the notorious and tenacious Marshal Mark Young.

"Almost home now!" McCarty shouted to the others, and they smiled back.

Fifteen minutes later the four outlaws entered Knifeblade Pass, riding four abreast. They held their horses to an even trot while they made their way between the large mounds that formed the north and south ridges. As they neared the west end Elzy Lay said, "First time I ever came through here, I was riding with Butch Cassidy!"

Waymore laughed. "From now on you can brag that the most important time you ever came through Knifeblade Pass, you were ridin' with the famous outlaw Gus Waymore!"

Just as McCarty and the others joined in the laughter, a taut rope appeared out of the dust, entangling the legs of the trotting horses. All four animals went sprawling forward, catapulting their riders to the ground.

The horses quickly got up, none seriously injured. As the men scrambled to their feet, cursing and slapping at their dust-covered clothing, they looked around and tried to figure out what had happened. Just as they spied the rope lying slack along the ground, they saw in the settling dust the broad-shouldered form of a man standing before them, gun in hand, a U.S. marshal's badge on his chest. Though they'd never seen him in person, all four knew who he was.

In a half whisper Mike Landy exclaimed, *"Mark Young!"*

Tom McCarty felt a wave of hatred as he faced the man. "Well, we finally meet," he said, forcing an even tone.

"Yes," breathed Young, struggling to suppress the anger he felt toward the man who had dared to harm Molly

Dunne. In a controlled voice he said, "We'll do this one at a time. McCarty, reach down and lift your gun with your fingertips and toss it off to your left."

As McCarty was moving his hand slowly toward the gun Elzy Lay suddenly noticed that his own gun had fallen from his holster when he tumbled from the horse. It was lying in the dust not six feet from where the marshal stood. There would be no chance to shoot his way out of this.

McCarty eased the revolver out and gave it a toss. It landed some ten or twelve feet to his left. Meanwhile Gus Waymore and Mike Landy were signaling each other out of the corners of their eyes. Abruptly both of them clawed for their guns. Young's weapon spoke twice in deadly fashion, dropping the men in their tracks. At that split second McCarty made a dive for his gun.

Young saw the move but did not want to kill the outlaw leader. Quickly he fired and plowed dirt just ahead of McCarty, who hesitated, then lunged for the weapon again. This time Young fired at McCarty's gun and sent it spinning away along the ground, its cylinder smashed and useless.

While the marshal was occupied with McCarty, Elzy Lay managed to grab the reins of a nearby horse. He vaulted into the saddle and kicked the horse forward. He didn't look back as he galloped toward the west, but he heard the crack of a revolver and simultaneously felt a stab of pain in his left shoulder. He managed to stay in the saddle and keep his horse at full speed as he passed through the mouth of Knifeblade Pass and raced on toward the Hole-in-the-Wall.

Mark Young watched the outlaw ride off in the dust. He knew he could not go after him without losing the bigger prize, Tom McCarty, and so he turned back to the dark-haired outlaw leader, who stood with a revolver in his hand. It was not his own mangled revolver, but Elzy Lay's.

There was a wicked glint in McCarty's eyes. "By my count you just fired your last shot, Marshal."

"You count to five real well," Young said with a thin

smile, "but are you so sure I didn't load the sixth chamber? Sure enough to risk your life?"

McCarty stared at the ominous muzzle of the revolver in the marshal's hand, then glanced down at the gun in his own. Suddenly he yanked his hand up, earing back the hammer and then squeezing the trigger. Before he had completed the motion he heard Young's revolver discharge with a deafening boom, followed by the whine of a bullet at his left ear. The slug tore away the earlobe, and McCarty's whole body jerked, causing his own gun to fire wide of its mark. The gun slipped from his fingers as he instinctively grabbed at his bleeding ear.

By the time McCarty realized what had happened and spun around to look for the gun, Mark Young had already come up with it and was standing only feet away, Elzy Lay's loaded gun in his hand.

"Now you're going to tell me exactly what you did to Molly Dunne and why," Young demanded, stepping closer.

"I'm not telling you a thing, lawman," McCarty said with sand in his voice.

"I asked you a question, McCarty!" bellowed Young. "I get an answer right now or the next bullet I fire will be between your eyes!"

McCarty could see the fury etched on Mark Young's face, and he knew the marshal would carry out his threat—badge or no badge. "Okay! Okay!" he blurted. "I'll tell you!" The outlaw went on to confess his role as Walter Smythe, including his murder of Sam Dunne and the way he'd manhandled Molly Dunne.

When the story was finished Mark Young stood staring at McCarty, feeling his temper boil. He holstered the gun in his hand and began to unbuckle his gun belt, all the while picturing McCarty's boot in Molly's ribs and his fist in her face.

McCarty's mouth sagged open in fear and surprise as the marshal laid the holster on the ground. Realizing that the lawman intended to take out his anger with his fists, he felt a sudden desperate hope. *All right!* he thought. *Now I have a chance!*

Young removed his badge and dropped it next to his gun belt. Through tight lips he said, "For the moment,

McCarty, I'm not a U.S. marshal but merely the friend of Molly and Sam Dunne." He removed his hat and dropped it to the ground. Looking up at the outlaw, he added, "I see that Molly left some marks on your face. Now I'm going to finish what she started."

McCarty rolled his shoulders, flexing his arms. He'd met few men who could match him in a fight, and he was certain this time would be no different. Leering wickedly, he hissed, "You'll be sorry you threw that gun away. I'm gonna rip you apart!"

McCarty immediately bolted toward the marshal. The sudden charge caught Young slightly off balance, and he was knocked by a hard right to the head that rocked him back on his heels. As he quickly shook it off he saw McCarty aiming another punch at his face. Stepping to one side, he bobbed his head to dodge the blow, then drove a savage left to McCarty's midsection. When the outlaw jackknifed from the impact, Young followed with a stinging right to the point of the chin. McCarty reeled back, then gained his balance and charged in again.

Young clipped him on the nose, following with a blow to the ribs. McCarty staggered slightly, and Young belted him on the mouth, splitting his lips against his teeth. As McCarty tasted blood he managed to tag the marshal with a wild punch, then took another blow to the midsection that lifted his feet off the ground. The earth seemed to fly up and slam him on the back.

Mark Young stood over him, sucking for breath. "Come on! I'm not through with you yet!"

McCarty rolled over, shaking his head. He knew he was whipped unless he could find a way to hurt Young quickly. Spitting a mouthful of blood, he took a deep breath, leaped to his feet, and barreled head down toward his adversary. He caught Young square in the midsection with his head, bowling him over and knocking the breath from his lungs.

The two men rolled in the dust, and McCarty came up on top. Eyes wild, he knotted his fists and pummeled the marshal in the belly. Young felt the pain shoot out in all directions, and nausea settled in his stomach. He arched himself and threw off the outlaw, but as he rolled to his knees McCarty lashed out his leg and kicked him in the mouth. It was the marshal's turn to taste blood.

McCarty stood and shot another kick at Young. This time Young seized his foot and wrenched it unmercifully. McCarty howled in pain and fell. Young let go of his grip and scrambled to his feet, puffing hard as he waited for the outlaw to get up. As soon as he did Young stepped in and chopped him savagely on the nose. McCarty went down hard, his nose spurting blood. On his back he looked up groggily at the half dozen images he was seeing.

Young thought of McCarty's boot in Molly's ribs. Stepping close, he hissed angrily, "This is for Molly!"

Tom McCarty had never been kicked by a horse, but he thought he had been when Young's boot connected with his rib cage. All the breath went out of him, and he flopped on his back, hearing a long moan that seemed to come from far away. Then the noise faded as McCarty felt himself falling into a dark, whirling void.

Rain had begun to fall on the night of July 7 as Cory Bell shared supper with Anna Laura Leslie and Molly Dunne. When the meal was finished Cory pitched in and helped with the dishes. As soon as the kitchen was clean Molly retired to her room, purposely leaving her sister and Cory alone.

A pair of kerosene lamps gave the sitting room a warm glow as the young couple sat down on the sofa. The brightness from an occasional flash of lightning filled the room, and the steady rainfall added a soft patter to the night.

Cory turned to face Anna Laura, and she smiled gently. For several minutes they remained silent, trying to read thoughts in each other's eyes.

Finally, Anna Laura said, "Cory . . ."

"Yes?"

"Do you remember that a few days ago I said I wasn't ready to fall in love?"

"I sure do. I've prayed that you'd change your mind and fall in love with *me*."

"You really did?"

"Yes, and when you called me *darling* after I shot Bob McCarty I felt sure my prayer was being answered."

Her eyes widened. "I called you *darling?*"

Cory's brow furrowed. "You don't remember?"

Looking away, she stammered, "Well, I . . . I . . ."

Feeling a touch of disappointment, the young cowboy stood and walked to the rain-spattered window, where he stood staring out into the darkness. Presently he heard soft footsteps behind him, then Anna Laura's delicate voice spoke his name.

"Cory," she said, moving close as he turned to face her, "I am not ready to fall in love now either."

Cory nodded solemnly, trying to accept it.

A smile tugged at the corners of her mouth. "I'm not *ready* to fall in love, Cory—because I already have."

Cory swallowed hard. "You mean. . . ?"

"Yes, Cory darling, I love you."

Cory Bell took her into his arms, and their lips came together in a long, tender kiss.

Chapter Twelve

T he sky was clear as U.S. Marshal Mark Young rode into Sundance just before ten o'clock on the morning of July 8. Beside him Tom McCarty rode with his hands cuffed in front of him. His normally handsome face was a mass of cuts and bruises. One eye was swollen almost shut, and his nose was bent and broken.

People came out of saloons and stores to get a look at the infamous outlaw as word spread through town that Marshal Young had caught him.

When the riders reached the sheriff's office Jim Naylor came out and greeted Young, who explained that he would take McCarty to Doc Breslin's office for treatment. Naylor then informed him that Bob McCarty was under the doctor's care for a gunshot wound and was handcuffed to a bed. McCarty's ears picked up when he heard that his nephew was still alive, but though he wondered how Bob had been wounded, he remained silent.

Moments later the marshal led McCarty into the doctor's office. Breslin was seated at his desk. He looked up over his half-moon glasses and smiled. "Well, Mark," he said pleasantly, running his fingers through his silver hair, "I see you got him. This has to be Tom McCarty. Even with his swollen face I can see the resemblance between him and his nephew."

"This is McCarty, all right," Young replied. "He's got

some sore ribs you might want to check, and I'm pretty sure his nose is broken."

Breslin looked at McCarty and shook his head. "Looks like you ran into the wrong end of a stampede." Turning to Young, he said, "Let's take him to the infirmary in the back. That's where his nephew is."

The doctor led the two men down a narrow hallway. Pushing open a door on the left, he gestured for them to enter first. Young and McCarty smelled the strong odor of medicines and antiseptics as they stepped into a large room that contained two metal beds and an operating table.

Bob McCarty lay upon one of the beds. At the sight of his uncle he sat up quickly and exclaimed, "Tom! What happened to you?"

"Long story," McCarty replied glumly.

After Young shackled McCarty to the second bed he told the doctor that the sheriff would come by in a couple of hours or so to take McCarty to the jail. Then he left to meet with the sheriff, after which he planned a visit with Molly Dunne at the Circle D.

In the infirmary Doc Breslin said to Tom McCarty, "I've got to get some supplies. Be right back."

As soon as the doctor left, Bob pressed his uncle for details of what had happened. McCarty filled him in, then asked where Bob and Anna Laura had been when they were supposed to have left for Sundance with Molly, Elzy Lay, and McCarty. Bob lied, saying that he was merely out for a ride with Anna Laura when Cory Bell and a Pinkerton detective suddenly appeared. He went on to claim that he managed to kill the Pinkerton but in the process was shot by Cory, and he left out that Cory Bell had come upon him trying to rape Anna Laura.

Though McCarty was not inclined to believe his nephew, he figured it no longer made any difference. He merely shook his head and said grimly, "Somebody spilled their guts to that detective. Had to have been one of my men. No one else knew the plan to take over the ranch. Really bothers me, wondering which one of the gang was a traitor. Never would have been Elzy, so whoever it was is dead, I suppose."

"The man who spilled his guts is not dead," Bob pronounced solemnly.

"What do you mean?"

"It was Willie Chance. The detective said so, just before I shot him."

"Willie Chance!" blurted McCarty. "I never even thought about him! Well, one thing's for sure. When we get out of here I'm looking Willie up. He's gonna pay!"

As Mark Young headed up the street toward the sheriff's office a small crowd was gathering. Hurrying over, he saw Sheriff Naylor trying to calm a woman who was nearly hysterical with grief.

"Somebody's got to go up there and bring him down!" the woman was imploring.

"What's going on?" asked Young.

The woman looked up, and Young recognized her as Clint Yarrow's wife, Helen. She immediately pulled away from the sheriff and sank her trembling fingers into Young's shirt. "Oh, Marshal Young!" she cried. "It's my boy, Danny! He's up on Devil's Tower and can't get down! He's going to fall—I just know it! Somebody's got to bring him down!"

Squeezing her shoulders, he said, "Mrs. Yarrow, don't worry. Everything will be all right." Turning to Naylor, he asked, "Jim, what's the story?"

The sheriff laid his hand on the shoulder of a ten-year-old boy who stood nearby, and introduced him as Gordie Ulster. Gordie had just ridden into town to tell Mrs. Yarrow that he and Danny had taken a horseback ride out to Devil's Tower. Danny, also ten years old, had been inspired by Bill Rogers's daring feat to climb the oak pegs, then had become frightened. Now he was stuck on top of the tower, afraid to climb down.

"Somebody's got to help my boy get down!" cut in Helen. "Clint would do it, but he's in Cheyenne. Oh, Marshal, as scared as Danny is, he'll fall if he tries to come down!"

Young was thoughtful a moment, then said, "Seems to me the natural man for the job is Bill Rogers. I can get him on the way to the tower."

"Won't help," Naylor said flatly. "I was just telling

Helen that Bill got his leg shot up in the gunfight with the McCarty gang. There's no way he can climb."

"That's right, Marshal," spoke up a lean-bodied cowboy, moving in close. Young recognized him as Allen Chaney, one of the Circle D ranch hands. "Took a bullet in the thigh," Chaney continued. "He can't even walk, much less climb."

By this time a large crowd had assembled. Jim Naylor raised his hand for silence and said, "Any of you men ever done any mountain climbing?"

At first no one answered, then a voice called out, "For an inexperienced man to go up there and try to bring the boy down would be suicide!"

"He's right," put in Deputy Ken Eastman. "You saw the trouble Rogers had. Those pegs aren't secure. The boy may not weigh much, but a full-grown man . . ."

"Well, we can't just leave Danny up there," Young proclaimed. "Somebody has to try."

All eyes were suddenly trained on Mark Young. It was as if his statement was an act of volunteering.

Helen Yarrow wiped away tears and looked expectantly at the stalwart lawman. "Oh, Marshal Young, *would* you?"

The die was cast, and Mark Young knew it. With a grim smile he said, "I'll go up after your son, Mrs. Yarrow, but you must understand that I've never done any climbing like this. I can't guarantee anything."

"I understand," she responded. "I certainly don't want anything to happen to you. But if you don't try, Danny will fall for sure."

Young turned to Gordie Ulster. "Gordie, are you sure Danny isn't trying to come down alone?"

"I'm positive, Mr. Young," he said with assurance. "He was very scared and was crying. I shouted up that I'd go for help. I also signaled in case he couldn't hear me. I know he understood. He waved back. I'm sure he won't try it alone."

Young asked Sheriff Naylor to accompany him to the tower, then told Ken Eastman to transfer Tom McCarty from the doctor's office to the jail in a couple of hours. He added that the deputy should take along two or three townsmen to assist, since McCarty was dangerous even in handcuffs. The deputy assured him that he would do it.

When the two lawmen escorted Helen Yarrow and Gordie Ulster out of Sundance, word of Danny's plight spread like wildfire through town and beyond. Even the Circle D was soon informed of the upcoming rescue attempt, as cowhand Allen Chaney mounted up and rode hard for the ranch, eager to carry the news.

The head of Devil's Tower was etched dramatically against the clear Wyoming sky as the four riders approached the southeast base and dismounted. Mark Young shielded his eyes and traced the vertical line of the dark oaken pegs to the very pinnacle of the tower. Then he cupped his hands around his mouth and shouted, "Danny-y-y-y!"

It took a moment for the breeze to carry the sound upward, but presently Danny Yarrow's head appeared at the edge. Helen breathed a sigh of thanks that he was all right, then joined with the others as they waved to the frightened boy. Danny waved back.

Young quickly shed his hat and gun belt, wrapped his saddle rope over one shoulder and around his chest, and began his ascent. As he made his way upward he was glad that he did not have to do it the way Bill Rogers had. It was much easier with the pegs already driven in place.

The marshal moved slowly, careful not to look down, testing each peg before trusting it with his weight. About forty feet up he found one peg to be quite loose. With some effort he bypassed it, making a mental note to be careful of it on the descent.

In just over an hour Young was nearing the top, when he became aware of a growing commotion down on the ground. He didn't need to look down to realize that spectators were arriving to watch the rescue, or at least its attempt.

The wind plucked at his hair as he came within twenty feet of the spot where the young boy waited, his fear-stricken face glancing over the edge.

"You all right, Danny?" Young asked, sleeving sweat from his forehead.

"Yes, sir," the boy answered timidly.

As Young bellied over the rocky lip Danny made a feeble attempt to help him, then burst into tears as he began to apologize profusely for what he'd done and the trouble it had caused. Moving away from the edge, Young stood and put his arms around Danny, pulling him close.

After Danny was calm, Young stepped back to the edge and looked down. As expected, he saw wagons, buggies, surreys, and people on horseback. He estimated that at least one hundred were there already, and he could see little dots of travelers strung out toward Sundance.

Turning back to the boy, he said, "Okay, Danny. We've got to go down together. Are you afraid?"

Swallowing hard and trying to smile, Danny said, "I won't be, as long as you stay close to me."

"Good. Now, I'm going to tie one end of this rope around you and make a loop at the other end. I'll slip the loop over one of the pegs and move it from peg to peg as we go down. That way, if you lose your footing or anything, the rope will hold you. I'll start down first. As soon as I'm over the edge I want you to come feetfirst. I'll be right there to guide you onto the first peg. Don't look down, even at me. I'll be right under you all the way. We'll take it one peg at a time. All right?"

Danny took a deep breath and nodded feebly. Young patted his shoulder, then unraveled the lariat rope and tied one end in a harness around the boy's chest. He played out about ten feet of rope and cut it with a jack-knife from his pocket, then knotted a sturdy loop at the end. As he worked he reassured Danny that within an hour or so he would be on the ground in his mother's arms.

"Are you ready?" Young asked with a reassuring smile.

The boy nodded. "Yes, sir, I think so."

"Good. Then let's go home."

The marshal lay down on his belly and swung his legs over the edge of the tower. The first peg was only a foot from the surface, with the next one two feet beyond that. In a moment Young was standing upright on the ladder that Bill Rogers had driven into the fluted column of rock.

With his shoulders and head still above the lip of the tower, Young reached forward and grasped the loop at the end of the rope, then leaned over and slipped it onto the oak peg at his feet. Straightening up, he signaled Danny to lie down and crawl feetfirst toward the edge. The boy hesitated, then cautiously complied. Young helped him find the first peg with his foot, then stepped down a peg to give Danny room to continue. Within a minute they were both standing firmly on the ladder, with Danny's feet just above the marshal's hands.

As they cautiously made their way down the ladder Young paused periodically to slip the rope off the peg by his hands and replace it on the one at his feet. Each time he took the opportunity to compliment Danny on what a fine job he was doing and to remind him not to look down. Soon they were moving in steady rhythm, making rapid progress down the sheer wall of Devil's Tower.

More than a hundred spectators watched the slow and careful descent as Marshal Young guided ten-year-old Danny Yarrow to safety. When they finally touched the ground the crowd surged forward, with Helen Yarrow at the lead. She scooped her child into her arms, tearfully hugging and kissing him as she repeatedly blurted out her thanks to the man who had risked his own life to save her boy.

Mark Young stood on shaky legs, for the first time realizing how exhausted he was, as cheering people swarmed around him, slapping his back and pumping his hands. The world around him was in a swirl as he struggled to focus on the sea of unfamiliar faces. Then one face came forward out of the mass and began to take form, and as he recognized Molly Dunne, all the others seemed to fade away.

"M-Molly?" he muttered, his voice cracking.

"Oh, Mark!" she exclaimed, stepping closer and embracing him. "Thank God you're all right!"

Young held her close, reveling in the touch of the woman he secretly loved. As he released her he was about to say something, when Anna Laura Leslie came rushing forward and gave him a hug and kiss on the cheek.

"That was such a gallant and unselfish thing to do!" she proclaimed. "You could've fallen to an awful death with just one slip! You're absolutely the bravest man on earth!"

As Anna Laura released Young she noted that his gaze

remained fixed on her sister—and she thought she recognized the look on his face. Slipping away, she walked over to where Cory Bell was standing and whispered something to him. He nodded and disappeared into the crowd.

A few minutes later Cory returned to where Anna Laura was waiting. They spoke together for a moment and then approached Mark Young, who stood next to Molly while receiving congratulations from admirers.

"Mark," Anna Laura said, catching his attention, "I was wondering if you might do me a favor?"

"Why, of course, Anna Laura. What is it?"

"Cory and I would like to ride back to the ranch with some friends, but we didn't want Molly to have to make the ride alone. If you're heading that way . . ."

Anna Laura hesitated, and as if on cue Young put in, "Why, I'd love to escort Molly back to the Circle D." He turned to Molly and added, "That is, if you don't mind."

"Mind?" Molly asked, slipping her hand through his arm. "I'd be delighted."

The sun was throwing long shadows across the Belle Fourche Valley as Marshal Young drove the Circle D wagon southeast from Devil's Tower, with his horse tied on behind. He and Molly rode in silence for several minutes, and then both started to speak at once and abruptly stopped. Each tried to get the other to speak first, and finally Young agreed, saying, "I was going to say that it's nice to have this time together. Perhaps Anna remembered that I wanted to speak with you when I got back, and I appreciate her giving me this chance." He paused a moment, then added, "What were you going to say?"

"Everyone's talking about your bringing in Tom McCarty, and I wanted to know how you caught him."

Young gave Molly a brief rundown on McCarty's capture, taking care not to mention the bloody fistfight.

As he finished, Molly smiled and said, "From what folks have been saying about the way McCarty looks, it sounds like he went a couple of dozen rounds in a prizefighting ring and came up the loser. If that's so, I'd just like whoever taught him a lesson to know that I'm much obliged."

Young smiled sheepishly, neither admitting nor denying what had happened.

As the wagon rolled along and the sun dropped lower Molly laid a hand on Young's arm. "You've been such a good friend, Mark," she said tenderly.

Young cleared his throat. "That's exactly what I've been waiting to talk to you about, Molly—our friendship."

Turning toward him on the seat, she asked, "Is there something wrong with our friendship?"

"Nothing at all," he assured her. "But there's something I have to tell you. Would . . . would you mind if I pull the wagon off the road for a few minutes?"

Molly eyed him quizzically. "Of course I don't mind."

Young guided the team off the road and pulled up under a stand of Rocky Mountain junipers that were bunched along a tiny brook. Wrapping the reins around the brake handle, he turned to face her head-on. Licking his lips nervously, he said, "Now, Molly, you would never have heard what I am about to say if Sam had lived. Is that clear?"

She nodded, her deep blue eyes searching his.

Young wiped the back of his hand across his mouth. "I'm going to be quite blunt," he said with a tremor in his voice. "Molly . . . I am in love with you."

Her eyes widened. "Mark, I—"

"I've always been in love with you, Molly—ever since we were kids—and that love has never died. I hate myself for one thing. I never told you how I felt back when we went out together for a while. You know, the dances and parties. Somehow I never could spit it out. Maybe I was afraid of getting hurt—afraid that you'd say you liked me as a friend but had no romantic feelings for me. I almost told you a couple of times, but then Sam walked into your life."

"Mark, I—"

The words were coming like a flood, and Mark Young could not hold them back. "I've always wondered what would have happened if I'd told you that I loved you. Maybe . . . maybe things would have worked differently. But of course, it all went out the window when you met Sam. Molly, I've carried a torch all these years. I tried to squelch it. I told myself that you were Sam's wife and that I had no right to have these feelings for you. But try as I did, I couldn't snuff out the flame. So I just stayed away most of the time. That was the only way I could keep my heart from being crushed. I . . ."

Young saw tears glisten in Molly's eyes. She reached down and took his hand. With quivering lips, she said, "Mark, if you had told me how you felt before Sam came along, I think it would have made a difference."

Looking at her in disbelief, he muttered, "It would?"

She squeezed his hand. "Like many of the other young women back then, I felt myself falling in love with the handsome Mark Young. You were so popular—which is why it was always a surprise that you never married. I had no reason to believe your feelings were anything other than those of a friend."

"Molly, I . . . I wish I had known. I—"

"I secretly pined for your love, Mark—but so did all the other girls. And then Sam came along. He was so bright and charming, and he had eyes only for me. I really did love him. We had a wonderful marriage."

Young nodded thoughtfully and smiled. "Yes, I know you did. He was very special—and very lucky to have you as his wife."

Molly lifted her hand and gently touched his cheek. "All of that is water under the bridge now. We can't turn back the clock or the calendar. The good Lord has seen fit to take Sam, and he's gone forever. I must go on with my life. Both of us must look to the future."

Mark Young looked at the way the light of the lowering sun was glistening upon Molly's jet-black hair. She seemed more beautiful than ever before.

They sat silent for several minutes, words suddenly distant and out of reach. Then Young whispered, "Molly—"

Before he could say any more she lifted a forefinger to his lips. "Mark, let me say one thing first." She took a deep breath and continued, "The old flame that used to burn for you must have been smoldering down deep. I would never have realized it if Sam had lived. I loved him as much as any wife could love a husband. But . . . but now I sense that old fire welling up within me."

Young's heart was pounding.

Reading his thoughts, Molly said, "I should really wait a few months until I remarry. But if you'll wait for me, Mark, I'll be yours." With a coy smile she added, "Who's doing the proposing here? Me or you?"

With a wide grin Mark Young pulled her close and tenderly said, "I love you, Molly, darling. I love you more than I have ever loved anything in my life. Here and now I make the formal proposal. Will you marry me?"

Tears flooded Molly's eyes. "Yes, my love," she whispered in reply as she laced her fingers behind his head and gave him her lips and her heart.

Earlier that afternoon, while Mark Young was still climbing Devil's Tower, Deputy Ken Eastman and two armed townsmen ushered outlaw Tom McCarty from the doctor's office to a cell at the jail. The seven drunks still occupied the four cells, so Eastman opened the door of the cell occupied by only one man, who was sleeping on one of the two cots.

When the deputy motioned McCarty to enter the cell the outlaw said, "Aren't you going to take off these cuffs?" He raised his hands, which were handcuffed in front of him.

"Nope," replied Eastman dryly. "Keep them till Marshal Young returns. They're his cuffs. He can take them off."

McCarty swore as the barred door clanked shut behind him. As the deputy and his assistants left the cellblock McCarty looked around the small cell. There was a cot on each side with a single latrine pot in one corner and a water jug on a small table beside it. The cell had a twelve-inch-square barred window, through which a narrow shaft of light provided the only illumination.

McCarty eased down on the unoccupied cot and glanced over at his cellmate. The man was short and thin. He was asleep on his side, facing the wall, totally oblivious to what was going on around him.

A quarter hour passed. McCarty was trying to think of a way to escape from his predicament when his cellmate rolled over in his sleep. McCarty gasped with surprise, unable to believe his eyes. There lay Willie Chance! McCarty's fingers opened and closed like talons. Fate had delivered the little man into his hands.

The other prisoners were relatively quiet, murmuring occasionally among themselves. Now and then the pair in the cell directly across from McCarty looked over, examining the new handcuffed prisoner. Just then Willie Chance stirred, his eyes fluttering. One of the prisoners across the way called out, "Hey, Willie! Wake up! You got company!"

The little man sat up, rubbing his eyes. "What say?" he mumbled.

It was then that Chance became aware of another person in his cell. He blinked, then focused on the face. Even though McCarty's features were bruised and swollen, Willie immediately recognized him. His heart froze.

"Hello, Willie," McCarty said coldly, his upper lip curling into a wicked leer. "I understand you had a little talk with a Pinkerton man, Willie."

Chance's eyes bulged with terror. His lips moved, but he was too frightened to make a sound. Rising shakily from his cot, he moved to the far wall of the cell. Slowly he inched along the wall, scraping it with his back, as if a few more feet of distance would protect him from McCarty.

The outlaw leader stood. "Hear how quiet it is, Willie?" he said, smirking as Chance looked nervously around and realized that there was no sound coming from the sheriff's office. "No one's out there. The sheriff's at Devil's Tower, and the deputy's gone. No one's gonna help you, Willie." Turning to the other men, he said, "I'm Tom McCarty. One of you squeals, I'll find a way to get you."

McCarty started toward Willie Chance, who threw up his arms and bleated, "Please, Tom! I—"

In a flash McCarty swung his manacled wrists over the little man's head, pulled him away from the wall, and slid behind him. With a burst of strength he yanked the short chain between the handcuffs tight against Chance's throat, crushing his Adam's apple. Chance gagged as McCarty bore down savagely on his throat. Within a minute his face went blue and his eyes bulged heavily in their sockets.

McCarty held him in the same position for a bit longer to make sure he was dead, then laid him on the cot. A moment later, the front door of the sheriff's office was heard opening and closing. Someone was in the outer office.

"Deputy! You there?" McCarty shouted.

The door to the cellblock opened, and Deputy Eastman called out, "Somebody in here want me?"

"Yeah," McCarty replied. "I think you've got a sick man here. You better take a look at him. He may be dying!"

The young deputy stepped over to the cell and glanced at the ashen-faced man lying on the cot. He dashed back out to the office and returned with the keys. Just before he inserted the key in the lock he pulled his revolver and aimed it at McCarty. "Move back in the corner," he ordered.

The outlaw obeyed. He watched calmly as the deputy entered the cell and approached the body on the cot. When McCarty saw the young man flinch at the horrid look on the dead man's face, he leaped forward with lightning speed and threw the cuffs over Eastman's head. This time he brought the chain up so violently that he snapped the man's spine, killing him instantly.

McCarty lowered the deputy to the floor of the cell and went through his pockets. He grinned triumphantly when his hands closed around the small key Marshal Young had given the deputy. A few seconds later McCarty had the handcuffs unlocked and removed from his wrists. As the other prisoners watched in awe, McCarty removed the deputy's holster, strapped it around his own waist, snatched up the revolver, and fled from the jail.

Chapter Thirteen

Molly Dunne was awakened by her sister late at night after returning from Devil's Tower with Mark Young. She was surprised when Anna Laura told her that Young had just returned from Sundance and was waiting downstairs to speak with her. Molly slipped into some clothes and went down to meet him. Her joy quickly faded when he told her that Tom McCarty had escaped jail, freed his nephew from the doctor's office, and disappeared.

Young said they were no doubt heading for the Hole-in-the-Wall, and he had to leave at once to try to catch them before they reached that haven. He told Molly he might be gone for quite some time—as long as it took to catch McCarty—then he kissed her and rode away, promising to keep her informed of what he was doing.

The weeks passed, during which Molly received several letters from Young describing how the McCartys had managed to elude him. Convinced they were at the Hole-in-the-Wall, his only choice was to stay near the outlaw haven until McCarty decided to come out and return to his life of crime.

In late August Molly received a letter postmarked Kaycee, Wyoming. Young wrote that, according to rumor, Tom McCarty had managed to slip out of the Hole-in-the-Wall on the west side and had headed south into Colorado, where he was forming a new gang with his nephew. Young was leaving Kaycee in pursuit.

"My dearest, Molly," his letter concluded, "know that my love for you grows stronger every moment. It is that love which gives me the strength to go forward each day. It is that love which will soon bring me back to your arms."

On the morning of September 3, 1893, Marshal Young approached Delta, Colorado, hot on the trail of the newly formed McCarty gang. He had picked up their trail in the Rattlesnake Hills south of the Hole-in-the-Wall and had followed them to Saratoga, Wyoming, arriving just after they had robbed a bank and crossed the border into Colorado. At Grand Junction they had robbed another bank, leaving one teller dead. Pursuing them from Grand Junction, Young had almost been fooled when McCarty had made it look as if they'd gone into Utah. But the experienced eye of the U.S. marshal soon detected the ruse, and he cut south, quickly picking up their trail again.

Several witnesses at Grand Junction had given Young a good description of the gang's horses. There were six men, and three of them rode blue roans; two were on bays, and one rode a striped dun. Following their trail, he drew close enough to catch glimpses of the six riders in the distance several times. They were headed straight for Delta, and he was sure they intended to rob the town's only bank.

It was noon when he guided his horse down Delta's main street, his eyes exploring both sides of the dusty thoroughfare. He stiffened in the saddle when he saw the last of the six outlaws enter the bank. Their horses were tied loosely at the hitch rail. Young grinned. The outlaws were so sure of themselves that they hadn't bothered to leave a man outside as a lookout.

He reined in at a spot directly across from the bank and slid from the saddle. Turning to a man who was passing on the boardwalk, he asked, "Is the sheriff in town?"

"Yep," the man replied with a nod. "Just passed Sheriff Goode and his deputies down the street."

"Go get them!" Young exclaimed. "Tell them U.S. Marshal Mark Young told you there are six outlaws in the bank right now—the Tom McCarty gang. Have Goode arm as many townsmen as he can. Hurry!"

Moving as fast as he could, Young enlisted men on the street to help him clear all the horses from the hitch rails within fifty yards of the bank, including those belonging to the outlaws. He sent another man up and down the boardwalks to get all the citizens off the street.

Less then a minute later Sheriff Frank Goode and a pair of deputies came charging down the street to where Young was directing operations. Though they had never met, the sheriff recognized the famous U.S. marshal from pictures in the newspapers, and he immediately put himself and his deputies at Young's disposal.

Within minutes women and children were huddling in shops and stores, and the men were crawling behind boxes, barrels, and the corners of buildings, revolvers and rifles ready. Young stationed himself behind a rain barrel in front of Mamie's Dress Shop, across the street from the bank. In a hoarse whisper he told the women inside the shop to move back as far as they could and to get down on the floor. He heard one young mother tell her child to come away from the window.

The sheriff was kneeling nearby, behind a wooden crate. Word had been passed to all the men in the street that they should not open fire unless the marshal gave the word or the outlaws started shooting.

"How many men do we have out here?" Young asked Goode.

Glancing around the street and then up at the two men on the roof behind him, the sheriff replied, "Looks like about twenty-five or so."

At that moment two rapid shots were heard from inside the bank, followed by a third. The door flew open and the outlaws came bursting out, guns in hand. All six were on the boardwalk before they realized their horses were gone.

As someone inside the bank closed and bolted the door Mark Young raised up enough to be seen. "Give it up, McCarty!" he shouted. "We've got an army out here! You haven't got a chance!"

The gang stood frozen in their tracks. Tom McCarty had his gun in one hand and a stuffed canvas money bag in the other. His face registered shock at discovering that the marshal had hunted him down, despite his elaborate efforts at masking the trail.

"What'll we do?" one of the gang members asked McCarty in a half whisper, his eyes roving the street.

Before the outlaw leader could respond his nephew Bob shouted, "You'll never take us, lawman!" Then he raised his revolver and fired at the marshal.

Young ducked as guns started firing everywhere. He glanced around the edge of the rain barrel and saw that the outlaws had dived behind barrels and boxes and were returning fire. Only Bob McCarty remained standing on the boardwalk. He was shooting wildly at the rain barrel Young was crouched behind, trying to drive a bullet through to the marshal.

Young ducked back as a bullet struck the barrel just above his head. He rolled and came up on the other side, his gun raised and cocked. Taking quick but careful aim, he squeezed the trigger. A black spot appeared instantly on Bob's forehead. Blood sprayed the bank door behind him as his knees buckled and he fell forward.

Young heard a high-pitched shout, followed by an ominous thud as one of the men on the roof behind him slammed into the ground. Across the street one of the outlaws screamed, raised up from behind a crate, and fell dead on top of it.

Guns continued to blaze, filling the street with smoke. Mark Young had turned around and was leaning against the barrel as he reloaded his revolver, when suddenly he saw a little girl emerge from the nearby dress shop, apparently unnoticed by her mother. The child wandered out into the street, directly toward the line of fire.

Snapping the cylinder in place, Young holstered his gun, flung his hat to the ground, and bolted after the child. Bullets chewed the dirt all around him, ricocheting and whining angrily. The little child saw him coming toward her and stopped, and just then a woman's voice could be heard screaming, "My baby!"

Young bent down, wrapped his arms around the child, and ran for cover. He was still in the open when he felt a bolt of fire lance through his right side. He rolled in the dirt, clutching the tiny girl in his arms. Bullets whizzed past him as he staggered onto the boardwalk and stumbled through the door of Mamie's Dress Shop.

Young was vaguely aware of a frantic woman grabbing the child from his arms. Then the world blurred, and all he could sense was the deep, burning pain that spread from his side to fill his entire being. The pain washed over him, and then even that feeling faded as everything went black.

When Young finally regained consciousness, he saw two men standing over him. He shook his head to clear the vision and slowly recognized one man as Sheriff Frank Goode.

Young started to speak, but the unidentified man laid a hand on his shoulder and said, "Rest easy. You're in my office. I'm Dr. Lawrence Harrison."

"B-but McCarty . . . what happened?"

"We wiped out the whole gang, Marshal," spoke up Goode. "All except for Tom McCarty. He got away—with a good load of the bank money too. We went after him with a posse but couldn't find him."

"But how?"

"Damned if he didn't take a flying leap right through the front window of the bank. About the time you took that bullet, I'd say. While we were pinned down out front he escaped through the back door of the bank, grabbed a horse, and beat it out of there."

"I'll find him," Young said through tight lips.

"Not for a while, you won't," said Dr. Harrison, who went on to explain that Young had taken a bullet in his right side. The slug had been removed, but the damage was extensive enough that he would be laid up for another two weeks. If he was going to return to Sundance within the next month, he would have to do it by stagecoach. It would be at least two months before he could ride a horse again and take up Tom McCarty's trail.

Sighing resignedly, Young said, "Am I well enough to write a letter, Doc? There's someone who needs to know about my whereabouts and condition."

The physician smiled. "I think you can handle that."

At the Circle D ranch on the morning of September 8, one of the cowhands knocked on the door of the big ranch house. Anna Laura Leslie opened the door and greeted him.

Touching his hat, the man said, "Mornin', Miss Anna. The boss asked me to deliver this to you precisely at eleven o'clock."

Anna Laura quizzically eyed the envelope in the man's hand, then reached out and took it. "Thank you," she said, hastening to open it as he walked away. She immediately recognized the handwriting of Cory Bell:

> My Darling Anna,
> You will probably think me childish, but you have so often mentioned the courage of Bill Rogers and Mark Young in climbing Devil's Tower. Now that we've pledged our love and lives to each other, I feel that to measure up fully I must show the same courage displayed by these two fine men.
> If you leave the ranch by noon, you should arrive in time to see me reach the top.
> Desiring to be all you want in a man, I forever remain . . .
>
> Your loving Cory

Anna Laura was shaken. She had not realized that she'd made so much of Rogers and Young climbing the tower. Since her sister was in town that morning, she scribbled a hasty note saying where she'd gone, then saddled her horse and rode like the wind toward Devil's Tower.

Squinting as she drew near the lofty tower, Anna sighted the column that contained the oak pegs and followed it up and down. Cory was nowhere in sight. She had left the Circle D well before the time stated in the note, so Cory could not have already reached the top. She hoped he had not yet begun his climb and that she would have time to talk him out of it. But as she neared the base of the tower she spied his horse standing alone, tied to an aspen tree near the bottom of the ladder.

Jumping from her horse and scrambling over the huge boulders that made up the base, she topped the crest and saw Cory Bell lying at the bottom of the sheer rock wall.

"Cory!" she gasped, running over and dropping down beside him. "What happened?"

Forcing a weak smile, he said, "I got up about thirty feet and a peg came loose. I think my left leg's broken."

"Oh, my darling Cory!" Anna cried. "I'm so sorry! But you didn't need to do this. I love you for what you are! You proved your courage when you saved me from Bob McCarty!" She kissed him soundly, then said, "Come on, darling. We'll make a splint and I'll help you down to your horse. We've got to get you to Sundance."

Later that night at the Circle D ranch Molly Dunne undressed and slipped into her nightgown. She was alone in the big ranch house, having received word from Sundance that Anna Laura had brought the injured Cory Bell to the doctor's office and would stay in town overnight, then return with Cory the next day.

Before retiring for the night Molly sat down at her dressing table and spread open the letter that had come from Mark Young that day. By the thin light of a kerosene lamp she read it for the third time and breathed a prayer of thanks that the bullet in his side had done no permanent damage. Folding it and placing it back in the envelope she sighed and whispered, "Yes, my darling, I'll be waiting eagerly for your return. Those three or four weeks will seem like an eternity, but I'll be here with open arms."

Yawning, Molly blew out the lantern and slipped between the sheets. She was just falling asleep when she was startled awake by a loud thump from somewhere downstairs. Shaking her head to clear it she opened the drawer of her bedside stand and removed a loaded .32 caliber revolver. As she quietly put on her robe she heard several small knocks and a scraping sound, which seemed to come from the library.

Molly pulled back the hammer of the revolver and

cautiously made her way out into the hall and down the stairs. She headed down the hall to the open door of the darkened library. She looked inside, where the moonlight framed a shadowy figure slipping out through an opened window.

"Hold it!" Molly shouted, raising the revolver.

The stranger immediately spun around, raised a hand, and wildly fired a handgun. Molly jumped away from the doorway as the bullet thudded into the jamb. When she glanced back into the room the stranger was gone.

Molly ran over to the window in time to see the figure of a man running across the yard. She raised her revolver and fired five rapid shots. The man staggered slightly, then disappeared into the shadows. A moment later she heard the sound of a horse taking off at a gallop, its hoofbeats quickly fading into the night.

Molly dropped down into a chair beside the window. She suddenly felt the revolver shaking in her hands and stared down at it, then let it drop to the floor. In the distance she could hear doors slamming and the shouts of men running toward her from the bunkhouse.

Tom McCarty rode away from the Circle D at a full gallop, one hand clutching the reins, the other pressed against his bleeding right hip. He could feel the stinging pain where Molly Dunne's fourth bullet had found him, and he cursed the woman for all the trouble she'd caused.

Slipping the reins under one arm, he reached behind him and patted the canvas bag hanging from the saddle. The money he'd taken from the Delta bank when the rest of his gang had been slaughtered was still there. Then he patted the two envelopes inside his shirt—the thirty thousand dollars he had just retrieved from Molly's library.

It's all been worth it! McCarty thought as he grasped the reins and kicked the horse to a faster gallop. He had had enough experience with gunshot wounds to know that his injury was not serious—so long as he found a place to hole up and treat it. But he was afraid that might not be easy with Mark Young on his trail.

Tom McCarty was completely unaware that the U.S. marshal had been wounded in the Delta gun battle; that

vas why he'd ridden so hard back to the Circle D to get
iis money. Amazed at the uncanny way Young had tracked
iis gang to Delta, he had planned to retrieve the enve-
opes and ride as quickly as possible to the only place safe
or him or any other outlaw—the Hole-in-the-Wall.

But now McCarty faced a double threat. His leg was
njured and needed attending, and in a matter of minutes
. posse of Circle D cowhands would be hot on his trail,
vith Mark Young perhaps not far behind. With this wound
ie knew he could not outrun them to the Hole-in-the-
Vall. Biting his lip against the pain, McCarty told himself
hat he must find a place nearby to hide and outwit both
he posse and Mark Young by doing the unexpected.

Anxious to get out of the flatlands, he headed toward
he nearest hills—to the northwest. As he rode the stab-
)ing pain did not let up, but the flow of blood seemed to
low. He was hoping the wound was not too deep. Glanc-
ng behind him periodically, he searched the moonlit land-
cape, relieved that as yet there was no movement.

McCarty considered going to some nearby ranch. If the
Circle D hands or Mark Young overtook him, he would at
east have hostages with which to strike a deal. Keeping
iis horse at a full gallop, he continued riding northwest as
ie watched for a ranch.

The desperate outlaw had just about given up hope of
naking it to freedom when he saw a dark black shadow
owering upright against the pale-gray horizon. Suddenly
ie remembered that he was heading toward Devil's Tower—
vhere a young cowboy recently had climbed to the top
ipon a ladder of oak pegs.

Laughing to himself in spite of the pain, McCarty clutched
he wound and pushed the horse onward toward the black
nonolith ahead. "Devil's Tower!" he cried aloud. "Mark
'oung will never look for me there!"

Quickly the outlaw devised an ingenious plan. If he
:ould obtain enough food and water, he could climb to the
)p of the tower and hide there while his wound healed.
Meanwhile Mark Young would find no trace of him in the
rea and would take the search elsewhere. Then when
McCarty was fit to travel he could climb down, steal a

horse, and ride west for California, where the money he was carrying would allow him to live like a king.

McCarty had been past Devil's Tower on several occasions and remembered a small ranch just south of it. He was coming upon the tower from the southeast, so he angled his horse to the left and headed in the direction he thought the ranch to be. A few minutes later he spied a small cluster of buildings, and he pulled up well before them.

Dismounting, McCarty tied the horse to a fence rail and took a moment to examine his wound. As he thought, it was painful but relatively minor. The bleeding had all but stopped, but still he tied his bandanna tight around his thigh before grabbing his canteen and heading on foot toward the ranch buildings.

He quickly located a storage cellar beside the main ranch house and was relieved to discover it unlocked. He made his way inside and, using a wooden match, managed to find a candle on one of the shelves. In the thin candlelight he gathered enough food to last him a week, careful not to take so much of any one item that it would be missed. Grabbing a burlap sack from a pile in the corner, he stuffed the items inside, blew out the candle, and left.

Filling his large canteen at the well, McCarty hurried back to his horse and headed for Devil's Tower.

It was still a couple of hours before dawn when Tom McCarty arrived there. He circled the base until the oak pegs came into view. Dismounting, he gathered up the burlap sack of food, the canvas bag of money, and the canteen and placed them on the ground at the rocky base of the tower, near where the ladder of pegs was driven into the upright stone.

Wrapping the horse's reins loosely around the saddle horn, he slapped the animal hard on the rump. He watched as it headed toward the Belle Fourche River, stopped to drink, then slowly forded the river and disappeared into the forest beyond. He neither knew nor cared where the animal wandered. It was the third horse McCarty had stolen since escaping the shoot-out at Delta, so that even when someone found it, there would be no way to link it to him.

With effort McCarty shouldered his supplies, climbed he rocky base, and approached the tower. Using a short iece of rope he'd salvaged from the saddle he tied the wo bags together and made a loop at the other end of the ope. Then he started up the ladder, hanging the bags on ach peg as he went.

The sun had risen over the eastern horizon as the out-aw neared the top. His wound had opened up and was leeding again, but McCarty paid it little attention as he oncentrated on the task at hand. He had not heard any iders in the area, and he wanted to reach the top before nyone came upon him still climbing the tower.

By the time McCarty finally pulled himself over the dge of the towering precipice, he was so drained from he physical exertion and loss of blood that he almost rgot where he was. His head was reeling so much that e felt as if he were on a raft in the middle of a rolling sea.

Straining to keep his senses, he turned around, reached own, and hoisted the sacks over the edge, dragging them way from the jagged rim. Then he lay back with his head gainst the bags and watched the clouds spinning wildly verhead.

At last I've outfoxed the great U.S. Marshal Young! IcCarty thought, his dry lips curling into a smile. *I'll just wait few days, climb off this rock, and be a rich man forever!*

McCarty closed his eyes but could still see the clouds hirling above him as he fell into a deep, exhausted sleep.

Several hours later Sheriff Jim Naylor arrived at Devil's ower with Clint Yarrow, young Danny's father. They de as close as their horses could get to the ladder of oak egs, then dismounted. Clint removed from his saddle-ags a hammer and small saw, each with a long leather ong that allowed it to hang around his neck. Leaving the neriff with the horses, he removed his denim jacket, limbed the boulders to where the ladder began, and arted his ascent.

When he reached the spot where a peg had come out nder Cory Bell's weight, resulting in the near-fatal fall, e called down, "This high enough?"

"No!" Naylor shouted back. "Better go about twice that

high. We don't want any Sunday daredevils throwing a rope up to where you are and looping a peg. Go on up!"

Minutes later Clint was nearly one hundred feet up the sheer face of the tower when he heard the sheriff call for him to stop. He waved down, then started his descent, hammering the pegs loose or sawing off any that were wedged too tightly in place.

Now no more kids'll get stranded and no more legs'll get broken, Sheriff Naylor thought as he watched Clint make his way down the bottom hundred feet of Devil's Tower, stripping it of pegs and dropping them one by one to the ground below.

Epilogue

On September 24, 1906, a crowd of over two thousand people gathered at the base of Devil's Tower. They had come from throughout Wyoming, Utah, Montana, Nebraska, Colorado, and the Dakotas to attend ceremonies conducted by President Theodore Roosevelt. Devil's Tower was about to be proclaimed the first national monument in the United States.

A further attraction was twenty-three-year-old Dan Yarrow. Thirteen years before, at the age of ten, Dan had climbed the face of Devil's Tower on oak pegs previously driven by daredevil cowboy Bill Rogers. What few pegs were left in the upper portion of the tower had long been rendered useless by wind, rain, and snow. On this historic occasion Dan would use sharp steel stakes to scale the tower's vertical face in celebration of the new national monument.

Bright-colored fliers were handed out to the crowd, declaring that no one had climbed to the top of Devil's Tower since ten-year-old Danny Yarrow had been rescued by U.S. Marshal Mark Young in July of 1893.

A carnival atmosphere prevailed, with a sixteen-piece brass band in attendance. There were food and drink stands, along with barkers selling pinwheels, stuffed toys, and photographs of Devil's Tower. An aging huckster named Doc Witherspoon was also present with his new magic show, which operated out of a freshly painted and now obsolete Abbott and Downing stagecoach.

Newspaper reporters were on hand, along with several photographers. Horses, carriages, buggies, surreys, and wagons were gathering. There were also a number of "horseless carriages" arriving, frightening horses and children as they backfired.

Mark Young and his family arrived in a Circle Y ranch surrey, followed by a second surrey bearing Cory and Anna Laura Bell and their three children.

Pulling the surrey to a halt Young stepped down. He wore a U.S. marshal's badge and was still quite handsome, though his hair was flecked with gray and tiny wrinkles had formed at the corners of his eyes. As he helped Molly down he squeezed her shoulders and gave her a kiss.

Eight-year-old Melinda giggled and said, "Daddy, must you and Mommy do that all the time? I want to get down."

While Young lifted his daughter out of the surrey ten-year-old Mark, Jr., hopped out and made a beeline for Dan Yarrow, who was surrounded by a group of admirers.

Sundance's mayor, Clint Yarrow, and his wife approached the two Circle Y surreys. "Howdy, Mark, Cory," said Clint. "Who are these two beautiful females you're riding with?"

"Oh, just a couple of strays we found along the way," replied Young with a grin. Molly gave him a playful scowl.

Clint was called aside by one of the town's citizens. As Molly and Helen Yarrow greeted each other Young walked over to the brightly colored stagecoach that stood nearby.

Doc Witherspoon was barking out the amazing features of his new magic show when he spotted the tall man approaching. Pushing his hat back on his head he smiled and said, "Well, I do declare! Unless these old peepers are deceiving me, here comes Uncle Sam's favorite lawman!"

Young grinned and shook Witherspoon's hand. "What happened to your Indian River Elixir, Doc?"

Witherspoon chuckled and replied, "Well, son, the river done dried up! So I'm doing magic!"

"Seems to me that's what you were doing before," Young commented dryly.

Witherspoon laughed and began his spiel again.

Turning away, Young was starting back toward Molly when his eye caught a familiar face. It was Pinkerton detective Jack Clancy.

Clancy had spotted the marshal at the same instant, and a wide grin spread across his face. Hurrying over, he shook Young's hand and said, "I see you're still in the business."

"Yes." Young nodded. "I do some ranching on the side, but I still wear the badge. How about you?"

"Oh, I'm in real estate now up Cheyenne way. Gave up the detective business after a certain U.S. marshal had me jailed over in Kaycee." Squinting slightly, he added, "Law enforcement isn't the same as it was in those days, eh?"

"Not quite," Young said, shaking his head. "The real excitement went out at the turn of the century. But I still like it. I guess I was born to wear a badge."

Chuckling, Clancy asked, "You still locking detectives in jail?" Without awaiting an answer, he gently cuffed Young on the shoulder and said, "I owe you a lot, Marshal."

"Oh?"

"Sure. Because of you I can tell my grandchildren I was once in jail with the famous outlaw Butch Cassidy!"

Just then Dan Yarrow and Mark Young, Jr., came over, and Young introduced them to Clancy.

Continuing his conversation, Jack Clancy said, "Speaking of Butch Cassidy, Marshal, do you think the reports about him and the Sundance Kid are really true?"

"You mean that they were killed in a gun battle in South America five years ago?"

"Yes."

"No way of knowing," commented Young, hunching his shoulders. "Some people say they've seen Cassidy around, but there's never been any proof."

Cocking his head, Clancy said, "You never did catch Tom McCarty after that Delta, Colorado, bank holdup, did you?"

"Nope. McCarty remains the one dark blot on my record. He's the only outlaw I ever set out to bring to justice who eluded me. I hunted him off and on for six years afterward, but there was never a trace of him. It was like he vanished from the earth."

"Any speculations?"

The marshal nodded. "He may have gone to South America. Wouldn't surprise me if that's where Cassidy and Sundance got the idea."

Dan Yarrow spoke up. "It's too bad about that one dark blot, Marshal. I wish you'd been given the satisfaction of bringing McCarty to justice. If any outlaw ever had it coming, it was him."

"That's for sure," agreed Young. "But more than anything I would just like to know what happened to him."

Suddenly a whoop went up from the crowd. President Theodore Roosevelt had just arrived in a well-polished, open-top automobile. The vehicle pulled up beside a platform that had been built for the occasion. American flags were draped over it, and one flag hung on a pole, flapping in the breeze. The brass band played a rousing tune as the president mounted the platform.

Mayor Clint Yarrow introduced the Chief Executive of the United States. Then Roosevelt stood before the crowd with his straight-backed military stance and made a brief speech formally pronouncing Devil's Tower America's first national monument. The crowd cheered, and the band struck up "The Star-Spangled Banner."

After the president took a seat on the platform Clint Yarrow stepped forth and told the story of Bill Rogers's climb on July 4, 1893, and of his son's subsequent ascent of the tower several days later. Pointing out Marshal Mark Young in the crowd he said, "There's the man who rescued my ten-year-old boy, folks! I hope the marshal will not have to rescue him again!"

The crowd laughed, and several people slapped Mark Young on the back.

The band began to play as Dan Yarrow made his climb up the hazardous face of Devil's Tower, driving steel pegs as he went. Mark and Molly Young took a seat on a blanket beside Cory and Anna Laura Bell, while both sets of children played nearby.

Four hours later, while the crowd watched in silent awe, Dan Yarrow neared the top. From far below he could hear a drum roll begin. His mind flashed back to that frightful day thirteen years before when he'd been stranded up there. Today there was no fear. All had gone well, and the descent held no threat.

The drum roll built to a thrilling crescendo as Dan hoisted himself over the edge. Once again the band broke into "The Star-Spangled Banner." At that point Dan was supposed to unfurl the large flag fastened to his back, just as Bill Rogers had done thirteen years before. He stood and was reaching behind his neck to untie the flag when a ghastly sight met his eyes.

Before him lay the skeleton of a man, sprawled face down. A rotten leather gun belt was looped around the spine, and there was a rusty gun in the holster.

Yarrow was so taken with the sight before him that he had forgotten the crowd below. Slowly he became aware of the band playing in the distance. Hastily he removed the flag from his back and unfurled it. Lifting it to the wind, he stepped to the edge of the tower and let it wave, while the crowd roared with excitement.

After a few moments Dan folded the flag and returned to where the skeleton was lying. He wondered who this unnamed man might have been and when he'd made the climb. It had to have been many years ago, since he no doubt had used Bill Rogers's pegs. So it must have been between the time Dan had climbed them as a boy and his father had pulled the first hundred feet of pegs. But why had this man stayed up here and died?

His curiosity aroused, Dan began looking around. Shortly he spied a rock shelf, and in its shadow lay a strange-looking object. He reached down and picked up a dirty, partially eroded canvas bag. He slapped at the bag, dislodging the outer layer of dust, and discovered faint letters that read: MERCHANTS BANK, DELTA, COLORADO.

Dan Yarrow's jaw fell as the truth struck home. The skeleton was Tom McCarty!

Grinning excitedly, Dan tied a rope to the canvas bag and slung it over his shoulder. Stepping to the edge of the tower, he stood looking down at the milling throng below. Somewhere among that crowd was Mark Young.

Have I got a surprise for the man who wears the U.S. marshal's badge! Yarrow thought as he eased himself over the rim of Devil's Tower and began his descent.

Author's Note

After Devil's Tower was proclaimed a national monument by President Theodore Roosevelt on September 24, 1906, it was climbed intermittently for several years by both men and women. On October 1, 1941, daredevil George Hopkins parachuted to the top of the tower from a rented airplane. After landing on its relatively flat surface, Hopkins realized there was no way to get down. He was marooned without food or water for six days until an experienced climber went up and got him.

Records of climbs have been kept at Devil's Tower since 1937. In 1963 the one-thousandth climber checked in, and in 1970, the two thousandth. Since 1977 more than one thousand make the climb every year.

Devil's Tower remains one of America's most striking phenomena. The giant monolith still stands in northeastern Wyoming, lifting its majestic head to the blazing sun by day and reaching toward the seven stars of Pleiades by night.

THE BADGE: BOOK 2
THE FACELESS MAN
by Bill Reno

By age seventeen, Jim Blackburn has seen a lot of life. For it is on that birthday that his entire family is gunned down by the vicious Hegler gang. And it is on that day that he swears to strap on a gun and hunt them down one by one, until all five Hegler brothers lay cold in their graves.

Jim seeks out the famous gunfighter Spence Landford and learns the fast draw. Then he assumes the name Jim Black and sets out on his mission of vengenace, disregarding Landford's advice to give up the gunman's path before that inevitable day when he will be confronted by the faceless man—the gunman who will outdraw and kill Jimmy Blackburn.

One by one Jim hunts and kills the Heglers. Thinking his work done, he lays down his gun and fulfills his dream of becoming a lawyer. But fate is not through with Jim Blackburn, and he finds himself facing a stream of gunhawks intent upon proving their skill by killing the famous Jim Black.

Facing the greatest challenge of his life, Jim puts on a badge and straps on his gun in order to save the people he has come to love. But this time he knows he will confront his faceless man. Because unknown to the people he serves—even to the woman he loves—Jim Blackburn is going blind.

Read **THE FACELESS MAN**, on sale December **1987** wherever Bantam paperbacks are sold.